To D

Enjoy

David

David Brewerton is an award-winning journalist born and brought up in the East End of London, but with a passion for sailing small boats on the rivers and estuaries of East Anglia. *Dancing to Domino* is his second novel.

DANCING
TO
DOMINO

DAVID BREWERTON

Matador
Unit E2 Airfield Business Park,
Harrison Road, Market Harborough,
Leicestershire. LE16 7UL
Tel: 0116 279 2299
Email: books@troubador.co.uk
Web: www.troubador.co.uk/matador
Twitter: @matadorbooks

ISBN 978 1 80313 312 6

British Library Cataloguing in Publication Data.
A catalogue record for this book is available from the British Library.

Printed and bound in Great Britain by 4edge Limited
Typeset in 11pt Minion Pro by Troubador Publishing Ltd, Leicester, UK

Matador is an imprint of Troubador Publishing Ltd

To Vi and Jack, my late parents,
who never trod on my dreams.

"Can one ever escape the claims of a troubled past, and how does one act when those claims demand a final answer? In David Brewerton's compelling new novel, Jack (or should it be Jacques?) Boyer is drawn from his retreat as a loner on a boat moored in the Essex marshes into a reluctant confrontation with these life-defining questions. The search for answers takes him deeply back to the post-war East End of his youth and on into the challenges of an uncertain future. With its sharply observed cast of unusual characters and its vividly evoked locations, this intriguing mystery story also unfolds a moving drama of self-discovery."

Lindsay Clarke, Award Winning Author

"An absorbing story about the way the past never truly lets us go and is seldom quite what we remember. The characters spring vividly to life and the settings are beautifully evoked. Dancing to Domino will remain in the readers' mind long after the last page has been turned."

Mike Walker, Author of 'The Epic of Tumanbay'

Acknowledgements

Where does one start with acknowledgements when one has leaned heavily on so many talented people to bring an idea into print? Throughout this project I have received so much encouragement, but would particularly like to mention two fine literary mentors, Lindsay Clarke and Mike Walker and a dear "friend in writing" Kathy Berriman.

Patricia, my wife, sent me back to my study if I appeared to lose impetus and my dear daughter in law, Jo did the first edit of the draft manuscript. The experts at Troubador made the journey to publication as terror free as possible.

So to you all, thank you.

One

Somebody was watching him. He glanced up at the sea wall. Nobody he recognised, collar turned up, hands deep into the pockets of his overcoat, his face mostly hidden beneath the brim of an old-fashioned trilby hat.

Jack Boyer would remember the date, Sunday 9 October, because it was John Lennon's birthday. He would have been seventy-six, but for the assassin waiting outside his New York apartment.

But on that birthday, shortly after nine in the morning, Jack had work to do. His thoughts were far from Manhattan.

When he'd marked the date in his diary the sun had been shining and autumn simply a golden memory of previous years. Come the day and it was pissing down. He'd spent a good hour setting out the boards, too busy to notice what was going on up on the sea wall. How long had that man been standing there, just staring? So what? If he wanted to hang about in the rain, that was his problem. Jack had too much to do to worry about strangers.

The last of the tide trickled away. Red and green buoys lay flat on the shiny mud. Boats normally afloat left high and dry, leaning at crazy angles. Now for the real work. He made his precarious way around the old scaffold boards to the stern of his pride and joy, *Duchesse Anne,* fifty tonnes of steel and wood that patrolled the seaways before becoming his home.

Over twenty-five years of living aboard, Jack had reluctantly grown used to people watching him work – the price of being moored alongside a public footpath near a popular pub. Usually he would pretend not to hear if they called out stupid questions and comments. Now and again an interesting conversation would come his way, but not often. He glanced up to the sea wall again. The man hadn't moved. Why didn't he just sod off?

Jack turned his back and picked up the lance of his pressure washer, to begin blasting away the weeds and barnacles that had made a home on the old boat during the warm summer. They came away easily, but it was miserable work. The boards became more slippery with each successive blast of cold drizzle. His hands were wet and freezing. Water from the pressure washer made matters even worse. At any moment he could end up face down in the mire.

Above the noise of the compressor he heard a shout.

"You're Jack Boyer, aren't you?"

Jack released the pressure and turned.

"Who wants to know?"

"I do. I've got a message for him. Is it you?"

"Leave it up there somewhere. Under a stone or something. I'll look at it when I'm finished here."

Jack squeezed the trigger. The water cascaded over the rudder, revealing the red paint that had been hidden beneath a year's growth of weeds.

"The boss said I was to wait until you'd read it. He said it's important."

Again Jack paused and turned to face the man, who could have been sent by Central Casting for a *film noir* walk-on part. He did, however, look vaguely familiar.

"Who's your boss, then?"

"Mr Russell."

"I don't know any Mr Russells."

"He says you do."

Jack laid the lance down on a board, made his way back across the planks and climbed up the sloping concrete of the river wall, stopping a couple of metres away from the man. The visitor's cashmere overcoat and leather shoes were so out of place that Jack felt the urge to laugh. But there was something about the man. Had they met before, a long time ago?

"So, what do you want? Where's this message that's so important?"

The man reached inside his coat and held out an envelope.

"I'm to wait while you read this."

"So you said. And what if I don't fancy reading it now?"

"I dunno. I'll have to ask."

Jack sighed. The man was only obeying orders. He took the envelope and ran his finger under the flap. Inside he found a handwritten letter:

Dear Jack,

I thought I ought to tell you that Stan is in hospital with pneumonia. I would be pleased if you could go and see him, and my driver will take you. He is in Newham General.

I hope you are keeping well.

Kind regards,

Brian Russell

Bloody hell. Brian Russell. Russ. Fancy Shoes was right, he did know him, but never expected nor wanted to hear from him again. But Stan. Stan, in hospital? A sharp gust threatened to tear the letter from his fingers. Jack forgot the other man was standing just a couple of feet away, watching his every move. Then he spoke. "I'm to take you straight to the hospital."

Jack read the letter again and looked him straight in the eye.

"You may not have noticed that I'm just a bit busy right now."

"How long you gonna be? I'll wait in the car."

Jack put the envelope in the front pouch of his overalls.

"Look, Mr whatever your name is, you don't seem to understand. You can tell Mr Brian Russell that if I do decide to go to the hospital, I will go under my own steam and at a time of my own choosing. Is that clear enough for you?"

"I'll have to check with Mr Russell. Won't be a minute. The name's Glover, by the way." He walked carefully down the steps into the car park of the Old Smack Inn, unlocked a black Range Rover and climbed in. After a couple of minutes, the Range Rover spun its wheels on the Old Smack's gravel and was gone.

Glover? No wonder he looked familiar. Roy Glover, of course.

East London, 1948

"Now then," said Auntie Emm, pouring a few drops of yellow stuff into the basin, "let's get a proper look at you."

She dipped a small piece of cotton wool into the warm

4

water and dabbed it gently on Jack's swollen lip. He felt his tears welling up again, and tried to stop himself from crying by reading the powdered egg packet beside him on the table.

"Explorers, diggers and hunters," he managed, "requiring fresh bread will find Bird's Concentrated Egg Powder excellent for making light wholesome bread while engaged in expeditions." But he couldn't hold them back. How could he ever go on expeditions if he couldn't stop crying?

"There, darling, it's not like you to cry. Come here, let's give you a hug." Auntie Emm leaned across the table and pulled his head gently to her. Jack put his arms around her waist. She stroked the back of his head. "OK now?"

Jack sensed she was about to pull away, and held tight to her, taking deep breaths, trying to suppress his sobbing. He didn't want to cry any more. Russ could come in at any moment.

"Sorry," he muttered. He dug his fingers into the waistband of her thick woollen skirt. "I do have a dad, don't I, Auntie?" he whispered, so softly, almost to himself.

She stroked his head and pulled him tighter against her.

"Of course you do, my luv. And a *maman* that loves you. And then there's Stan and me. You're a lucky little blighter, Jack Boyer." She pulled away and dabbed at his lip. "Now then, tell me what happened. Dry them tears and tell me all about it."

"Russ said I'd never had a dad, and that one day I'd find out for myself."

"Take no notice of him, my luv. Of course you've got a dad."

"So where is he? Why don't I ever see him? Is he ever coming back?"

"So many questions, young man. As I said, take no notice. Your lip will be sore for a day or two, so no kissing the girls. Now then, let's have a look at that knee. What were you doing to end up in such a state?"

Jack straightened up.

"We were over on the sandhills, taking it in turns on Frankie's old bike. I was halfway down the big hill when Russ suddenly jumped out in front of me."

"Why would he do that, then?"

"I don't know, Auntie. But I swerved and that's when I fell off."

The back door rattled. Russ mustn't see him crying. He buried his face against Emm's blouse. Through slitted eyes he could see Russ standing looking, his mouth open. Then he turned and went back outside, closing the door behind him. Jack pulled away from the safety of Auntie Emm. He sniffed loudly and rubbed his nose with the back of his hand.

"Better now, my little hunter?" She tore a piece of clean white cotton from an old sheet she kept in a kitchen drawer, dipped the corner into the water and gently dabbed his face. She handed the piece to him. "Now dry your eyes."

She picked up a fresh piece of cotton wool and carefully began wiping away the congealed blood and dirt from his leg.

"Looks worse than it is, thank the Lord. We'll soon have you patched up right as rain. Don't want to frighten Maman when she comes for you."

She patted his leg dry. One cut continued to ooze a little blood, but mostly there were just grazes. Auntie Emm found a large Elastoplast.

"There you are, young Jack. Good as new." She held out her arms. "Let's get you down from there."

"Can I stir the cake, Auntie?"

"Of course you can. Just let me put the milk in first."

"Why do you have to cook cakes, Auntie?" he asked, as he watched her slide the cake tin into the oven. He ran the wooden spoon around the basin, getting as much of the raw mixture as he could. "Cakes are much nicer like this."

"You and your questions. Off you go outside and see what that Russ is up to in Stan's shed."

He was halfway out the door when he heard the roar of Stan's Royal Enfield.

"There's Stan," said Emm, grabbing the kettle off the stove and filling it from the tap. Her black plimsolls squeaked on the polished lino floor. Good old Stan, with his smiling face, jam doughnuts brought home from the bakery and rides on the motorbike and sidecar.

At the sound of Stan's return, Russ burst through the back door, sending it crashing back against the sink.

Emm caught his arm as he tried to rush past.

"Just a minute, young man," she said, swinging him around to face her, "I want a word with you before you go tearing off anywhere."

Russ, clearly surprised at the sharpness of Emm's tone, stopped in his tracks, his mouth open.

"What?" he said.

"Jumping out like that and making Jack fall off the bike."

"I didn't jump out. He was chasing me."

Emm turned to Jack, standing beside the kitchen table.

"Well," she said, "were you?"

"Yeah, but he was saying nasty things about Maman."

The front door banged. Stan. As ever, he arrived with a broad smile on his face and a paper bag in his hand.

"Put the kettle on, Emm. Once I've had a cuppa let's all go out for a spin. It's a wizard afternoon." He turned to the boys. "What you two looking so miserable about? Anyway, here's a couple of old doughnuts to put a smile back on your faces."

Emm let go of Russ's arm.

"You two," she said, "you'll be the death of me. Take one each and make yourselves scarce outside while I make Stan a cuppa. And no more fighting. Understand? And if you, young Russ, want to go out on the bike with Stan, you'd better go and ask your mum."

Russ grabbed a doughnut and made a dash for the front door.

"Back in a minute," he shouted.

*

Jack watched the Range Rover disappear up the lane and shook his head. He was cold and wet, and what little enthusiasm he previously had for pressure washing *Duchesse Anne* had completely deserted him. He just wanted to get back into the warm, out of the drizzle. But even if he abandoned work for the day, the scaffold boards would need to be stacked back up on the sea wall, and the pressure washer dragged back on board. He could, however, take a break. The tide would not reach the foreshore for at least another hour, or more likely two. And then decide: carry on or put it off until the next day.

He made his way down the steeply sloping gangway into the boat's wheelhouse, laid the letter on the chart table and went below. He first filled the kettle and set it to boil. He flicked open the doors of the little iron stove and only then did he dare take off his coat. Who would have thought that early October could be so cold and miserable? Only that morning there'd been quite a few gale warnings in the shipping forecast. It wasn't going to get any better for a while.

The kettle boiled. He added a little water and swilled it around to warm the teapot. One spoon of tea went into the pot. The spoon was part of a set, a present from Margate that had included a wooden caddy. Stan had brought it back with him one day as a present for Emm. It had Margate's coat of arms on the handle: a sea horse at the top and below that a curious image of a lion's head attached to what looked like a Viking ship. Jack couldn't remember why he now had the spoon, or what had happened to the caddy. He poured the water into the teapot, stirred it once and put the lid back on.

He set the pinger to three and a half minutes and climbed the short steps to the wheelhouse, sat himself in the swivel chair and stowed the letter in the chart table drawer. What a weird morning. Roy Glover, dressed up like a cinema gangster, hand delivering a letter from Russ, somebody Jack never expected ever to hear from or see again. After what Russ did, he didn't want to set eyes on him ever again.

But Stan? Stan was not so easy to dismiss. So far as he knew, none of what happened back then could be laid at Stan's door. On the contrary, Stan and Emm always looked after him when Maman had to make one of her trips to wherever it was she went.

He still did not know where she went. When he asked, they brushed him off with non-answers. They said she went to look after people. What was that supposed to mean? What people? Where?

Did Stan and Emm know? Emm would usually say she went to see a man about a dog, and that he asked too many questions. Stan just said women were funny creatures and it was best not to ask. But Jack was sure it had something to do with his father, another mystery. Who was he, and why had he never met him? Something else they weren't saying.

But they all loved him, and cared for him, and surely it wouldn't be asking too much to go and see Stan in hospital?

Pneumonia in old people is serious. It's not called the old man's friend for nothing.

The pinger sounded from below. He went down, poured a mugful of tea and carried it back up to the wheelhouse. The debris from his morning's work, unhelpfully interrupted by Roy Glover, lay around the old boat. He couldn't sit there too much longer, just thinking. He had to get back to work, or at the very least go back down to the mud and pick up the boards.

The tea was still too hot to drink. He looked again at the stuff scattered around the boat. It wasn't going to take too long to clear. With luck it could all be packed away before his tea got cold. And the rain had stopped.

He zipped up his coat. What a bloody cheek that Russ had. He didn't ask for any of this. Not now. Not ever. When Jack stormed out of all their lives nearly half a century ago, he made himself a promise that he'd never go back. What was done was finished. Over. No looking back. He told himself he'd outgrown them all anyway, and it was probably a lucky escape.

He slid open the drawer and read the letter again. It didn't actually say that Stan wanted to see him. So was it Russ trying to pull the strings? Typical. He'd obviously not changed one little bit.

When he stepped out onto the deck the cold, damp air was strangely comforting. Now, there was work to finish, and he reckoned he had just enough time to finish before the tide returned. And then he could reward himself with lunch at the pub.

He started the compressor and climbed down onto the foreshore. Returning to the stern, he blasted weed and barnacles off the twin screws. Would the screws ever turn again, powering *Duchesse Anne* downriver and out into the estuary? The engines could do it, he knew that. Right now, he could go up into the wheelhouse, turn the key and, one after the other, the two old Perkins would roar into life without missing a beat.

One thing was certain: if he did decide to go, he would do so without Russ's help. Under his own steam and at a time of his choosing, as he'd told Russ's messenger. Roy Glover! A nasty piece of work, like all his family. Why on earth would Russ want to get together with him?

Finishing at the stern, he laid the lance down. Only then did he notice Alison watching him from the sea wall. She waved. It would be good to stop again, to sit and drink coffee in the wheelhouse with her. Get out of the cold and wet. But he had a lot to do before the tide returned, and he'd already had one interruption. So he simply waved back and turned his attention to the keel. What he saw was not good. The black pitch that protected the steel was flaking away. He released the trigger. The water stopped. Poking around with the old engineer's screwdriver he always carried when working confirmed what he already suspected: within the next year or two *Duchesse Anne* would have to be hauled out, shot-blasted, have some of her thinning plates replaced, then repainted and repitched, and put back into the water. And that meant money, big money, even if he did much of the work himself.

Across the river a children's birthday party was under way around a barbecue on the beach. He stopped for a moment, listening to the excited shouts of the kids and the clink of bottles as the dads sunk a few beers. The drizzle didn't seem to bother them.

Two

A week after it arrived, the letter still lay in the chart table drawer where he'd left it. Until that letter, he'd not heard from Russ for forty years, and he liked it that way. He didn't need to know about Stan's illnesses. If Stan had pneumonia, well, there was nothing he could do about it. Even if he went to see him, a flying visit to his bedside wasn't going to make him better. And where did Russ fit in? Why had he taken it upon himself to track Jack down, just to give him bad news?

And would Stan even want to see him? After all, they'd had forty years to get in touch, to explain what happened, and hadn't bothered.

But he couldn't go into the wheelhouse without knowing that the letter was lurking there, waiting for him to slide open the drawer and read it again and again, even though he knew every word. He had asked Alison what she thought, and she said he should probably go and visit the old man. But it wasn't that easy. What was there to say to Stan? And what if he bumped into Russ at the hospital? Or Roy Glover. He didn't want to see any of them. As for Bel herself, what could he say to her after what she did?

A few weeks later, winter proper hit East Stone. A run of sleety and rainy days followed by stormy nights made him question, for the first time ever, whether he should still, at his age, live on a boat. He didn't want to end up with pneumonia like Stan, but then, Stan had worked all his life in the bakery where exposure to the dust must have played havoc with his lungs. But *Duchesse Anne* demanded a lot of love and attention. Not to mention cash. Maybe he should think about living ashore.

He spent most of November writing his columns for the local paper, sitting in the pub and, when the weather wasn't too bad, going for long walks. He tried to plan his outings to coincide with the times that Alison would walk her black Labrador, Millie, along the sea wall. Some days they would meet and walk all the way to Tollesbury. They might have a bowl of soup together in the little cafe. Occasionally, there was still some work to be had at the boatyard.

One morning he slid open the drawer, took out the letter, tore it into pieces and watched them float downriver on the ebb tide. He didn't keep either Russ's address or telephone number. The dilemma was not so easy, however, to get rid of. To visit or not? Had Stan pulled through, or had he died? There were few mornings when the old man was not in his waking thoughts.

East Stone went into its usual winter hibernation. The Old Smack's outside tables that all summer had seen people clinking glasses and eating from the seasonal menu, were now piled one on top of another, underneath blue tarpaulins lashed down with cheap polypropylene rope. The bar echoed with his footsteps when he entered. Clump, clump across the bare wooden floor. Rarely did he enter to a buzz of conversation. The only bright spots were the open fire and Katie's welcome.

One bright December morning, he was halfway to Tollesbury with Alison when a flight of geese came winging in from the estuary. In recent days he'd been cheered by the sight of the greylags returning from the north to overwinter on the East Anglian marshes. He'd even thought he might get out his old Beretta again, but worried about how Alison and Katie might view him going wildfowling.

But it was the perfect time of year and the breeding season had been good. It was now or never.

"You know what, Ali," Jack said, "I think I'm going to take up shooting again."

Ali stopped and called to Millie to be clipped back onto her lead, as if the very mention of shooting had put her dog in danger.

"You, Jack? Really? I can't imagine you ever killing anything. Do you even have a gun?"

"Of course I have a gun. A very nice one as it happens. Old, but still as accurate as the day it was made. They last for ever if you look after them."

"What will you shoot?"

"Geese. Something we can eat."

They resumed walking, the dog between them. Jack didn't have to wait long for further reaction.

"At least there's plenty of them, so maybe losing one or two from a flock wouldn't be tragic, even if they have flown all the way from Iceland just to end up on your plate. Just don't ask me to go with you."

"Ah, but what about roast goose? What would you say to that? All that lovely fat for the potatoes."

Alison tucked her arm in his.

"Now you're talking, Monsieur Boyer. That's an entirely different matter."

That afternoon he spent oiling and polishing his beloved twelve bore. He'd made the decision: when the weather and the tides were right, he'd put it to use. And then maybe he'd be able to forget all about Russ and Stan again and get on with his life.

East London, 1952

"You won't see him, no matter how long you stand there, Boyo," Russ yelled, above the roar of the boat train heading for London. Jack had no idea Russ and Frankie had arrived. He wished they hadn't. Sometimes it was better to be on your own. He threw a stone at the train and missed.

Jack swung down from the tall iron fence that ran alongside the railway.

"Anyway, I was just watching the trains. Who told you I was here?"

"No one. Just guessed where we'd find you. No point in hanging about here all on your lonesome, Boyo. Watching for him, were you?"

"Who?"

"The dad you ain't got."

"Who says I haven't got?"

"Where is he, then?"

"Still away."

"What, hiding from police? My dad was killed fighting for king and country, he was."

"So was mine," said Frankie, who usually stood well back when Russ and Jack started one of their arguments.

Russ put his arm around Frankie's thin shoulders.

"Dads to be proud of, eh, Frankie? Not like some I

could mention. Even his mum don't know which bloke it was got her up the spout."

Jack grabbed hold of Russ's arm, spinning him around. Frankie stumbled forward, reaching for the fence to stay on his feet.

"Say that again and I'll punch your head in," Jack shouted.

Russ shook himself free.

"Keep your flipping hair on. Only joking. Didn't mean nothing by it."

"I told you. Just shut up about my mum. And my dad. One more time, and I mean it."

"I said, didn't mean nothing by it." Russ sniffed and kicked a stone along the path.

"Well, just watch it."

"OK. OK. I heard you first time."

The three boys walked on, Russ in front, Frankie limping along beside him, Jack bringing up the rear, hands thrust deep into his pockets. Why couldn't Russ just shut up? Leave him alone? But Russ always had to pick on somebody. Sometimes it would be Frankie. He'd say Frankie's dad was in prison up north because he'd run away from the Germans. He'd made up a joke. "What do you call Frankie's dad?" A pause, and then he would say, "Frankie Coward." Jack should have stopped him, but he never did. And Frankie never stood up for himself.

No matter what Russ said, Jack knew the truth about his dad, even though he'd never seen him. Obvious. Secret missions. Hunting down Nazis.

Jack had seen special soldiers like him, up there on the screen at the Coronation, dropping by parachute behind enemy lines. As the blue cigarette smoke curled up into the beam from the projector, he'd watched them blow up bridges and trains. Creep up on the Nazi guards and rabbit punch them into oblivion. He knew. He just knew. But it was all top secret. One day he'd come back, and then Russ would be sorry.

Another train rumbled along the tracks, labouring its way up and over the flyover. Truck after truck full of coal.

"Give us a ha'penny," Russ suddenly demanded. He pointed at Frankie. "No point in asking him, 'cos he's never got two to rub together."

Jack said nothing.

Russ sighed.

"I suppose I'll have to use my own, then." He took a coin from his pocket and flipped it into the air, catching it in one deft movement. "Come on," he said. "Let's get there before the next one."

The boys hurried downhill to the place where there was the loose railing. Russ squeezed through.

"Hurry up if you're coming," he said. "I can hear the next one." He crouched down and put his ear to the rail. "It's on this line alright." He put his coin onto the line and, just as the train emerged from under the Rabbits Road bridge and let out a mighty whistle, dashed to the side of the tracks.

The train hurtled past, the driver waving his fist at the boys. Russ rushed to pick up the flattened halfpenny, which had doubled in size, but immediately dropped it.

"Flamin' red hot. If that had been dynamite, that train would have been blown to smithereens." He picked up the prize with a dirty handkerchief.

"That's what my dad was doing, in the war," Jack said, as Russ emerged back on the path.

"Was he, Boyo? So what's he doing now the war's over?"

"Can't tell you, but you'll see, when he comes back. And then you'll be laughing on the other side of your face."

The boys resumed their haphazard progress.

"Do you have to go there, Boyo?" Russ asked, kicking a stone downhill.

"Where?"

"Pargeter's."

"Think so. Maman says it's what's best for me."

"What you talking about?" Frankie asked.

"School. Next term. I'm going to Pargeter's."

"Even if you pass for the grammar?"

"Either way," Jack answered, wishing it wasn't true. "Anyway, you and Russ will probably go to the tech in a couple of years, and we wouldn't be together then anyway."

"My mum says you must be made of money to be going there," Russ said, "Will you come back at weekends?"

"Dunno," replied Jack, as another train steamed past. "I don't want to talk about it. Let's go and find some golf balls."

Three

Katie's heels clicked across the bare boards.

"Can I bring you another one, Captain?" she asked over his shoulder.

He swung his head around and gave her a broad smile.

"No thanks, Katie, I'll be heading back in a minute."

She threw a small log onto the fire, and a shower of sparks floated up towards the blackened beam that supported the chimney breast.

"You look pleased with yourself this evening, Captain," she said, rubbing her hands down her jeans. It was more of a question than a statement.

"Do I? Well, I've just decided to get out my gun and see if I can still shoot straight."

The barmaid touched his shoulder as she turned back towards the bar.

"You're a strange one, Captain," she said.

Jack took the final mouthful from his glass, blew a kiss to Katie and began the short walk across the car park and over the river wall to *Duchesse Anne*. The air was still and the moon round and clear. A poachers' night, if ever there was one. He thought about his plans. It would be good to step out along the little-known twisting paths across the marshes further down the estuary. How long had it been since he had seen a bird fall from the sky, already dead? When the crack of a shot over water came from his own gun?

Early winter – the best time of the year. But if really severe weather came through, the birds would be under too much pressure for honest sport. If he was going to do it, he'd better get cracking.

Two days later, he rose before dawn, filled a flask and walked off down the dark river wall munching a bacon sandwich, brown sauce dripping down his chin and his spirits higher than they had been at any time since that wretched letter had arrived. He walked for nearly an hour, as the sky turned from black to grey. When the first slithers of pink could be seen, he clambered down the river wall and took an almost hidden path out towards the incoming tide.

Could he still do it? His eyes were not so good now. He had to be sure of a clean kill. Nothing else would do. Could he still hit his target?

He found a gully, clambered down, took out his Beretta, giving it a final rub with the yellow duster he kept in the bag, and slipped cartridges into both barrels. A flight of ducks, heard before they could be seen, approached from the river. He brought up the gun, heavier than he remembered, adjusted his stance, selected his target, pulled the gun in tight against his shoulder and began counting down to the moment when, aiming just ahead of the chosen bird, he would squeeze the trigger. Eighty yards, fifty. Squeeze.

But his fingers didn't move, and the flight passed safely overhead, heading inland to forage among the newly ploughed fields.

"I need some practice," he muttered to himself. "Can't risk a winging." He climbed out of the gully and looked for a likely target. Thirty yards away, the remains of an old bridge, destroyed by the villagers when it was feared the German Army might choose East Stone as the place to launch an invasion, stuck up out of the mud.

He settled his stance: left leg forward, the right back with the foot at ninety degrees. Gun pressed hard on his right shoulder. It felt comfortable. Familiar. Why had it been so long? He picked out the top six inches of a blackened post, took a deep breath, and squeezed. Three inches of rotten wood flew into the air and, moments later, an assortment of birds soared up, their early morning scavenging interrupted by a sound that they seemed to know, instinctively, meant danger. He lowered the gun, enjoying the familiar smell of hot oil and gunpowder.

There was still the other barrel. Jack selected a mallard heading towards him, counted it into range, and watched it fly inland. He could have done it. He could have downed the mallard. Hadn't he hit the post, bang in the centre of his target area? He could still shoot. What stopped him?

He took his stance again, raised the gun to his shoulder and centred on an old tyre, lying half submerged at the bottom of the creek bed. It was a good fifty or sixty feet away. OK, it wasn't a moving target, but if he could just hit the top third, well, it proved something. He squeezed and saw the tyre twitch as the pellets hit home. Next time, next time he would bring down a goose.

He loaded the warm gun back into its bag and made his way back to the river wall. God, it was good to be out early again. Too many mornings he'd lain in his bunk like a sulky teenager, but this morning he could breathe clean salty air into his whole being. He sat on the path, his legs stretched before him, and poured a cup of tea from the flask he carried in the old General Post Office bag that had accompanied him on his shooting trips for heaven knows how long. Next time. Next time, he was sure.

But the second time, a few days later, was simply a repeat of the first. What the heck? He'd rediscovered the pleasure of early mornings: the rise of a watery sun over the grey–green river, the cries of the oystercatchers and the beat of flights far above his head. He shot at decaying posts, old tyres, rotting boats, but he did not really need more practice. He could still hit a bird at fifty feet, but he no longer wanted to. Something had changed. But, surely, it could change back, like the turn of the seasons.

A third time, he set off as before. Flocks of brents, newly returned from their summer in Russia, make attractive targets, but only with a good clean shot at a single bird. Jack despised those hunters who pointed their guns into the air and hoped for the best: sure, they might bring one or two down, but there was no skill involved and too much cruelty.

Returning home at lunchtime, this time with the gun unused in its bag, Jack found an envelope lodged behind *Duchesse Anne*'s windscreen wiper. The oversized scrawl and the expensive paper did not need a signature to identify the sender. He dropped his bags down on the deck and, with trembling hands, ripped open the envelope. It's about Stan. It must be. A relapse. Why hadn't he gone to see him in hospital when he received the first letter? He unlocked the wheelhouse door and propped himself up on the stool in front of the wheel. There were two sheets.

My dear Jack,
I was sad we didn't hear back from you. The good

thing is, Stan picked up alright and is now safely back home. He had had a good summer to fall back on, dozing in the garden or watching old films, and I'm sure that helped. How he will get on now the weather has turned is anyone's guess. We'll just take one day at a time, and see what happens. He is in good spirits, and that's the main thing.

He would very much like to see you, and for that matter, so would I. Life is too short to spend playing the blame game so if you could find it in your heart to pay us a visit, you'd be sure of a warm welcome.

As I said before, just pick up the phone and I'll send the car.

Very best wishes,
Russ

Jack carefully folded the sheets and put them back in the envelope. Only then did he notice that there was no stamp. But he did notice the address at the top of the paper. One of the best addresses in East London, where the gardens back directly onto woodland forming part of Epping Forest.

Russ had clearly struck lucky somewhere along the line. But then, he usually did.

*

Jack stood at the counter in the Old Smack watching Katie pour perfect pints for the only other two customers in the pub. He picked up his glass and took a long draught. He'd been up since before dawn, and in the normal way he would have told himself he'd earned a decent pint and a good lunch. But this wasn't in the normal way of things and he wasn't there for the food or the ale. He needed to find out who had tucked that wretched letter under *Duchesse Anne*'s windscreen wiper.

Why did it matter? The letter was there and had done its dirty work. The joy of the morning had been shattered in an instant.

What if Russ himself had put it there? What if, instead of being out there on the marsh trying to decide whether or not to take up wildfowling again, he'd been sitting quietly in the wheelhouse reading his charts and Russ had appeared on the foredeck? If he'd looked up and seen Russ's round smiling face staring through the window at him? What would he have done? Pushed him over the side? Picked up his gun and ordered him off the boat? Invited him below for a cup of tea?

Now here he was sitting uncomfortably on a bar stool desperate to know how the letter got there but unable to ask Katie if she knew anything about it without appearing to be a fussy old git.

"You found your letter, then?" she said, returning to his end of the bar to ring up the till for the other customers' drinks.

"Oh, yeah. Did you see who delivered it, by the way?"

"I did."

"Sorry?"

She looked up from the till. Jack waited for one of her melodramatic sighs.

"I said, I did. I popped it across after some chap came asking after you. If I'd known you were coming in I could have saved myself the walk."

"What chap?"

"No idea who he was. Smartly dressed. Gammy leg. That's all I noticed, really. Came in, asked if I knew you, and where your boat was. I started to explain and then thought, with that leg he shouldn't be climbing up and down the sea wall, and risking his life on your rickety old gangplank, so I said I would drop it off for him. He seemed a bit reluctant, to be honest.

"He said thank you, nice enough, ordered a coffee but then didn't stay long enough to drink it. Didn't say much. Nice car, though."

"What did he look like?"

"I told you. Gammy leg. Nothing special about him. Could be a chauffeur. Cockney."

"Was it a big chap in a cashmere overcoat?"

Katie sighed.

"Captain, listen, I told you. He was just an ordinary sort of bloke with a bad leg. Not big, not small. Just average. But as I said, he drove a really nice car."

"What sort? Was it a black Range Rover by any chance?"

"No. More like a Jaguar or something like that. Maybe a Lexus. I don't know. Dark blue. Or maybe green. What does it matter? Now, if you've finished the third degree, are you ready to order? We had some mussels fresh in this morning from Mersea. Where are you sitting?"

Jack eyed a copy of the *Daily Mail* on the counter, and thought better of it.

"I'll have the mussels. And chips. I'll sit where I always sit," he grunted, heading for the seat by the fire, wishing he was no longer there.

So was it Russ who drove all the way down from London, looking for him? Just to tell him that Stan was back home, having made a miraculous recovery from pneumonia? It made no sense.

However irritated he felt by Russ's incursion, he was relieved on one level that Stan hadn't died. But the fact remained that he didn't want to see any of them. Especially not Russ or Bel. Fifty years hadn't healed the wound.

Over on the other side of the bar two middle-aged men

25

were talking about going fishing. It sounded like a business lunch, for the discussion veered off past fishing glories into delivery schedules and prices. Jack didn't want to listen, but one of them had a voice that demanded to be heard. He wished they would just go away, or shut up.

"Here you are, Captain." Katie put the mussels and chips down in front of him. The chips were in a miniature galvanised bucket. He tipped them out onto the plate. Why did even decent pubs insist on serving simple food in bizarre containers? Weird.

He often teased Katie about it but today he wasn't in the mood. He tried to picture Stan as an old man, and for a while nothing came. But the mussels were good. Very good, in fact. He downed the rest of his pint and tried to catch Katie's eye. Usually he didn't drink at all at lunchtime, or if he did, limited himself to one pint. But today he fancied a second, particularly as the two bragging fishermen had pretty much stopped talking as they tucked into their sirloins and chips.

He pictured Stan as he was when he last saw him, before the wedding, and then tried to adjust for the passing of time. He wouldn't have lost that cheeky smile, surely? His hair, if he still had any, would be white but his eyes would be clear. Jack pictured a dapper old chap, neatly dressed in a nice jumper and cord trousers. Whatever he looked like, Jack was sure Stan would still be the good-natured cockney "sparrer" he always was. A winkles for Sunday tea man with a witty answer to every question.

It would be good to see him, really good. But he couldn't face the others, no matter what. So that was that.

His second pint arrived. Katie removed the empty plates and the bowl piled high with mussel shells.

"Would you like the paper, Captain?" she asked over

her shoulder as she headed back towards the door that led to the kitchen.

"Not if all you have is the *Daily Mail*."

She disappeared through the door without replying. Across the room, the other customers had finished eating and were putting on their coats to leave. The one with the demanding voice went to the bar to pay. The other one walked up to Jack's table and offered him a newspaper.

"Today's *Telegraph* if you would prefer it. It was a Jag, by the way."

"Sorry?"

"The car the gammy leg bloke was driving. Dark blue Jag."

Jack took the paper and murmured, "Thank you."

Two minutes later, both the men had gone. The fire crackled in the grate. It was beginning to grow dark outside.

*

Back on board *Duchesse Anne*, Jack lit the stove and read the letter again. Well, Russ could just sod off. First Stan was supposed to be at death's door. Now he was better. Not bad for a man in his nineties.

He went out on deck. Beyond the river wall, behind the lattice of horse chestnut trees, the coloured lights of the Old Smack flickered on, spreading a glow into the darkening sky. The river ran swift and dark. He returned to the wheelhouse, wishing he had a cigarette to smoke, even though he hadn't touched one in twenty years. He cleared condensation from the glass and switched on the windscreen wiper. Midstream, the number 8 buoy blinked its green light. The kettle whistled, summoning him back to the snug warmth of the cabin.

So, how had Russ made his money? Jack typed "Brian Russell" into Google. There were any number of Brian

Russells, none of whom seemed likely. Dozens of faces stared out at him from the screen, none of them the Russ he knew. Until, on the second or third page, there he was: "Brian Russell, Chairman, Russell Homes". That was him, alright, the boy's face still visible underneath the puffy skin. That smug, self-satisfied expression on his face that so many people, including his own *maman*, would describe as charm.

So Russ had become a property developer, and a successful one at that, it seemed.

No surprise there, then. Russ always ended up smelling of roses, no matter whom else he left in the shit.

Russ was not especially clever but, boy, was he determined. What Russ wanted, Russ got. Unless he'd changed over time, he would persist until Jack gave in. There would be more letters. But Russ was not the only one who could be determined.

Worrying about what it was that Russ wanted was not, however, going to help. From his CD rack he pulled out Mozart's *Requiem*. The hi-fi might be getting on a bit, but it could still pump out enough volume to hurt his ears. The Choir and Orchestra of the Academy of Ancient Music roared through *Duchesse Anne*'s old hull. The stove clicked as the heat built up inside. He pulled the cork on a nice bottle of red and set it on the little rosewood table beside his chair.

After his lunchtime *moules frites*, he did not need to eat another meal that day. He had a nice wedge of Montgomery cheddar in the fridge. That would be enough with an apple, a cox from his own tree at the allotment, and some fresh bread. Jack had baked nearly all his own bread since he retired from the local paper eleven years earlier. A kilo of strong flour from the mill at Kelsale, a packet of easy-blend dried yeast, a bit of hard work and you can produce the best bread you can find anywhere.

He poured the flour into a big mixing bowl, which he put on the top of the stove to warm. Mozart was, as ever, working his magic. Jack lit the oven on the little butane stove. In an hour's time he would be able to enjoy the wonderful aroma of baking bread. Meanwhile, he would open up his bag and put the gun away, clean his boots and try to decide whether or not he would go shooting the next day.

While he left the dough to rise he went up to the wheelhouse, turned the master switch to "port", and put in the ignition key. First to the right. Count twenty to warm the plugs. Turn the key to the left. Beneath his feet, the first engine roared into life. He pushed back the throttle, listening as the revs dropped to a comfortable burble. He repeated the starting procedure for the starboard engine.

Oil pressure on both engines was excellent. The tanks were half full of diesel, enough to take him across the Channel. All he had to do was cast off. Let go forward. Drop back and let the stern line take the strain. Tweak the wheel to starboard. Wait while the stem edged out into the current. Then let go aft before she turned too far. Full ahead both engines. Simple. Anyone could do it.

He switched on the Decca, and then the radar. The green line revolved around the screen. There were the few yachts still on their moorings, but nothing moved on the river.

He shut down the engines, switched off the radar and the Decca. So, Russ wanted something. Tough. Jack Boyer was not bending to Brian Russell's will. He went below and attacked the dough, stretching it out and knocking it back again.

Stan had worked in the local baker's all his life. Dear Stan. Jack didn't owe Russ anything, not a single thing after what he did. But Stan was a different matter. He couldn't just ignore him, could he?

Four

Jack arrived on Alison's doorstep, his breath floating upwards into the still, cold, morning air. He noted the neat garden, the ramblers newly pruned and the lawn edged, and paused, inhaling deeply, absorbing the scent of newly turned soil, getting his breath back.

Before his hand touched the shiny brass knocker, a smiling Alison O'Rourke opened the door.

"Jack, come on in," she said. "I've just made a fresh pot."

He pulled off his gloves and, ducking his head to avoid the low beams, stepped into the warmth of the little sitting room, which he'd often imagined, but never before entered. He felt too big for the space, afraid he might knock something over.

"Hope I'm not too early? I did warn Katie that I'd be round about now. You didn't need it, I hope? Because I could always go by train…" He was babbling.

Alison touched his arm, as a mother might to calm her child.

"No, Jack, I don't need the car today." She followed Jack's gaze around the room, as if she, too, was seeing it for the first time. Jack did the same when he allowed anybody to go below on *Duchesse Anne*, striving to see her through the visitor's eyes. Alison began to move things around on the coffee table.

"She just drops the keys anywhere when she comes in. You wouldn't believe how much time we waste looking for them." She moved a newspaper, that day's *Daily Mail.* "Oh, here they are."

Jack made to take them, and then realised they were not actually being offered. He caught a glimpse of himself in the mirror above the little enamelled stove, in which, despite the early hour, a fire burned behind tiny mica windows. His face was red and his hair needed cutting.

"Thanks, Alison, I'll get out of your way now. Do you need it back by any particular time?"

"No, anytime will do. I'm not going anywhere and Katie is working lunchtime and tonight. Now, what about that cuppa?" She closed her hand around the keys and put them in her apron pocket. Jack unwound his scarf and followed her into the kitchen. The table was set with two places. Butter in a little dish, marmalade, cups and saucers, a jug of milk, the scent of toast. The dog asleep in her basket. "Let's take your coat," she said. "Now. Sit yourself down. Have you had breakfast?"

"I don't want to, well, impose. The table's already set for you and Katie."

Two slices of healthy-looking bread popped from the toaster. Alison laughed.

"That's not for my daughter. She just grabs something as she walks through the kitchen, and never before half past nine. I just thought you might like something after your walk up the hill, and before you set off, for London, isn't it?"

"Oh, yes." Jack paused. "I need some bits and pieces for the boat." He sat down. The kitchen clock ticked almost in time with the snoring of the dog. Alison put more bread into the toaster.

"How about a nice boiled egg?"

He glanced at his watch.

"That's really kind of you, but, honestly, a piece of toast is quite enough to keep me going." He tapped his belly. "I already had a bowl of porridge this morning. Before I left." He didn't add that he had then poured it over the side of *Duchesse Anne* because he was too wound up to eat it. But sitting here in Alison's kitchen he could feel himself beginning to relax. Why not accept her hospitality, stay and dip buttery soldiers into a bright yellow yolk, sip tea and gossip about village life? But there was no backing out.

The little car, an elderly Renault, started first time. While the engine warmed, he scraped frost from the windows. He pushed the driving seat back as far as it would go, put the Grateful Dead into the stereo, and backed carefully off the drive, pausing to wave to Alison watching from her window.

He had no need for maps. This was his own patch, or used to be. The destination was one of the smartest roads in East London, where big detached houses backed onto the woods. He'd delivered papers up and down that road, possibly even to the house where Russ now lived. Lonnie Donegan had one of the big houses – he took the *Times*, the *Daily Sketch* and *New Musical Express* and *Melody Maker*. But in the three years that Jack delivered newspapers to the King of Skiffle, he never once saw him. Not a glimpse.

Sooner than he wanted, Jack found himself crossing the Rabbits Road bridge over the Liverpool Street mainline. He parked beside the gates to the City of London Cemetery, another place to which he once delivered newspapers. It had taken all his courage to push open the side gate on a misty morning and enter the domain of the dead.

It was also where Ma Vinney had been laid to rest.

He planned to walk the rest of the way, down the bridle path where, fifty years earlier, he and Russ could slip through a gap in the railings to put their penny pieces on the railway track. But the path wasn't the pleasant route it had been. It was rough underfoot. Littered with empty lager cans. Fast food debris. After 200 yards, he'd had enough and turned back.

When he got back to the car, he stood for fully two minutes jiggling the keys in his pocket. He didn't want to take the car, but time was moving on.

Two minutes' drive took him to the top of Shaftesbury Crescent. The black and white tea shop on the corner had become a betting shop. That must have upset a few people. The street was not, after all, particularly wide, and with cars parked on both sides, there was scarcely room for two vehicles to pass. But it was still lined with plane trees and the houses were built to impress. Curved "in and out" gravelled drives fronted the solid Edwardian architecture of bay windows and elaborate gable ends. This was where criminals and footballers lived. Parked out front were black Range Rovers with tinted windows, Porsches and Mercedes jostling for space with the builders' vans.

He drove slowly, watching for the numbers. Just as he remembered, the evens were on the right, where the owners could slip through their own back gates, directly into the woods to walk their pedigree Alsations or pit bulls. Number 42 looked as quietly prosperous as all the others. Through the metal gates he could see a dark blue Jaguar.

After following the road around the sweeping curve he

found a place to park. He switched off the engine. What now? So Russ lived in a big house? He already knew that. Unless he was prepared to knock on Russ's door, he'd done all that he could. A wasted journey.

But if he sat there much longer, some enthusiastic busybody from Neighbourhood Watch might call the police. That he couldn't risk. He started the engine and turned it off again. Better to walk. To stroll past Russ's house in the hope of getting a peek into the windows. It meant, however, running the risk of being seen, or even bumping into Russ or any others of the crowd who used to hang around together. Roy Glover, for instance. Or, even worse, Bel.

Could he cope with that? No, of course he couldn't. He was just a sad old paranoid bastard who was too stupid to let go of a version of the past that bathed him in righteous hurt. However unlikely, Russ may just want friendship. So why couldn't he just walk quietly up to Russ's front door, ring the bell, and see what happens?

He climbed out of the car, stretched his back and locked the door. But he didn't walk, or even stroll, past Russ's house, let alone knock on his door. Instead, he took a circuitous route that avoided most of Shaftesbury Crescent and brought him out on the busy road that ran alongside Wanstead Flats.

Half a mile away, across the scrubby grass, beyond the pond, was the shop that had once been Ma Vinney's. The same shop where Bel had worked on Saturdays, just a few doors away from the prefab in which she lived. Jack hadn't been near the shop since the night Ma Vinney died. Even when he finished his National Service, after all the horrors he had seen and done in Cyprus, he never ventured within half a mile of the place.

But today, he felt drawn to it. He could maybe lay the

ghost of the whole Ma Vinney cock-up. Walk right up, bold as brass, push open the door, go in and buy something. A bar of Dairy Milk maybe. And then, at least, the journey would not have been a total waste of time.

He waited for a gap in the traffic and dashed across the road. Striding out across the grass his legs seemed to get longer. He could breathe more easily. He could smile at the little hills, the "Sandhills", which had once seemed so steep. Something positive could come out of this day after all. It wasn't going to be comfortable, but then he didn't need comfort. He needed closure.

He walked to the top of the bigger of the two hills. The Flats was an island of green in a sea of houses with Marley-tiled roofs. Once he had dealt with Ma Vinney, he would tackle the Russ issue. Simply knock on Russ's door: "I was just passing so thought I'd look in to see how Stan was doing."

And if Bel happened to be there, well. "Thanks, Bel, I would love a cup of tea."

As he drew closer to where the shop and the prefabs had been, he could see that it had all changed. The pair of semi-detached cottages in front of which the shop had been built was no longer there. Neither were the prefabs. In their place a block of low-rise flats had arrived. There were no demons to confront – they'd been swept away to make way for council housing.

He turned and headed back towards the cemetery, where, with luck, he might be able to get that cup of tea he was not going to get from Bel. But the bounce had already gone from his step, and the day seemed dull again, as if a cloud had gone over the sun.

The cemetery cafeteria was surprisingly busy. He ordered tea, and sat at an empty table, watching other customers with their black ties and sad faces, wishing he was back beside his river. He pushed the tea away – it was far too hot and he wanted to get on the move again. One last look at the house, he told himself, and back home. No need to knock on the door. Nothing lost. But then he had another idea.

Fifteen minutes later, he was back at Shaftesbury Crescent, passing Russ's house in the car. Nothing had changed in the intervening hour or so. He drove as far as the park entrance, stopped and put on the black beret bought in Brittany many years earlier. He wound his scarf around his neck, covering his nose and mouth. It was cold, after all, so it shouldn't attract attention.

Little in the park was how it used to be. The boats had gone from the concrete pond, along with most of the water. The dribble that was left had frozen solid. Along the path behind the houses, fallen leaves and heavy rain had created a mush, rutted with enough tyre tracks to suggest that today's kids were as keen as their grandfathers had been on riding their bikes through the dark tunnels of trees.

He passed the first of the garden gates. Why did someone bother to put a hardened steel chain and five-lever padlock onto a gate in the final stages of rotting away? He slurped or crunched on, depending on how hard the ground had frozen. Either way, slipping over felt more a certainty than a possibility. He counted down the house numbers. Most gates were overgrown or simply nailed up.

But 42 stood out. Newly varnished and with the number proudly displayed alongside a "Private Property" sign in bright red. A gentle push: locked. Footprints and wheel tracks in the mud showed that the entrance was regularly used.

By standing on a log, he should just be able to peep over. He looked up and down the path, listening hard. But other than the occasional rustle of the few leaves still to fall from the trees, and the distant hum of the M11 motorway, nothing stirred. He stepped up onto the log and steadied himself by holding onto the top of the gate. A few feet at the bottom of the garden had been allowed to go wild. Beyond, he could see a lawn dotted with trees, a pond with a fountain, smooth paved paths. A weak December sun reflected off a Victorian-style conservatory spanning the full width of the house. To one side stood a garage, while to the other was an extension big enough to be a home in its own right.

He was about to leave, to push the log back into the undergrowth, when somebody came out of the garage and, without hurrying, began walking towards him. A limp gave him away as the deliverer of the letters Katie had described. It was not Russ.

Jack stepped off the log, kicking it to the side of the path. Slipping and sliding he hurried back, looking for somewhere to hide. He heard the buzz of an electronic lock and ducked behind a dead tree. A male voice called out, "Anyone there?"

Jack didn't dare move until he heard the click of the gate being relocked. Only when he stepped out from his hiding place did he spot the CCTV camera mounted above the gate, pointing right at him. Without a sound, it swung slowly away.

Pargeter's School, 1954

Jack wrote the last *passé composé, j'ai joué*, onto the test paper and looked at the clock above the teacher's head. Why did it move so slowly? Still another ten wasted minutes before the bell would ring and lessons would be over. He couldn't wait to get into his whites and out to the nets. He was on form for a perfect season, and summer would not go on for ever. Next year he should make the first team.

A knock on the classroom door sounded sharp against the torpor of the warm afternoon.

"Come," snapped Jones, the French teacher. Everybody turned their head to see who it was, grateful for any interruption to the tedium of being tested on French grammar. The door opened a fraction; a bony hand appeared through the crack, beckoning to the teacher.

At the end of a long hot day the absence of a master allowed a much-needed break. A couple of boys came up to Jack's desk to help with questions they couldn't answer. Others started flicking ink pellets. An arm wrestle left undecided earlier was restarted. Porter pulled out a copy of *Health and Efficiency* and unbuttoned his flies.

Jones reappeared and the noise subsided. He looked straight at Jack, raising his eyebrows.

"*Tu as fini?*"

Jack jumped to his feet.

"*Oui, Professeur.*"

"Thought you would. Not much of a test for you, was it, Boyer? Anyway, bring your paper here and pop along to the headmaster's study, there's a good chap."

Jack picked up his paper and took it to Jones' desk. Boys started to whisper.

"Settle down now, it's nothing to get excited about," said Jones.

Outside the classroom he found Miss Pointer, the school secretary. She gave him a smile and went ahead. Jack felt a knot in his stomach. So what did the Old Man want him for? Had somebody reported him for smoking or seen him over the fields when he should have been at prep.

"Don't worry," she said, clicking along a few feet ahead of him, "you're not in trouble."

He followed her down the long corridor, enjoying the cool breeze coming through the open windows. A sudden burst of shouting from outside. He rubbed his hands on the back of his shorts as they turned the last corner and were confronted by the solid oak door to the headmaster's study. Outside stood a boy from the fifth year, holding the blue cloth-bound punishment book, in which Jack's name had appeared only twice. So far.

Miss Pointer tapped on the door, opened it and strode in. Jack waited.

"What you up for?" said the boy.

Jack was about to reply when he heard a muffled "Come in, Boyer" from within. He pushed open the heavy door and there, sitting one each side of the headmaster's desk, were Stan and Emm. Stan had on his suit, Emm her best summer dress. But it was not what they were wearing that he first noticed, it was the expressions on their faces.

He concentrated on a small round tray on the desk and tried to close his ears. There were three teacups, a milk jug and a teapot. One of the cups had lipstick on it, the same bright red as Emm's. She leaned forward and brushed a stray lock of hair from Jack's eyes.

The head half smiled at Jack, picked up a pencil, and twirled it between his fingers.

"It's about your mother, Boyer. I'm afraid there's been an accident."

St Pabu, Brittany, France, 1954

The battered green Citroen crested a hill, passing a village

39

sign. After two days' travel, they had reached St Pabu. Below them, like dominoes standing on end, stood row upon row of tombstones. So many graves for such a small village.

A knot of people had gathered at the crossroads, obviously watching for the arrival of the old car and the boy from England that none of them had ever seen. The car slowed to a halt outside a bar and the driver climbed out, stretching his back.

Jack had imagined a graveyard like the City of London Cemetery. Green grass, old trees, ancient warm yellow headstones tipping at crazy angles, tombs surrounded by rusting iron railings. Mellow walls, the sound of summer birds. The chapel in the middle. Instead, here were hard black stones, set alongside straight paths of grey gravel. Not a single tree interrupted the angular layout. No sound could be heard other than hushed chatter of the crowd and the slow dismal ring of the church bell. There must have been somewhere better to leave Maman, surely, but it was too late now. Emm, sitting silently in the back, leaned forward and squeezed his shoulder.

"Best foot forward, love. Make Maman proud of you in front of her family. What do you think happens now?"

Jack could smell the wine on Emm's breath. The driver had insisted they stop at a bar somewhere between the hotel in Brest and the village. Dutch courage, Emm said.

Healthy, country faces peered in through the windows. A young man, not many years older than Jack, tapped on the window. Jack began winding down the glass, but the young man shook his head and opened the door.

Jack climbed out. A very old woman came forward, her arms outstretched, and pulled him into a tight embrace. Emm remained stock still in the back of the Citroen. Somebody opened her door and it was her turn to face the crowd.

"Thank you, Jacques," the old lady was saying, "thank you for bringing her home." She hesitated, closed her eyes and swayed a little, backwards and forwards as if she was about to faint. She held tightly onto both his hands, pulled him closer and whispered in his ear. "And you are such a fine boy. We never knew. After the war, she came home sometimes. We never knew why she went away so suddenly. Why didn't she tell us?"

It was only then that he noticed the horse-drawn carriage on which rested the coffin. The young man who had opened the car door took up a position next to him and offered his hand. He spoke in French.

"I am Yann, one of your cousins. I will tell you what to do. First we follow the carriage to the church and then walk behind when the coffin is taken to the grave. You throw a handful of earth onto the coffin and then we all go for lunch."

Emm was hanging onto Jack's arm.

"What's he saying?" When Jack explained, she seemed to relax a little.

The whole thing took far less time than Jack had expected. The curious thing was, he didn't shed a tear throughout the service, and came close to it only when he threw the earth down into the grave.

Lunch was at the bar and seemed to involve the whole village. Emm had been taken over by one of Jack's elderly relatives who spoke reasonable English, and Jack was sat next to Yann.

At the end of the meal, Yann signalled to Jack that they could leave the table.

"Come," he whispered, "there's something I want to show you." Without another word, the two boys slipped away, through the open door and headed downhill.

At the river bank they came to a ramshackle shed at the top of a cobbled jetty. Yann went inside and emerged with two pairs of stiff yellow trousers.

"Put them on over your clothes, and then we'll find you some boots," he said. "You look like one of us now, Jacques, except, *mon ami*, you are too tall and too blond. Careful, now, as we go down. The ramp is slippery."

Small boats bumped each other as they lay tied to iron rings set in the jetty. Waves lapped gently against their painted hulls. Across the river, trees hung over the bank. Why had Maman left this beautiful place for the shabby East End of London? Swapped a big, warm and comfortable family for a lonely life in Manor Park, doing whatever menial work she could find?

The boats were rough and ready, not at all like the ones on the park lakes back in London. Some had masts and thick canvas sails folded against their bottom boards, others were simply rowing boats. A few had outboard motors. A smell of seaweed, fish and petrol filled his nostrils.

Near the end of the jetty, Yann stepped down into a small sailing boat that was a little cleaner than the others. Jack followed him into the boat and was told to sit beside the mast. Yann handed Jack a rope and told him to pull. As he pulled, Jack watched, fascinated, as a brown sail rose up the mast, flapping in the light breeze. Before he realised quite what was happening, Yann had untied them from the jetty and they were moving out into the river.

Jack grasped the sides of the boat as it leaned to the breeze. The sail stopped flapping and they were speeding towards the open sea. Jack relaxed. Yann knew what he was doing.

"Where are we going?"

"To check the pots. Papa will be too drunk to sail this

evening, after all the wine. We still have a living to make. Do you like crab?"

Within a few minutes they were beyond the steep wooded banks of the estuary and the boat began to bounce in the waves. Jack glanced at his cousin, confident in the stern, who handed him a wooden pole, worn smooth by years of use, at the end of which was a rusty hook.

"When we come beside the flag, you catch the rope under the buoy with the hook, OK? Go to the front."

A yellow triangle of cloth, more rag than flag, fluttered in the breeze on the end of a short stick, no more than fifty yards away. They were still speeding along, so how on earth was Jack meant to catch the rope? Suddenly, Yann pushed the tiller right over. The sail began to flap and the boat stopped, the flag within easy reach. Jack captured the rope, handed it to Yann who hauled until a round basket appeared just below the surface.

Yann pulled it aboard. Inside four brown creatures with a multitude of legs and claws struggled over each other, claws snapping at thin air.

"Can you help me get them out?"

Jack looked at the prehistoric creatures and shook his head.

Yann put in his hand and picked up the first crab, its legs thrashing and pincers snapping. Its body was the size of a dinner plate.

"Is that really a crab?" Jack asked. He remembered when he and Maman caught the train to Leigh-on-Sea, and sat outside a shed from which fishy steam billowed. She ordered a crab and when it arrived it was no bigger than a saucer. She started to laugh and then just burst into tears. Now he knew why.

Other small boats emerged from the river mouth, heading off in various directions.

"The meal must be over," said Yann. They went from flag to flag, until they had about twenty crabs in the box. The little boat skipped across the waves.

Jack belonged here, out on the estuary, the spray on his face, the wind in his hair and a box of restless crabs at his feet. Not at a snooty private school in London. He never wanted to go back.

Five

Four days after his visit to Wanstead, Jack found himself halfway down the sea wall, club hammer in hand, strengthening *Duchesse Anne*'s moorings. A storm had been brewing in the Western Approaches for days, and it was on the move. A real hoolie.

As he worked, he planned his next *Anglia Life* column. "Savage Beauty: Storm in the Estuary".

The crack of a twelve bore sent the waders up in the air. What an afternoon to be shooting: the birds making their return from the mudflats and sandbanks to roost, flying low because of the weather. Perfect. Some lucky beggar was out there on the marsh, enjoying himself.

It could have been him out there. It should have been. It was worth another try, surely?

He brought the hammer down hard. One point eight kilos of cold forged steel impacted on the length of white-painted scaffold pole, which sank another inch into the earth. The nearby waders again took flight, circled and returned to the mud. Jack stared downriver. Crabtree Island was barely visible through the murk. The poplar tree that had stood beside the sea wall since Jack first came to live at East Stone creaked and groaned in the strengthening wind. It would not see many more winters. Not many more storms.

A flight of geese appeared beyond the far bank. A second crack, softer than the first, sounded across the marshes. Jack put down the hammer and stretched his back, looking for the Labrador or spaniel rushing to retrieve a brent or a graylag from the water's edge. He saw neither. They must be shooting right over at the creek. Odd how far sound carries sometimes.

The first few fat raindrops smacked down onto the dusty path of the sea wall. Behind the dank aroma of mud and seaweed, Jack could smell the approaching storm. He could taste it in the air. Along the tideline, oystercatchers and redshanks picked frantically, eating all they could find before they would need to seek shelter. The shrouds on the dinghies behind the sea wall smacked against their masts.

A fierce squall raced upriver. The light was fading and Jack was getting wet. But it was glorious – the howling of the wind and the sting of clean rain against his dry skin. Beyond the marshes, past the army firing range, he could make out the orange glow of the little seaside resort where, decades ago, he and Russ had enjoyed so much innocent naughtiness. Cheating the Penny Grab machine on the pier, stealing postcards, reprogramming jukeboxes after somebody else had paid their money.

But he'd done enough work for one afternoon. *Duchesse Anne* was not going anywhere, no matter how fierce the storm. He picked up his tools. Time to put that shepherd's pie into the oven and open a simple red before settling down to enjoy the gentle rocking of *Duchesse Anne* and the roar of the gale powering and colouring his column.

His hand was on the handle of the wheelhouse door when he heard a car coming down the lane. Curious, he stood and watched. Headlights briefly lit up the front of the Old Smack. In the fading light he could make out the unmistakeable shape of a Jaguar XJ as it came to a stop outside the pub. The driver got out and went to the pub doorway.

Jack reached inside the wheelhouse door and, without taking his eyes off the pub, groped around until his hand found the binoculars he always kept on the chart table. Light spilled from the open pub door. Vapour spewed from the car's exhaust. Through his binoculars he saw the driver turn and walk back to the car. Jack had not been able to see his face, but the man had a pronounced limp. The car turned smartly around. Jack watched as its tail lights danced up the bumpy lane as far as the smooth tarmac, then grew smaller and disappeared as the Jaguar accelerated away into the night.

He slid the wheelhouse door open, closed it behind him and went below. He lit the stove and the butane cooker. Russ was not going to make him change his plans. He peeled off his muddy *vareuse* and trousers, stuffing them into the washing machine. He took a shower and dressed.

Already the waves on the river were man enough to make themselves heard through *Duchesse Anne*'s heavy hull. Some gusts of wind puffed smoke back into the cabin. He looked along his collection of CDs. If ever there was a night for *Ride of the Valkyries,* this was it, even though he didn't usually play anything by the anti-semitic son of the Leipzig policeman.

He cranked up the volume until he could no longer hear the storm outside and began to write. Only when he had finished the first draft of his column, eaten his pie and consumed half the bottle was he going to go and get the latest bloody letter. He'd had enough of dancing to Russ's tunes.

Around nine o'clock, he closed the lid of his laptop, pleased with his work. He wanted to help readers appreciate what it was like to revel in the harshness of nature, to feel, but not fear, its power. To convey to them the extraordinary taste you find on your lips when exposed to a storm at the coast. The piece was nearly there. Wagner had given way to Schubert a couple of hours earlier, as he thought some *Impromptus* might be a better accompaniment to his supper.

He waited until the final chords of the "Number 4" faded away and put another couple of logs into the stove. The cabin would be warm when he returned.

The pub was empty. Who in their right mind would want to turn out on a night like that: freezing rain propelled by gale force winds? Only somebody who needed to be there. To collect a letter, say. And there it was, propped up against the Arrowroot biscuit jar. Why not simply walk to that end of the bar, pick it up and put it straight on the fire?

Katie looked up from her *Giant Book of Sudoku Puzzles*.

"Wasn't sure even you would be in tonight, Captain," she said, putting a pint glass – a straight glass, rather than the chunky tankards that most people seemed to prefer – under the Norfolk Wherry pump. "Nasty old night, eh?"

Jack smiled.

"Depends on your taste, Katie dear. I love it. Fantastic. As a matter of fact, I've just spent the last two hours or more writing my column, trying to describe what it is about a storm on the coast that is, well, magnificent."

She slid the pint across the bar.

"You're a strange one, Jack, to be sure. It's on the house, by the way."

"Any particular reason?"

"I want tonight to be the first evening that I've put absolutely nothing at all into that till."

Jack took his first mouthful.

"And you say I'm the strange one!"

Katie picked up her pencil and resumed puzzling. The cream envelope lolled up against the biscuit jar, like some truculent teenager. The old clock ticked the seconds away. A strong gust sent woodsmoke into the bar. The windows rattled. Jack examined his own reflection in the polished glass behind the bar.

"Want to do one?" Katie asked, pushing the puzzle book his way. Surely she'd remember soon that a letter had been delivered for him. He didn't want to ask for it. Why ask for something you didn't want?

"Thanks," he replied, picking up the pencil and flicking the book open at random. Katie walked to the far end of the bar and lifted the flap that would allow her into the public side of the room. This had to be it – she would have to walk right past the Arrowroot jar, would remember the letter and bring it to him. For a moment, it looked as if she would pass right by the jar without pausing. But she stopped, picked it up and slid herself onto the stool beside his, placing it face up on the counter.

"There you are, Captain, somebody loves you. Besides me and Mum's dog, anyway."

Jack did his best to smile, picked up the envelope and tapped it, edge on, on the counter. Should he open it now, in front of Katie, or simply slide it into his waistcoat pocket? He did neither, but tapped it on the counter again.

"Was it the chauffeur, or whatever he is, brought it? Like last time?"

"Same as before, Captain. Her Ladyship must be right keen on you to keep sending him down like this."

"In your dreams, Katie. If you only knew."

He folded the envelope in two and put it into his

waistcoat pocket, pulled the puzzle book towards him, opened it at the first unattempted puzzle and began to look for a pattern in the numbers, aware that Katie was watching his every move.

He downed the last of his pint and looked up from his puzzle.

"Am I allowed another pint, or will that muck up your determination to put nothing in the till tonight?"

The pub door swung open and one of the shipwrights from the yard strode in, coat dripping water, but his face split with the broadest smile.

"Might have guessed you'd be in here, Jack Boyer. When I saw there was a bit of a breeze blowing I thought I'd better just run down and have a check on the moorings. A pint of the usual, please, Katie love."

"All OK, then, John?" Jack asked, grateful to escape the puzzle book.

"All good, Jack." He smiled. "Didn't even need to get the launch out. Another for you?"

"I wouldn't say no."

"And one for yourself, Katie love."

Katie called time early, shortly before ten o'clock. Jack said goodnight to John. He stood outside, listening to all the sounds of a dying storm, while watching John walk back up the lane, home to his comfortable wife, the few remaining minutes of *News at Ten* and maybe a small Scotch to round off the evening. Jack pulled his coat around him but the wind, although strong enough to have brought down a carpet of loose branches from the old trees, was not cold. The feel of a true southwesterly. Wet and warm.

From the car park he could hear the slap of waves against the jetty, the sough of wind in the trees, the angry clank of halliards against masts and the squeaking of the old pub sign as it swung back and forth, back and forth. He took the envelope, identical to the other two, from his waistcoat pocket. It had to be faced. He slid his finger under the flap, pulled out the single sheet of expensive cream paper and, by the light of the porch, began to read.

Dear Jack,

We were pleased to see you looking so well the other day. You've taken care of yourself. We tried to catch up with you before you left, but neither of us can move very fast these days. Why don't you come and see us? We'd love that. I can send the car to get you.

Your lifelong friend,

Russ

The cold feeling began in the pit of his stomach. It spread down his thighs and up between his shoulder blades. He turned and walked slowly in the direction of the sea wall, the letter held tightly in his hand, as if his life depended upon it.

East London, 1954

The train stopped just beyond Stratford. Emm looked at her watch.

"Oh, get a bloody move on," she muttered. And then to Jack, "Anyway, I can't see why we've got to traipse all the way up to London to see some solicitor."

Jack looked up from his book, *Bleak House*, which had to be finished before he went back to school. The train jerked forward.

"We'll know soon enough, Auntie."

She looked at her watch again.

"Should still be in good time, no thanks to British Railways. Probably nothing to worry about, is it?" She took the letter from her bag and read it through. She patted his hand. Dickens' words were becoming difficult to absorb.

The solicitor's office was directly opposite Liverpool Street station. "Bernard and Company, Solicitors. Commissioners for Oaths". The door was next to a tailor's shop.

"Doesn't look much, does it?" whispered Emm as she pushed against the brown door. It didn't budge. She tried the bell push. Somewhere deep inside a bell rang and shortly afterwards a shadow appeared through the mottled glass. The door opened to the squeak of hinges crying out for oil. Before them stood a tall man with glasses so thick his eyes were the size of gobstoppers. So this was the mysterious Mr Bernard.

Bernard smiled and extended his hand.

"Mrs Donovan, so good to meet you. And Jack, please come along in. Make yourselves comfortable." They shook hands in turn and followed Bernard through to his dusty office. Two ancient dining chairs, one with the stuffing hanging out, stood in front of a large desk piled high with books and files. A fireplace displayed the remains of a long dead fire.

Emm perched on the edge of her chair, hands clutching her bag.

"So what are you reading, young man?" Bernard's deep brown teeth reminded Jack of the headstones in St Pabu. The office smelled of the same cigarettes as the buses that came from the docks. A packet of Capstan Full Strength lay open on the desk.

Jack showed him the book.

"*Bleak House*, sir."

"Aha. Did you know Mr Dickens was once a solicitor's clerk?"

"No, sir."

"Well, he was. You can tell that to your English master. Have you met Mr Perker?"

Jack swivelled around, expecting to see another person in the room. Seeing nobody, he shook his head.

"Then you should read *Pickwick Papers*." He turned his attention to Emm. "Now, what about some tea?"

Emm nodded, swallowed and managed a hoarse, "That would be very nice."

Bernard pushed a button on one of the telephones, the colour of which matched his teeth. Exactly.

"Yes, Mr Bernard?"

Without picking up the receiver, he asked the woman to bring in tea. Jack thought it might be fun, being a solicitor.

Bernard opened the file and appeared to be reading. They all sat without speaking for what seemed minutes, listening to the slow rhythm of a grandfather clock. Then the tea arrived and the woman made a business of pouring a cup each for Jack and Emm before leaving, shutting the door carefully behind her. Finally, Bernard snapped the file shut and took off his glasses.

"Now then, Jack, you're twelve now, is that right?"

Jack nodded.

"And how is school going? Are you keeping up alright?"

"Yes, sir." What on earth was school to do with him? Jack searched his mind for something he may have done wrong, but found nothing. So, perhaps he wasn't in trouble after all.

Bernard pushed a cup of tea towards Jack. As he leaned forward to pick up the cup, Jack was gripped by the fear he would spill it. He sat back, leaving the cup and saucer on the corner of the desk.

"Now, Jack, as you know, under the law, you are technically a minor. But, despite what the law might say, I believe you are old enough to make your own decisions."

"Am I, sir?"

"What I am hoping we can agree today, without the need to go before the courts, are the plans for your future."

What was he talking about? He looked at Emm.

"I just want things to stay as they are. With Emm and Stan."

Emm coughed and found a small space on Bernard's desk to put down her cup and saucer. Bernard raised his eyebrows.

"What do you feel, Mrs Donovan?"

"Stan and me, well, we want to be sure that the best is done for him. We've talked a lot about it." She reached across to touch Jack's hand.

When Bernard smiled, the wart on his cheek from which three black hairs sprouted changed shape. He turned to Jack.

"Fortunately, young man, my client intends to continue to finance your education at Pargeter's and has asked me to make appropriate arrangements to cover your general welfare."

Emm nodded. Jack looked from one to the other.

"My client has also indicated that if suitable arrangements for your care during school holidays cannot be made in England, he is prepared to finance your travel to and from France where, according to a letter I have received from a firm of notaries in Brest, your late mother's family would be pleased to care for you. For the short breaks," he continued, "we can arrange suitable care in England."

He turned to address Emm.

"It is quite usual, Mrs Donovan. It is something we do for many children whose parents are posted overseas."

"There's no need for that," snapped Emm. "He's got a home with me and Stan for as long as he likes. It's what Nicole would have wanted. We don't need any talk about his going to live in France or anywhere else for that matter. Not for the holidays or any other time." She picked up the cup and saucer, and without so much as a sip put it back on the desk.

"Unfortunately, Mrs Donovan, as far as the law is concerned we do not know what Mrs Boyer would have wanted, as she appears to have died intestate, without a will, that is."

There was a tap at the door and the woman brought in a mug which she placed before Mr Bernard.

"Your coffee, Mr Bernard."

Emm waited until the woman had gone.

"Well of course she didn't make a will. She didn't know she was going to die, did she? Not so young." Jack could hear the slight crack in Emm's voice. He wished she would not get so angry.

Mr Bernard smoothed away non-existent creases in his blotter.

"Well, as I said at the start, I think the decision should be Jack's to make. At least, for him to express a preference. Do you need time to think it over, Jack?"

Jack felt a trickle of sweat run down from under his arms. He looked across at Emm, her face white and her hands beginning to shake. Stan should have been there, too.

He wanted to be 400 miles away, back in France, where he could feel the salt spray on his face, a basket of angry crabs at his feet, the smell of burning seaweed in his nostrils. Allowed to drink a weak evening pastis in the rambling garden overlooking the river.

But beside him, sitting bolt upright, he could hear Emm repeatedly swallowing.

The clock ticked on and on. From its innards came the sound of the mechanism preparing itself to chime, and then the chime itself. Twice for the half-hour.

"There's no need to make a decision right now," said Mr Bernard. "Perhaps you could talk it over with Mrs Donovan and let me know in due course. Meanwhile, the arrangements with Pargeter's will stand."

Jack took a deep breath and looked at Emm.

"There's nothing to think about. As I said, I just want things to stay as they are." Emm reached across the gap between the chairs and touched his hand, but Jack had not finished. "But then, in the summer, could I spend a bit of time in France? I want to visit Maman's grave sometimes. And see my cousin."

Mr Bernard picked up the teapot and grinned.

"I am confident that will be acceptable to my client, but you understand I have to check first. Now, would you like some more tea, Mrs Donovan, while I explain the implications of your acting *in loco parentis*, as Jack's legal guardian? Jack, would you like to wait in the other room? We won't be long."

Jack stood up.

"Do you mind if I ask you a question?"

"What would you like to know?"

"You talked about your client. Who is he?"

Bernard stood up and opened the door that led to the other office.

"I'm afraid I'm not at liberty to discuss that with you at this stage, Jack. I'll pop in and see you before you go."

Six

One by one, the Old Smack's windows went dark until only the light in the porch remained on. The blue tarpaulins flapped and the old sign squeaked back and forth in the wind. Katie came out and was locking the front door when she seemed to sense she was being watched and spun around.

"Oh," she said, "it's only you, Jack. You gave me a bit of a scare for a moment. What are you doing, standing in the middle of the car park?"

He could say, "I thought I might have left my keys in the pub," or "I was watching a fox creeping along the hedge," or "I was just sniffing the air," but he heard himself saying, "It's these letters, Katie. They're from somebody I knew years ago, who wants to make contact again."

She took a couple of steps towards him and tucked her arm in his.

"And you don't?"

"Absolutely not."

"Do you want to talk about it? While you walk me back up the lane. It's not a nice night for a girl to be out on her own."

There was no point in arguing, and anyway, it was nice, Katie being so close, so connected. The wind caught her hair and blew it briefly across his face. He pushed Russ's letter deep into his jacket pocket.

They turned up the lane, the wind in their faces, Katie's hair now streaming out behind her.

"I feel like one of those wooden sculptures they used to fit on the front of sailing ships." She pulled away from him, leaned forward into the wind and allowed her arms to hang loose behind her. "There, Captain, how about putting me on the front of *Duchesse Anne?*"

"You'd get too cold. And in any case, she never goes anywhere. A bit like me, really, I suppose."

She took his arm again.

"So, do you want to tell me what it is about those letters that upsets you so? I'm sorry I made that joke about them, by the way."

"They are from somebody I knew when we were both just kids. You know what it's like, you drift apart, or fall out over something, you move on. And then he pops up. Right out of the blue. Making demands."

She stopped walking.

"What do you mean making demands? Money? Blooming cheek."

"No, not money. I don't know what. Something. He wants me to go and see him and another old chap who used to be a sort of foster father. He's not been well."

"Mum mentioned something about that. So, do you think you should go? Do you think that would stop the other chap bombarding you with letters?"

"I don't know, Katie. I just don't know."

Lights burned in the downstairs window of the cottage Katie and Alison shared.

"Do you want to come in for a moment? Mum will still be up. She never goes to bed until I'm home."

Jack looked at his watch.

"No thanks, I'll be getting back to the boat. But thanks for listening."

She squeezed his arm before letting go.

"And thanks for walking me home. Mum will be right jealous."

The stove was still warm when he returned home to *Duchesse Anne*. He opened up the air, put another couple of logs on and poured himself a generous glass of red. Then he took out his faithful Beretta 692, bought second hand how many years ago? One barrel above the other. Simple elegance. Deadly accurate in the right hands. Tomorrow, maybe, if the wind drops overnight.

Methodist Youth Club, East London, Easter 1957

Most of the kids had left the youth club for the night, leaving only a handful in the church hall. Jack and Russ had helped pack away the table tennis tables while the girls finished the washing up. Frankie had put away the record player. "Blueberry Hill" was nothing more than a sweet echo playing at the back of Jack's mind. The youth leader rattled his keys.

"Come on, campers, haven't you got homes to go to?"

Russ turned to Jack.

"I dunno what's the matter with you, Boyo. You've been dancing with her half the night and staring at her for the other half. She don't bite. But if you won't go and ask her, I will."

Jack tried to stop him but Russ broke free and sprinted

across the hall to where Bel, with whom Jack had actually danced no more than three times that evening, was still chatting to some other girls. The girls looked across to where he stood. There were some giggles, and then Russ was on the way back, both thumbs up.

"She said she'd be going in five minutes, and you could walk with them if you wanted."

"Well, thanks a lot, Rusty. You've made me look a proper drip. And who is them?"

"Keep your hair on, Boyo. It's only Bel and Dianne. And she lives in Fourth Avenue, so won't be with you two lovebirds for long. Then you'll be on your own, Boyo, and it's up to you what you get up to. Holding hands across the flats, eh?"

The girls began putting on their coats. Bel looked across at Jack and smiled.

Russ gave him a push.

"Get your skates on, Boyo, or they'll be gone. I'll see you tomorrow."

Outside, Jack found himself between the two girls, who continued their conversation as if he wasn't there. So when Bel did address a question to him, it caught him unawares.

"Have you broken up already, then?" she asked.

"Yes. I came home this evening. I don't have to go back until the Thursday of the week after Easter."

"Lucky you. We don't break up until next Wednesday and then we're back on the Monday. But at least I don't have to sleep there. Must be lonely."

"Oh, it's not too bad. And Stan always picks me up Friday evenings and runs me back Sunday afternoon, so I'm home every weekend."

"I can't wait to leave," Dianne said. "One more term and I'm out of there. Anyway, this is my road. See you tomorrow, Bel?"

"What about the Palais?"

"I'll ask my mum. She might say no. She's a bit off with me at the moment." Dianne broke away and walked quickly down Fourth Avenue.

Bel slipped her arm into Jack's.

"Now, tell me honestly, Jack Boyer, why has it taken you so long to ask to walk me home? Ever since the Christmas party I've seen you looking at me. Or was I just imagining it?"

Jack felt himself blush.

"I suppose I can be a bit shy sometimes. It's not that I didn't want to…"

He pulled his duffel coat around him, pushing his hands deep into the pockets. The day had been sunny but the night had turned chilly. Bel slid her hand down into his pocket to find his.

"Do you mind?" she asked. "My hands are freezing."

They walked on in silence for a while, past the station and over the railway bridge. He felt her thumb rubbing the back of his hand. He responded in the same way.

"Why do you go away to school, Jack?"

"My mum thought I'd have a better chance in life if I went there. I don't really mind. She wanted me to keep up my French. I have extra lessons, which I couldn't get at the grammar. Since she died I don't have a home of my own anyway. Emm and Stan can't have me there all the time, sharing Stan's little room."

Bel stopped by a bench under the trees. They sat close and Bel allowed her head to rest lightly on Jack's shoulder.

"What about your dad? Where does he live?"

"Oh, he's abroad somewhere. He doesn't get home very often. It's still to do with the war."

She sat up straight and ran her hands over her hair.

"Anyway, I'd better go in or my mum will be getting worried. Thanks for walking me home. If you fancy the Palais tomorrow night, pop into the shop. I'm working there all day."

They crossed the road, together but no longer touching, to the front gate of Bel's prefab. She went up on tiptoes, pecked Jack on the cheek and ran up the short path, door key in hand. Jack waited until the door closed and then turned slowly towards home, "Blueberry Hill" still spinning in his brain.

Emm and Stan were both at work, so when the doorbell rang the following morning Jack reluctantly put down his copy of *Flying* and went downstairs in his pyjamas.

Russ, of course. Who else would be at the door at that time in the morning?

"So there you are, lover boy," Russ said before the door was even half open.

Jack stepped aside and Russ wheeled his bike into the narrow passage.

"I guessed it would be you banging on the door this early."

"Done me paper round while you was still having your beauty sleep. Some of us have to work for a living every day, not just when we want a bit of pocket money on our hols. I don't 'spose most kids at Pargeter's have to do paper rounds. They get up when matron tells them and wait for cook to bring their eggs and bacon."

Why did he always have to sneer? It wasn't Jack's fault that he was sent to a boarding school. He tried to ignore him, but it wasn't easy.

"I thought you was gonna leave me perishing on the doorstep all day long. Don't stand there gawping at me. You too much in love to shut the flippin' door, then? You're letting all the heat out. I'll put the kettle on, shall I? They at work, then?"

Jack nodded as he followed Russ into the scullery, watched him fill the kettle and light the gas, as if it was his home.

"You just gonna to stand there watching me, then? Where's the blinkin' teapot? Come on, Boyo. I know you're all in love but jump to it. What was you doing when I got here? Dreaming of Bel?"

"I was reading a magazine, if you must know."

"What, *Tit-Bits*?"

Jack sighed.

"No, *Flying*. It's American. One of Stan's."

Russ made the tea and carried it into the back room. Jack flipped open the doors on the little stove and they sat there staring at it for a while. There was a gentle gurgling sound from the hot water system. Russ slurped his tea.

"How far did you get last night, then? After I left you."

"Mind your own business."

"So nowhere, then."

"I didn't say that."

"What, then? Holding hands?"

Jack nodded.

"Goodnight kiss?"

Jack grinned.

"Lips or cheek?"

"Lips."

"French kiss? Hands inside her coat?"

"Bugger off, Rusty. None of your business, is it?"

"So, no, then. Still, not bad, Jack the lad, proper kiss on your first date. When you seeing her again?"

Jack stared into the fire, where a dull glow was turning to yellow flames.

"We'd better shut the fire down or it'll be burned out before Emm gets home at dinnertime. I'm going up for a bath. There's Stan's *Mirror* there if you want to read it. And can you wash the cups up?"

The bathroom was full of delicious steam. Baths were not something allowed to the boys at school, except for the huge communal pit in the changing rooms, which was filled up only after a rugby match against a visiting team. It was worth training for the team, just to get a dip in the hot muddy water. Normally, the boys had to shower.

The water was cooling. Jack turned on the hot tap with his toe. Above the rattle and gurgle of the water, he didn't hear Russ come in.

"You lucky bugger," Russ said, "wish we had one."

Jack looked round.

"One what?"

"A bath, you silly bugger. What did you think?"

"You can get in after me if you like. Emm won't mind. Not if you use the same water."

Moments later, Russ had stripped off. Jack hadn't seen him naked since the summer, when they'd often shared a changing cubicle at the swimming baths, but then they were more intent on watching the doors opposite, across the pool, where the girls changed. They could see the tops of heads above the doors and feet below. They could occasionally see a jumper being pulled off over a head, and shoes and socks being put on or taken off, but the rest had to be imagined.

He and Russ were convinced that, if only they could find the right spot, they would be able to see more. So they had both learned to dive from the top board, launching themselves far out over the pool, head turned to one side, in the hope of seeing something. But they never did.

"Wash my back and then I'll get out so you can have the

water while it's still hot." Jack held up a dripping flannel and handed it to his friend.

"Where's the soap?"

"I don't know. Must be in the water somewhere." He began to feel around, searching for the bar of Palmolive.

Russ put his hand into the water and pretended to look for the soap, tickling Jack's feet. Jack could not stop himself giggling. Russ ran his hand up Jack's leg.

"Up here is it, hidin' under little Willie?" The boys convulsed with laughter. "Or maybe it's here," tickling Jack in the ribs.

Jack turned to try to get away.

"Stop it, Russ, there's water going all over the floor."

Jack found the soap and Russ gave his back an unenthusiastic rub. He lay back to rinse off and climbed out, returning to Stan's room wrapped in a towel. He lay on his bed and picked up the magazine.

After a few minutes, Russ, dripping wet, was at the bedroom door.

"Can I have the towel, Boyo? That was lovely. Can you have one every day if you want?"

Jack threw him the towel.

"Yup. As often as I like, when the fire's alight. Just so long as there's still enough hot water when Emm and Stan want it."

Russ, towel in hand and far from dry, sat down beside him.

"Look at me. All lovely and pink. Do you want to pretend I'm Bel?"

"What do you mean?"

"You know. Pretend I'm Bel just got out the bath. You could dry my back for me." He handed Jack the towel and turned his back. Jack began to rub it dry.

"Gently, Boyo. You don't want to rub the skin off. I'm Bel, remember."

Jack rolled the towel into a sort of ball and patted Russ's back.

"That's better. Do you want to practise kissing and that?"

"With you? Get off."

"Just shut your eyes and pretend."

Russ lay back and tucked his penis down between his legs so only a triangle of dark pubic hair could be seen.

"Now I'm Bel. What you gonna do?"

Jack hesitated. There was no real harm in it, after all. Plenty of boys got up to things after lights out. It's just that Jack had never wanted to.

"No. I don't know. I'm not sure."

"Go on, Boyo. It's just a bit of practice." Russ grabbed Jack's shoulders and pulled him down. Jack shut his eyes. Just pretending. Russ was surprisingly gentle, his lips soft. He nibbled Jack's ear.

"Go on, show me what you'd like to do with her," he whispered.

East London, Christmas 1957

Jack rushed from the classroom, up the stairs and burst into the cell-like room he shared with three other senior boys. He went straight to the window, anxious to get a sight of the little Bond Minicar that Stan had bought after selling his beloved motorbike and sidecar. And there was Stan, bless him, sitting in the little car, muffled up with scarf and a woolly hat, cigarette smoke curling into the still cold air. Russ sat beside him, one elbow casually resting on the door, also smoking.

Why did Russ have to come? Jack didn't want to travel home squashed sideways into the back of the tiny car, with Russ sitting up front in his cheese-cutter cap. But he was glad to see Stan, alright. He just wanted to get home. He banged on the window and waved, but they were too far away.

Jack bounded down the stairs carrying his small case, stuck with labels for the Golden Arrow, of which he was immensely proud. Halfway across the playing field, already showing the first signs of the night frost, Russ spotted him.

"Get a move on, Boyo," he shouted. "It's the party tonight and we'll miss 'alf of it if you don't get your skates on."

Breathless, Jack arrived at the car.

"What party?"

"As if you didn't know. The one you've been waiting for all year. So you can get your dirty little hands on Bel."

Jack peered anxiously around. Russ and his big mouth.

"Shut up, Rusty."

Stan put his arm around Jack's shoulder and gave him a squeeze before taking his case to put behind his seat.

"You're in the back, Russ, like I said. Jack, hop in the front."

Only then did Jack realise the car was brand new, with doors on both the passenger and driver's sides.

"Like the Bond, Stan. Very smart."

Stan patted the bonnet.

"Had to use hire purchase. But this new one is so much better than the older ones. New suspension and steering gear, electric start, the lot."

Half an hour later, Stan was bringing the car to a standstill outside Emm's house. Jack spotted Emm standing looking out of the little bay window. Beside her, coloured lights blinked on and off from a little tinsel Christmas tree. Even before Jack had a chance to get out, Emm was at the front door, arms outstretched in welcome, her legs hidden under a long floury apron. From somewhere behind him, Jack heard Russ shout that he'd be round at quarter past six and he'd better be ready.

"You get on and say hullo to Emm, son. I'll bring your case in."

Jack crossed the pavement into Emm's embrace.

"You're freezing," she said, "and little wonder, running about with the hood down in the middle of winter. What on earth were you thinking of, Stan?" Without waiting for an answer, and leaving Stan rolling the canvas hood back in place, she shooed him in to the house.

The youth club Christmas party would probably be the last he would go to, and he was going to make the most of it.

He was just finishing cleaning his teeth when there was a knock on the bathroom door.

"Alright, son?" Stan poked his head around the door.

"Glad to be home."

"Things OK with you and Russ, then? I thought there was a bit of a thing between you on the way home."

"You know he's always making cracks about me going to Pargeter's, as if it was my idea. And he's a bit full of himself since he started work."

"He's working on some houses quite near the school. He is a grafter, you can say that for him. Seems to get on alright with Bel's uncle. At least, that's what he said. You calling for Bel, then, son?"

"No, she said she'd see me there. She's bringing one of her friends from school. Hoping she might fancy Russ."

"'Bout time he found a girl of his own, if you ask me. He shouldn't always be hanging around with you and Bel."

"I don't mind, Stan. And he keeps an eye on Bel while I'm away during the week."

"Bit too much of an eye, some would say. You sure you can trust him, son?"

Jack laughed.

"No, not really. But I can trust Bel."

Stan looked him straight in the eye.

"That's right, son. That's how it should be. She's a good girl."

*

The church hall was decorated exactly as the previous year, and the year before that. Paper chains hung from the lights; a banner declared, *Jesus Was Born to Save the World*. A white sheet covered the trestle table where they normally put the record player. They knew what lay under it – sandwiches and biscuits, fruit jelly, some sausage rolls and a Christmas cake from Stan's bakery.

A handful of boys and girls were already there, boys one side and girls the other, sipping weak squash from white china cups. Steve Leather, the new youth leader, was in control of the record player, from which came the Everly Brothers' "Bye Bye Love". Steve, universally known as "Blather" on account of his tendency to witter on for ages about nothing in particular, looked up as Russ and Jack entered. He clapped a hand around Jack's shoulder.

"Great to see you, Jack. How's school? Still enjoying it?"

Jack mumbled something about the school while scanning the hall. Blather went off to rescue his records, which Russ was already separating into various piles. The Everlys were followed by something by Doris Day.

Around half past seven, Bel arrived, arms linked with a

girl Jack did not recognise. She looked around the hall. Jack put down his table tennis bat and headed across to her. Russ also put down his bat, but held back.

Bel smiled and offered her cheek.

"So you made it, then?" she said as he gripped her hand.

"Stan picked me up this afternoon in his new Bond."

Bel moved closer and smiled that smile that made his knees feel weak.

"He's so proud of it, isn't he? It's lovely to see you. Thanks for your letters."

"And yours. They always cheer me up."

They stood looking at each other, neither knowing what to say. Would it always be like this, lost for words when they first meet after a couple of weeks, each one trying to assess whether their feelings have changed? Jack lived with the dread that Bel would find somebody else, that the next letter would be a Dear John, or that she would confess something awful when they met.

Finally, she seemed to remember her friend.

"Oh, Jack, this is Keelin, the friend from school I wrote to you about."

Jack stared into a pair of green eyes, twinkling with mischief, emphasised by dark eyeshadow. She wore white lipstick and black nail varnish. So this was the new girl that Bel had decided would make the perfect date for Russ. Lucky Russ.

Jack looked across the room to where he'd last seen him, at the table tennis table, but he was gone.

The girls followed his gaze.

"Russ here?" asked Bel, trying to sound as if it didn't matter.

"Yeah, he came with me. We were playing ping pong when you arrived. I'll see if I can find him."

"No hurry is there, Keelin?"

Jerry Lee Lewis hit the piano at a run and "Whole Lotta Shakin' Goin' On" filled the room. Beside the record player, Frankie sat bolt upright on a wooden chair, his hair slicked back, tapping his foot. A couple of the girls started to dance.

Russ returned from wherever he had been.

"Oh, there you are, Russ," Bel said. "This is Keelin. From school."

Russ did one of his almost coquettish grins.

"So why haven't I seen you before?"

"Maybe I saw you first."

Jack burst out laughing. Keelin had got his measure in less than a minute. Jerry Lee Lewis gave way to Chuck Berry. Keelin dropped her handbag onto a chair, smoothed down her skirt and held out her hand to Russ.

"Come on, then, if I'm going to have to get to know you let's see if you can dance." She had a voice like Ruby Murray's.

Bel held out her hand to Jack. Her touch was just how he knew it would be, soft and warm. Above the sound of "Roly Poly", he could hear the rustle of her starched petticoat under her dress. The little silver crucifix Jack had bought her for her birthday hung at her throat. They spun their way through more Chuck Berry, more Jerry Lee Lewis, Paul Anka and Elvis. Then a wind-down before the sandwiches with Pat Boone's "April Love".

Bel nudged Jack to make sure he'd seen Russ, red in the face from his frenetic dancing, come to the food table, hand in hand with Keelin.

"Looks like she's having a good time, doesn't it?"

After eating, the group began to split again along gender lines, the girls moving off to the far side of the hall. Frankie, who had been in charge of the orange and lemon squash, grabbed a sandwich and came and stood beside Jack.

"How's school, then?" Frankie asked.

"Not bad. Be glad when I leave and can join up."

"What you trying for?"

"RAF. I'm in the cadets at school. Six months and I'll be training as a pilot. What about you, still over the City of London?"

"Yeah. Digging graves, cutting grass. They're gonna train me up in horticulture."

Jack squeezed Frankie's biceps.

"You must be stronger than you look."

"Nothing wrong with my arms, Jack. Just me blinkin' feet."

Jack tried to imagine Frankie deep in a grave, spadefuls of earth flying out.

"Must be a bit miserable, though, working in a cemetery?"

"Not really, there's always something going on. And they're a nice crowd, the blokes what work there."

"Wake Up Little Susie" signalled the food break over, but nobody moved. The girls carried on their chatter while the boys gathered around the record player. Eventually Keelin emerged from the group, and walked straight up to Jack.

"Do you fancy a turn, then?" she said. "Somebody's got to get this place livened up a bit."

Jack cast an anxious glance at Bel. She smiled warmly enough, as if to encourage him. But you could never quite know with girls, what they were really thinking and feeling. Keelin raised her eyebrows and cocked her head to one side.

"Well, yes or no, otherwise I'll have to ask Russ again. By the way, who's this?" She put a hand on Frankie's shoulder.

"This is Frankie. He's a mate of me and Russ."

Keelin moved her hand to Frankie's cheek.

"Well, Frankie, save me the last dance, will you?"

Leaving Frankie blushing beside the food table, they moved into the very centre of the hall just as the Everly Brothers finished. Hands loosely linked, they waited for the next record. As the opening strains of Bing Crosby's "White Christmas" wafted across the hall, the party erupted into laughter and then fell silent. Keelin put her hands on Jack's shoulders, then linked them behind his neck, pulling him close. Her breath was sweet on his face, her breasts pushing against his shirt, her hips swinging gently to the music.

"Let's give them something to talk about," she whispered, so only he could hear.

The song ended, and after much clapping and jeering, they pulled themselves apart and returned to their groups. When Elvis resumed, Russ dashed across the hall to grab Keelin, while Jack went more cautiously to Bel's side, gently taking her hand and leading her onto the floor.

"I told you she was fun, didn't I?" she said, as Jack pulled her towards him and then gently pushed her elbow so she swung under his raised arm, her skirt swinging so wide it brushed against his legs.

Eventually, the music ceased and Blather held up his hand. People began to form into a circle. This was the part that Jack loathed, Blather's be good message and a prayer.

"I could do with a fag," he said.

Russ looked around.

"Go on, then. No one will notice if you get out before we start."

The evening was mild for the time of year, a mizzle of rain creating a pleasing miasma around the streetlights. Jack stood in the porch, watching the traffic on the main road. Things were good between him and Bel, better even than in the summer. They were both growing up. From the other side of the door, he could just about hear Blather droning on about something or other.

The cigarette was down to its last inch when Blather stopped talking. Silence. That must be the prayer. Then came a burst of applause, followed by the unmistakeable opening chords of Jerry Lee Lewis's "You Win Again". The last dance. For certain. Jack dropped the remains of his cigarette and dashed back into the hall. The lights had been dimmed. Everyone was on the floor, moving almost as one to the melancholic chords. Where was Bel? There was Keelin, true to her word, with Frankie pressed up against her, swinging from side to side, their hips joined. Frankie looked happier than Jack had ever seen him. Finally he saw Bel's white dress with the huge red roses. Over her shoulder, Russ winked.

The sod. He must have been planning that all evening.

Seven

"Mr Boyer, Mr Boyer, are you there?"

Jack looked up from his book, Dirk Bogarde's *An Orderly Man*, surprised not only to hear somebody calling his name but also pronouncing it correctly. He rubbed a clear circle in the condensation on the wheelhouse window. A man, quite small, waited at the end of the jetty, struggling to control a huge umbrella, emblazoned with the motto "Russell Homes – You Know You've Come Home". Jack slid back the door far enough to poke his head out.

"Yes, I'm here. How can I help you?"

"I've got a message from Mr Russell." A hand appeared from under the umbrella, holding out an envelope. This was too much. For God's sake, would Russ never give up?

"Then you'd better bring it to me."

The man folded the umbrella and stepped onto the jetty, steadying himself against the wind, gripping the wet rope that served as a handrail. So who was it this time, running Russ's errands? There it was, unmistakeable – the limp. The penny dropped: Frankie Adams, the boy with the turned-in foot, now grown into the man he had seen only a few weeks ago, making his slow way across Russ's

75

back garden. He reached the wheelhouse door and held out the envelope.

"You'd better come in out of the rain, Frankie."

"Thanks, Mr Boyer. You remember me?" He leaned the umbrella against the bulkhead and stepped inside. Jack took the envelope. Frankie tried a smile. "Mr Russell said to say sorry to disturb you, but he thought you would want to know."

Jack stared at the small man, standing there, eyes downcast, shoulders hunched, with his back to the open door. Frankie's funny little face was still there, just visible behind a mask lined by the passing of half a century.

"To know what?"

"About Stan. It's all in the note, Mr Boyer."

Frankie finally looked Jack full in the face.

"Should I wait, Mr Boyer?"

"Frankie, what is all this 'Mr This' and 'Mr That' business? I'm Jack and 'Mr Russell' is Russ. We've known each other far too long for that sort of nonsense. And could you just slide the door shut behind you?"

Frankie turned towards the door.

"As you want, Mr Boyer."

"Jack, Frankie, Jack."

"I just thought. Well, some people don't like to be reminded of where they came from. And, as I said, I didn't think you'd remember me."

Jack swivelled on the tall stool bolted to the wheelhouse floor. Just beyond the windscreen, pools of rainwater weighed down the canvas hatch cover.

"It was you said it, Frankie, donkey's years ago. We were standing outside the school. Last day at Fourth Avenue, before we both went off to our new schools. 'You won't forget me,' you said. "Frankie Adams. FA. Like in the cup."

76

Frankie gave the same little half-smile he'd worn as an eleven-year-old. Was he always so small?

Jack glanced down at the envelope. He wanted to say, "Sit down, Frankie. Can I get you a cuppa? It is good to see you, you know, after so long." But he didn't know how.

"Now then, Frankie, what's all this about?"

Frankie shifted his weight from one foot to the other.

"It's about Stan. He's in hospital again."

Jack wanted more, but Frankie just stood there, running his hand over the smooth mahogany and brass of *Duchesse Anne*'s wheel and staring out at the river.

Rain hammered on the roof. Jack slid his finger under the flap of the envelope and unfolded the letter, noting the usual expensive paper, the printed address, the same spidery writing. The letter was just a few lines.

Dear Jack,

Stan is seriously ill again in Newham General. If you want to see him, I think you should go very soon. He has a chest infection and the doctors are not optimistic. He would like to see you.

Yours, as ever,

Russ

PS Frankie will take you to the hospital and back home again.

Jack tried to picture Stan as a sick old man, but the image that came was of the fit young bakery worker swinging his leg over the Royal Enfield and standing on the kick-start to bring the beast to life. Frankie turned away from the window.

"Mr Russell, I mean Russ, said I should take you if you'd like to go."

"And where is 'Mr Russell'? Lurking in his fancy car?"

Frankie shook his head, and stared hard at the floor. Jack hated himself. Why was he blaming Frankie?

"No. He's at home," said Frankie, so quietly Jack could barely hear. "Doesn't go far these days."

Jack read the letter again. Russ had finally breached his defences, as he knew he would.

Frankie peered down the companionway.

"You live here all the year round, Jack?"

Jack refolded the letter and put it back into the envelope. He tapped it on the chart table and made to stand up.

"Yes. Summer and winter."

A strong gust of wind shook the old boat. Frankie reached out to steady himself.

"Terrible day, isn't it?" he said.

Jack nodded.

"What shall I tell Mr Russell?"

"Thank him for letting me know and tell him I will go to see Stan this afternoon."

"Would you like me to drive you? He said..."

"I know what Russ said. You've already told me once and it's here, in the letter. I can find my own way, thank you."

Frankie slid open the door behind him and started to back out of the wheelhouse.

"If you are sure. He's in Bluebell ward. Second floor."

He stepped backwards out into the rain, looked up and met Jack's gaze. His face broadened into the little childish grin that was still familiar, then picked up the umbrella and started down the jetty.

Jack watched him and went to slide the door shut. None of this was Frankie's fault. He couldn't leave him limping off into the rain like that.

"Hang on a minute, Frankie. If you can wait a moment or two, I'd be grateful for a lift. If the offer still stands."

Frankie didn't turn until he reached the sea wall. He put up the umbrella. Jack could not see his face.

"I'll wait for you here. No hurry."

"No, Frankie. Come back aboard. I expect you could do with a cup of tea before you drive back."

Russ had won. Frankie might be the chauffeur, but Russ was in the driving seat.

*

At the doors to Bluebell ward, he stopped to clean his hands with antiseptic gel. A nurse came out and looked him up and down.

"Can I help you?"

"I've come to visit Mr Gibson. I just wanted to make sure he didn't already have visitors." She glanced over her shoulder.

"It's not visiting until four thirty."

Jack looked at his watch and turned to go. The nurse stayed at the door, holding it open.

"Come far, have you?"

"Well, far enough. I live in the wilds of Essex."

"So you must be the friend who lives on a boat. Mr Gibson has told me about you." The nurse smiled and opened the door a little more. "It must be lovely, living with nature like that." She paused. "Anyway, you can come in. Visiting is pretty flexible on this ward."

Jack took a step through the door.

"So there's nobody else here?"

"No, you're the first today. Mr Gibson's lucky, having so many good friends like you and Mr Russell. Rain or shine, he's here every evening." She walked briskly away. Good friends? She wouldn't say that if she knew he'd not been in touch with Stan for forty years. Not even a Christmas card.

Half the beds were empty, and there was little sign of life from those that were occupied. He went to the desk where two other nurses were staring into computers.

"Excuse me, but where will I find Mr Gibson?"

One of them looked up.

"There," she said, nodding towards one of the blocks of four beds. "The one with the red socks."

Jack followed her gaze. After fifty years, he didn't really expect to recognise him. But it *was* Stan. He could see that. His head was back on his pillow, headphones clamped over his ears, eyes shut. A strip of sunshine lay across the bed. The rain must have stopped at last.

"He's not asleep." The nurse smiled encouragement.

"You sure?"

"Watch his toes. It makes us laugh, the way he jiggles them to the music."

Stan's eyes flicked open. Would he recognise him? The old man pulled down the headphones so they hung loosely around his neck. He screwed up his eyes, appeared to stare straight at Jack for a moment, and replaced the headphones.

Jack walked the few steps to the bed, but Stan wasn't looking his way. What to say? He could think of nothing.

The nurse got up from her station, walked over and tapped Stan on the shoulder. He again pulled down the headphones.

"Stan, you've got a visitor. It's…?"

Jack finished the sentence for her.

"Jack Boyer… from years ago."

Stan tried to sit up.

"Jack! Well, I'll be blowed. Can't believe it. Is it really you, or am I dreaming again?"

"It's me. So, Stan, how you feeling?"

Jack moved closer. The nurses were watching. Why did he come? He bent down, his head now inches away from Stan's.

"I'm sorry it's taken so long," he said, his voice barely a whisper.

Stan tried again to prop himself up, but the effort was too much. He groped around until he found his iPhone.

"Not to worry. You're here now. Let's turn this off." There were tears in his eyes.

"What are you on? Spotify?"

"Apple Music. Come here."

Stan held out both hands, the same hands that had tamed a heavy motorbike or kneaded the dough in a dusty bakery but which were now little more than bones. They were cold to the touch.

He tried again to lift himself but sank back into the pillow. He released his grip, still surprisingly firm in one so obviously frail.

Jack bent down awkwardly and put an arm tentatively around Stan's shoulders. Behind him, he heard the ward door squeak open and the sound of footsteps.

Stan shook his head.

"Relax, son, he won't be here for another couple of hours."

Jack sat down. The two men were no longer touching.

"Is it that obvious?"

Stan didn't answer, and appeared to have dozed off. He must already be getting tired. They sat in silence for a while.

Stan again reached for Jack's hand. Jack felt a squeeze.

"I'm glad you came."

"So am I, Stan. I'm just sorry I left it so late."

"It's never too late, son. You made it, that's the important thing. How did you get here?"

"Frankie brought me."

"How come?"

"Russ asked him to. Sent him down with a note."

"He's a good man, Jack. Give him a chance. Give it a go."

"Give what a go?" Jack answered too quickly. Stan deserved better than that.

"We all make mistakes, son. And what's done is done. Can't be undone." He stared at the window, then fixed Jack with the stern look he remembered from childhood.

Jack pretended to concentrate on the monitor beside the bed. Systolic. Diastolic. Pulse. All of them bouncing about all over the place.

"It's not that easy, Stan."

Stan again squeezed Jack's hand.

"Remember the Bond, son?"

"How could I forget, Stan?"

Stan drew in a breath to speak again, but was caught by a spasm of coughing. Jack held a feeding cup of water to his lips. A transparent plastic tube delivered oxygen to his nostrils.

"Thanks, son."

"I remember you coming to pick me up from school, the Christmas after you got it."

"Russ was with us, wasn't he?"

"You parked in the middle of all the posh Jaguars and so on. We had some fun with that car, didn't we?"

Stan nodded and stared up at the light above his bed.

"Can you turn it off, Jack, it's getting in my eyes."

He found the switch.

"That better?" he said, resuming his seat by the bed and again taking Stan's outstretched hand.

Stan tightened his grip.

"Why don't you just go and see him, son? He'd love that."

"You know why, Stan."

"But it's all water under the bridge now, isn't it?"

"Not for me, Stan."

"It's fifty years. A lifetime ago. Time to call it a day, surely."

"And what, Stan? Say it didn't matter after all?"

"But who are you hurting, Jack?"

"It's not that easy."

"You always could be an obstinate little sod."

Stan closed his eyes and his breathing stopped. Jack was about to fetch a nurse when the old man took a deep, rasping breath, and life shuddered back into him.

"We promised we'd be together always."

"Who, Stan?"

"You, Russ, Bel, Emm and me."

"We could have been, but for Russ."

Stan turned his head away.

"It takes two to tango."

Jack was ready with a bitter reply, but thought better of it.

"The Famous Five. We wouldn't all fit in the Bond, would we, Stan?"

Stan tried to chuckle but the attempt ended in another coughing fit. Eventually it subsided.

"I'm serious, though, son," he said. He took another deep breath and managed to prop himself up on his elbow. "Look at us all. Me on my last legs, Russ not much better, Emm back in Ireland, and you hiding away on some old boat." He fell back onto the pillow. A tear rolled down his cheek. "Scattered to the four winds." He closed his eyes and released his grip on Jack's hand. "Scattered to the four winds."

Jack sat for half an hour more beside the bed, while Stan slept. Every so often, he would not breathe for ten or twenty seconds, and Jack would fear it was all over and glance anxiously at the monitor. Then Stan would shudder and gasp and a more regular breathing pattern would resume. It was like it was long ago, when he was a boy, home from Pargeter's for a few days, lying in bed as Stan slept. A nurse came by and checked Stan's pulse without waking him. She smiled at Jack.

"He's a lovely man, isn't he? Never complains about anything. Known him for a long time, have you?"

Jack nodded, his throat too tight to speak. The nurse touched him on the shoulder and moved on to the next bed, where a wizened old man lay inert, his eyes closed. He had no visitors, but a huge box of Milk Tray on the side table said somebody cared for him. Jack had arrived at Stan's bedside empty-handed.

As quietly as he could, Jack stood to leave, giving Stan's hand a final squeeze. Stan hadn't mentioned where Bel was. Was that deliberate? Where was she? He'd have heard if she'd died, surely.

He found Frankie waiting by the door of the marbled entrance hall, a pool of water around the tip of his big umbrella. He stepped forward as Jack reached the bottom of the stairs.

"I wonder, Jack, whether you'd mind hanging on a minute or two while I popped up to see him."

"Of course. Take your time, Frankie. I'm in no hurry. He was asleep when I left him. I'll get myself a cup of tea and the paper."

The Times had a noisy front-page story about the rising cost of looking after our ageing population, and Jack quickly bored. He completed the Quick Crossword. He felt curiously at home, perhaps because the little cafeteria was an East End time capsule where the women still called their customers "luv" or "darlin'". He went back to the paper, half his mind reading one of the weekly columnists and the other thinking about what Stan had said.

So why no mention of Bel? Where was she? Where did she fit in now, if she did?

Jack heard the uneven progress of Frankie's footsteps.

"Not too good today, is he, Jack?"

Jack shook his head. He had no way of knowing whether Stan was better or worse than he had been the day before.

"Sit down, Frankie. Let me get you something. Would you like a sandwich? A piece of cake? It looks home-made. I haven't eaten since breakfast myself, and I don't suppose you've had time."

Frankie sat down.

"Just a tea, please. If you don't mind."

Jack ordered two teas and two shiny buns.

"Take a seat, dear, I'll bring 'em over," said the woman behind the counter. Boiling water from a steaming urn hissed into her big aluminium teapot.

Frankie drummed his fingers on the table.

"Spit it out, Frankie, what do you want to say?" said Jack, his tone as gentle as he could make it.

"I phoned Russ while you were with Stan. He said to say he's really pleased you came."

"So am I, tell him."

The teas arrived and Frankie plopped a sugar lump into his cup. He began stirring slowly.

"And Russ said to say if you would like to go back to his afterwards he'd love to see you. Otherwise, I'm to take you home or wherever you want to go."

Poor little Frankie, now made to be the go-between.

"That's very nice of him, but I think I'll go straight home

if you don't mind. Can you drop me at the station? You've had a long day already."

"If you're sure? Russ did say I should take you back if you wanted."

"No. The station will be fine."

The two men sat in silence, each concentrating on the tricky job of buttering a soft bun with butter portions straight from the refrigerator.

"So you stayed in touch, Frankie?"

"I knew Stan from when we were kids. He drove for Russ before me."

"I didn't know Stan worked for Russ."

"Well, you probably know that Stan was made redundant. They closed the bakery."

Jack didn't know, but nodded all the same.

"Well, by that time, Russ was practically running Bel's uncle's firm. They were everywhere, DIY shops and fitted kitchens, sand and cement, and all the rest of it. He gave Stan a job driving one of the delivery trucks.

"Then Russ took over completely. He bought this big house in Wanstead, well, you've seen it, haven't you?" He grinned. "Anyway, to cut a long story short, it had a sort of granny annexe which Russ offered to Stan, if he'd become his driver. Chauffeur, if you like."

"And Stan agreed?"

"What do you think? He jumped at it. Driving a Jag instead of a truck. No lifting. And a front door of his own in Wanstead. What would you have done if you were stuck in a bedsit in Seven Kings?"

"And he paid for it by being at Russ's beck and call twenty-four hours a day."

Frankie took a long swig of tea, watching Jack from above the rim of the mug.

"It wasn't like that, Jack. Russ is alright. He's decent to work for. Not like some, I can tell you." He put the mug down. "Anyway, say what you like about Russ, and I know full well why you two don't get on, by the way, but when Stan got too old to drive, Russ kept him on as a handyman and let him stay in the annexe. Not many would do that. Not these days."

Frankie's speech was like a dam bursting, but he wasn't finished.

"Stan was like a father to the pair of you, wasn't he? Russ said the least he could do to repay him was look after him in his old age." He paused, as if weighing up what he wanted to add. "It's in his nature, isn't it, watching out for people?"

"Really?" Jack said, more aggressively than he'd intended.

"I know you won't forgive him, Jack, but he's not a bad man. I can vouch for that, and so can Stan. I'll be outside when you're ready to go."

He stood up and walked out, his tea and bun barely touched.

Eight

Weeks passed with no further word on Stan's progress. Shortly before Christmas, Frankie had phoned with an update. Against the odds, the old man had pulled through. So that was that, then.

One afternoon in early March, Jack was walking the half-mile from the station to the Old Smack, hands pushed down in his pockets. He did a small side-skip to kick a pebble down the narrow lane, just as he had as a boy on the last day of term. He missed the puddle he was aiming for, but it didn't matter. Long shadows cast by the still bare trees faded as the few street lights of East Stone flickered into life. The night was dry and clear, the moon full. He could just keep walking through the night, on and on until the frost formed and the sky began to lighten. But he was hungry.

Rounding the last bend where the road sloped down to the river, there were the comforting lights of the pub. In the moonlight, smoke from the chimney merged with the clouds far above. The smell of burning wood tickled his nose. That first pint would go down well.

Tonight, unusually, he planned to stay in the pub all

evening. Then, tomorrow, he would plug in his laptop and get to work.

But tonight *Duchesse Anne* would be cold. He'd been out most of the day. The fire would be dead. So he had the perfect excuse to take advantage of the Old Smack's steak night, when you could order up a decent lump of beef and a drink for £8.75. He'd finish the day in warmth and comfort. And he'd earned it.

"Let me guess," said Katie as he put down his battered old briefcase and edged himself onto a bar stool, "a medium rare sirloin and a pint of IPA."

"You've got it. And have one yourself."

"Thanks. You look pleased with yourself, Captain." She slid the glass across the counter and winked at him. "By the way, Mum will be here in a minute."

Katie had been matchmaking Alison and Jack, not altogether unsuccessfully, for months. He picked up the glass and took a mouthful. Perfect. He'd never had a duff pint at the Old Smack, and although the landlord himself rarely graced the bar with his presence, he did know how to keep his beer.

"Did you tell her I'd probably be in?"

"So," she said, ignoring his question, "how did it go?"

He took a sip of beer, smacked his lips.

"Well?" she asked again.

"They want a monthly column from me. Money every month. And I thought I was going to be fired."

"I told you, they wouldn't ask you in to fire you."

"And you were right, as ever."

Behind him, the pub door opened. Jack swung around on his stool and met Alison's eye. He'd been planning to sit quietly and work, to sketch out some of the images he would bring into his first piece. How would he describe haw frost

89

on a canvas hatch cover? Or the way a spider's web, sparkling in the early morning sunshine, flexed with the movement of the mooring warps on which it hung? The noise made by a steel hull squeezing up against wet rubber tyres with each lift and fall of the swell? But work could wait.

"What can your daughter get you, Ali?" he said. "Tonight the drinks are on me."

"A glass of red wine, please, love," she said, addressing Katie. "And you can order me a small fillet steak, medium, and salad." She opened her purse.

Jack put his hand over hers.

"As I said, it's on me."

"You can't, Jack."

"I can, and I will. I've had good news and I want to celebrate." He grinned, picked up Alison's glass before she had a chance to touch it and carried it across to a table near the fire. Alison followed and sat down.

"Now then, Mr Boyer, spill, as my daughter would say."

He caught a whiff of her perfume. It smelled expensive, but then he was no judge.

"They want me to write a monthly column for them. Life on the river. The characters who live by the water, the wildlife, the change of seasons, that sort of thing."

"Brilliant. Oh, Jack, well done, you must be pleased."

"I am. I can't wait to get started. I'm brimming with ideas."

Katie brought knives and forks, wrapped in paper napkins, to the table. Reaching into the back pocket of her jeans, she pulled out a cream envelope.

"By the way," she said, "this came for you earlier. I almost forgot."

Jack's smile froze. He held out his hand.

"You'd better give it to me, then."

Alison looked from Katie's face to Jack's. The pub went quiet. He felt everyone was staring at him. He folded the envelope in two.

Katie touched the back of his hand.

"Relax, Jack. That bloke with the gammy leg and the posh Jag didn't bring it. It came in the morning post, just after I'd seen you walk off towards the station."

Only then did Jack dare to look at the envelope in his hand. The handwriting was unknown to him. The stamp was French.

He let go the breath he'd been holding. The pub became noisy again, the warmth came back into the fire, and the anxious expressions on both Katie's and Alison's faces disappeared.

*

With a good meal inside him and, he felt, his relationship with Alison moved on a notch or two, Jack returned to *Duchesse Anne* shortly after ten, reluctant to go to bed. He felt the letter in his pocket and laid it on the worn mahogany of the saloon table. It could wait until morning. He looked at the dead fire, and shivered.

Bed really was the most sensible option. But in five minutes he could have the stove well alight. In half an hour he would be able to smell hot iron. A nice bottle of red waited to be uncorked. He set to work. Firelighters, a couple of logs, and a single match.

While the fire began to warm the cold cabin, Jack climbed back up to the wheelhouse, still muffled up in his coat, scarf and gloves. The flood tide had already lifted his old boat clear of the bottom, and every now and again *Duchesse Anne* would squeeze herself up against the jetty, drop back and then try again.

He rubbed condensation from the windscreen. Withies marking the best water into the marina stood black against the dark charcoal surface, streaked with silver from the moon. He clicked on the VHF, selected channel 16. All quiet. It wasn't the sort of night you would expect much activity. Channels 9 and 71 were more active with ships in and out of Harwich and Felixstowe ports. On 9, the Felixstowe pilot guided a container ship in at half-tide.

When he opened the companionway doors to go back below a waft of warm air touched his face. He poured a generous glass and sat in his favourite chair. The stove clicked. The river gurgled against the old steel hull. He slipped Crosby, Stills and Nash out of its well-worn cover and turned up the volume – he had no neighbours to complain.

Only then did he pick up and open the letter. He went first to the bottom to see whom it was from. Yann, one of his cousins, but not, as he had expected, to tell him that one of his aged Breton relatives had died.

Yann said a stranger from Frankfurt had arrived in the village asking questions about Jack. Apparently he was a private detective. After asking at the bar in the village, he'd found his way to the big house that now belonged to Yann. Somebody, Yann didn't know who, had already told him that Jack lived in England. Yann said he had told the man that he didn't have his address.

A visiting card was paperclipped to the letter. It simply had the name of a firm based in Frankfurt and the name of the man who had been asking the questions. Günter Bohlen of FPI GmbH. Why on earth would a private detective based in Frankfurt be interested in Jack?

He took a sip of wine and turned down the volume.

Let's think this through. It wouldn't be to do with Russ,

because Russ already knew where he lived. So it had to be about something else. But what?

The music played, but he was no longer hearing it. *Wouldn't you know we're riding on the Marrakesh Express.* Certainly not Jack. What if it was somebody enquiring about Ma Vinney? Not likely, but not impossible, even after the best part of fifty years. But Frankfurt? Where would Frankfurt come in? Russ of course did know what happened that night. Might he have told somebody?

Ma Vinney's son had always said the full story hadn't been told. What was his name? Angus, that was it. Or was it Ian? Whatever he was called, he had complained long and loud to the local paper that the police hadn't done a thorough enough inquiry. And he was right. Maybe he'd moved to Germany. Perhaps he'd decided to give the pot another stir. Who could blame him, after all?

What about DNA? Would the police have kept any evidence after all these years? Probably not. At the time, DNA was so new that its use as evidence was not appreciated. He looked at his watch. He needed to know more, but there was no way he was going to make contact with the man. Crosby, Stills and Nash had done their stuff. The stylus was clicking impatiently. He lifted the pick-up and turned off the unit.

Yann also suggested Jack pay him a visit in St Pabu, as it was several years since he last went. Why not? He might be able to find out a bit more about the mysterious enquirer. Waking up the laptop, he googled the name of the company on the card. His German was limited, but good enough to confirm they were some sort of tracing or enquiry agents.

It would be good to see Yann and nice to get away for a few days. He checked Ryanair and saw there was a flight to Brest two days later. He could pick up a car at the airport and pay his cousin a surprise visit. An adventure! He drained the last of his glass, switched on Radio 4 to listen to the shipping forecast and began to undress. But he wasn't going to sleep, not for hours.

East London, 29 December 1957

A trolleybus hissed by, close into the kerb. Russ grabbed Jack's arm and pulled him back, but it was too late. The trousers he'd borrowed from Stan's wardrobe had oily muck up both legs.

"That won't come off, either," he said. "Just about sums up the whole bloody evening."

Bel hadn't been there. In fact, he'd not seen her since that Christmas party. She said she had family visiting and was not allowed out. But was there something else?

Only a few twelve- and thirteen-year-olds had turned up for youth club in the chilly hall. The leader had been in a foul mood. That week between Christmas and New Year was the worst of the year. Half the shops were closed. Everybody was miserable. Even Russ had nothing much to say.

Russ kicked the base of a streetlight.

"May as well go 'ome, then. Fancy some chips?"

"I told you. I'm skint."

The boys walked on a few yards and then stopped to look in the window of Ron's Bargain Stores. Even Ron's bargains were way out of reach of either of them.

"I know," said Jack, "why don't we do it tonight?"

"Do what?"

"Pay Ma Vinney a midnight call."

"Don't talk barmy. We'll just get some chips and go home."

"What's barmy about it? Nobody's about on a night like this. It'll be a laugh."

"Nobody's about 'cos it's freezing bloody cold and anyone with any sense is sat down in front of the fire. I'm going home."

Jack put his face close to Russ's.

"That your last word, is it, big boy?" he said, before turning to walk away. "It was your big idea. Haven't got the bottle when it comes to it?"

Russ stuck his hands deep into the pockets of his duffel coat and began to follow.

"Jack, listen. It's pissing with wet snow and I've got work in the morning. Another time, maybe."

Jack stopped.

"Tonight, or never. You coming or not?"

"Not. You're on your own." Russ started in the direction of the Broadway. Ten yards on he turned to face Jack. "Look, just come and get some chips and forget all about it. Just 'cos Bel's gone cold on you you don't have to go off your head. We'll do it another time. Promise."

"I told you, tonight or not at all. And she hasn't gone cold on me, as a matter of fact."

"Then why wasn't she there tonight?"

"She's got her aunt and cousin or someone staying, and she's not allowed out."

Russ walked back to his friend and put an arm around his shoulders.

"If that's what she told you, then it's bound to be true. Come on, Boyo, I've enough on me to buy you a bag of chips, OK? Pickled onion make you change your mind, eh?"

Jack twisted away and headed off in the direction of the flats. What if Russ was right? That Bel had gone cold on him. How would Russ know? Only if she'd told him. He pushed the thought away. When he looked back, Russ was in the fish shop. This wasn't what they'd planned, all those weeks ago, when they'd sat on the bench opposite Bel's, rocking with laughter at the idea of listening to Ma Vinney snore while they stole her cigarettes.

No lights burned at the shop. Nothing stirred on the street. He walked on, past Bel's prefab where the lights were still on. He tried to imagine what was happening inside. Was she in bed? He turned, retraced his steps and ducked into the alley beside the shop. Deserted. He began the climb, easy at first but the sloping roof was slick with ice.

They were supposed to do it together. That was the point. He wasn't meant to be on a slippery freezing roof on his own. He stopped to listen. What was going on under the roof of Bel's prefab next door? How many times had Russ walked up that garden path while he was away at school? This week even, while Jack kicked his heels around at Emm's?

Over the road he could see the bench where it had all begun. A bus slid past in the distance. An owl hooted. An express train clattered over the points. The night boat train to Harwich. He'd promised Bel that one day they'd both be on it. Now he wasn't so sure.

He crawled towards the skylight and froze as a piece of cement clattered down the roof and into the alley. A light came on below. Jack stared down through the skylight and there was Ma. She looked up, straight into his eyes.

Jack dodged back into the shadows, but she must have seen him. Then came another sound, a bump, a crash, followed by silence. He didn't dare move. After what seemed like ten minutes, he again edged towards the skylight and looked down. Ma lay sprawled at the bottom of the stairs, her neck horribly twisted but her eyes wide open.

As quietly as he could, he scrambled down from the roof. Running through the streets at nearly midnight would attract attention, so he walked away as casually as he knew how. Five minutes later he was back in the high street. Dirty wet furrows had been left in the snow by the traffic, but it was bound to freeze overnight. The chip shop was closed. His clothes were splattered with muck. He would just have to say he'd slipped over.

The red telephone box near Ron's had a thick layer of snow on the roof. Jack pulled open the door and stood for a moment looking at the receiver. He could dial 999, tell them to send an ambulance to the shop, and then leg it. But what would be the point? Ma Vinney looked like she was dead already. No ambulance could bring her back to life, while making the call could get him caught. He closed the door and walked on, working out what he was going to say when, late and filthy, he finally got home.

Light from the porch reflected on the snow, throwing a long shadow behind Jack as he walked up Auntie Emm's front path, took off a glove, stuck his shaking hand through the letter box and fumbled for the key. He left his shoes on the doormat and hung his coat on the hall stand before putting his head around the back-room door. Stan was still up, sitting in front of the fire, reading *British Baker*. "Alright, son?" he asked, looking up.

"No, not really," replied Jack, rubbing his knees. "I tripped over the kerb in the snow. Hurt my knee. I think I'll go straight up."

"Why don't you have a bath? It'll help the bruise. There's plenty of hot water."

Ever since the bathroom had been installed, whenever there was a tankful of hot water, Stan tried to get somebody to have a bath. "Otherwise," he would say, "the water'll go to waste." He sometimes sent Jack next door to ask if they wanted one.

Jack tried to keep his voice steady.

"Good idea, Stan. It'll warm me up."

As the water hissed and spluttered from the tap, Jack began to undress. His fingers were still so numb from the cold, he struggled with the buttons. Was he shivering from the cold or trembling from the shock of seeing Ma Vinney sprawled at the foot of the stairs?

He shook in some of the bath salts he'd bought Auntie Emm for Christmas, tested the water with his hand and climbed in. The water felt good, but every time he lay back and closed his eyes there was Ma Vinney, one arm twisted into an impossible shape. Dribble ran from her mouth and her sightless eyes stared at him, the accused.

He sat up and busied himself with the scrubbing brush, first his nails and then his feet. When he was finished he again tried lying back, but with his eyes open. It was no use. Ma Vinney was there on the ceiling, watching him, asking why he hadn't even phoned for the ambulance.

After a few minutes he heard Stan make up the fire for the night and then come up the stairs. Jack didn't think he could get through a conversation with Stan, and remained in the bath for the best part of twenty minutes, topping up the water with fresh hot as it cooled.

When he reckoned Stan would be asleep, he pulled out the plug and watched the water disappear down the plug hole. Even when all the water had gone, he felt unable to move. Trapped in a world of white cast iron, haunted by Ma Vinney's eyes, he could feel the iron bath rapidly cooling. If he didn't get a move on, he'd be hit by another bout of shivering. Was this what it was going to be like for the rest of his life?

Should he get dressed again? Creep out to the phone box. But Auntie Emm would hear the front door. And it was too late. The evening could not be undone.

He pulled on his pyjamas and went into the bedroom he shared with Stan, who turned over and opened his eyes.

"Bad night, was it, son?"

"What do you mean, Stan? The snow?"

"No. The club. Russ. You know what."

"No different from usual, except I tripped over the sodding kerb and hurt my knees."

"Looks lovely, though, doesn't it, the snow, before anyone's walked on it?"

Jack took a deep breath.

"It's the quiet I like, Stan, when the snow comes down. All the noise seems to stop."

Stan propped himself up on one elbow, and in the light filtering in from the street Jack saw him smile. He dropped his voice to a whisper.

"I passed Russ on my way home. Surprised to see him on his own. Fall out over something, did you, son?"

Jack felt his stomach go cold.

"Sort of, Stan." Had his shaky voice given the game away?

Stan sunk back into his pillow.

"If you'd have been with him, I'd have given you both a lift home. But I thought, 'Let him walk,' so I just sailed past pretending I didn't see him." He paused, then turned to face the wall. "Funny little bugger, isn't he, that Russ? All big talk until push comes to shove, then he's nowhere to be seen." With that, Stan took a deep intake of breath and he was asleep.

Sleep, however, was much slower coming to Jack. Every time he was nearly off, he would jerk awake, as if stepping off a kerb he didn't know was there. He got out of bed several times, to stare out of the window at the snow coming down again, covering the tracks left by traffic. The snow would also cover the footprints he must have left in the alley. He heard the bell of a police car. It faded into the distance. But wherever he looked, there was Ma Vinney sprawled on the stairs, her nightdress all ridden up, showing her dimpled old thighs.

Eventually, just as the sounds of morning were beginning, he went off.

*

In those precious moments, which seem only to occur after a disturbed night, between being awake and being still asleep, when your limbs feel heavy and the bed is like a cocoon, everything seemed normal. The room looked the same as always. The house was quiet, for both Auntie Emm and Stan had left for work. Perhaps it had all been just a nightmare. Maybe Ma Vinney was in her shop as usual, grumbling at any customer who dared come to buy without the right money.

But, too soon, he was awake, facing the enormity of his sin. When he looked for his trousers, he found them in a shopping bag at the top of the stairs. A note was pinned on the bag. *Can you drop them into the cleaners.* When he looked down the stairs, Ma Vinney was spread-eagled at the bottom, her mouth open, ready to scream. Shivering again in the cold of the unheated bedroom, he dragged on his dressing gown and went downstairs, relieved he did not have to face anybody.

Another note from Auntie Emm written, like all her notes, on the back of a used Christmas card, lay on the kitchen table. She asked him to take his coat into the dry cleaners at the same time. The packet of cornflakes was set beside his bowl, as it was every day if she went to work before he was up. No police had come knocking on the door. Apart from the knot in his stomach, it could have been just any day.

He turned on the wireless and heard the closing song from *Workers' Playtime* as he poured milk onto his cornflakes. But he wasn't hungry. He stirred the mixture around until it was too soggy to eat, then went to the outside lavatory and tipped it all away. As he pulled the chain he heard a banging on the front door. Instinctively he pulled the toilet door shut and held his breath. They'd found him. In a moment the police would force the front door and come storming down the hall. "Boyer, you're nicked, son."

There was no point in running. He may as well leave the sanctuary of the lavatory and give himself up. Halfway across the scullery, which Emm had taken to calling the kitchenette since Stan had bought a glass-fronted cabinet and put in a sink unit, he saw the front door open.

"There you are, then, Boyo," shouted Russ, red-faced, as if he'd been running. He reached out to grab the collar of Jack's dressing gown, pushing his face forwards until they were just inches apart, staring into each other's eyes. "What 'appened last night? Did you do for Ma Vinney, 'cos if you did, I'm gettin' out of here? I had nothing to do with it, don't know nothing about it, understand?"

Jack pushed Russ away.

"Course I didn't. It wasn't my fault. She fell down the stairs."

"So, what happened, then? I passed the shop on me way to work and there was two police cars, and an ambulance parked up and a copper standing outside. Then I heard she'd snuffed it. So what did you do?"

So it was real, after all. Ma Vinney was dead, and it was his fault. His legs felt as if they would give way, and he felt sick again. He wanted to tell Russ, but the words wouldn't come. He needed the lavatory, even though there was nothing left inside him. He went outside and closed the door behind him.

After retching up bile, he returned inside to find two cups of tea on the table. Russ was smoking a cigarette.

"So, Boyo, are you going to tell me or not?"

Russ offered Jack the cigarette, which Jack took and drew on deeply before handing it back.

"So, what did you do?"

Jack put a spoonful of sugar in his cup, and then another. Tea slopped into the saucer.

Russ went to stare out of the window. Tiny snowflakes, more sleet than snow, blew around the garden.

"So you're saying you didn't touch her?"

Jack took a gulp of tea. His voice sunk to a whisper.

"Course not. I didn't even get in. She was wandering about and fell downstairs. I saw her go."

"How did you see her go if you didn't get in?"

"Through the skylight. I was still on the roof."

"You'd better start getting your story right. So tell me what really happened."

Jack slumped down onto a dining chair, and reached down for the leg of the table, twisting his hand around the barley sugar carving. When he was little, when Maman was away and Emm was looking after him, he liked to sit right under the table, his arms stretched out, running his hands up and down the carved legs. Stan would come home from the bakery and Jack would bark, or meow, until Stan fed him with a piece of cake or a bit of doughnut. Only then would he come out.

He took a deep breath.

"OK. I got on the roof easy as pie. Then I heard her moving about."

"So what did you do then?"

"What do you think? I jumped off the roof and ran for it."

"So you really didn't touch her?"

"Course not. It was like I said. I heard her moving around and ran for it."

"No good telling the Old Bill that if they come calling. If you admit you were there, that's it. Guilty. Ten years at the very least. You weren't there, got it?"

He stared at the front page of Stan's *Daily Sketch*, but all he saw was Ma Vinney's face and the headline: *Pargeter's boy: guilty verdict.*

"So where was I, then?"

"With me at the chip shop. Old Gordon was on his own there last night – if I tell him we were both there he'll believe me."

"What if someone saw me?"

"They made a mistake. Easy to do in the dark. Did you see anyone?"

"No."

"Well, then. Here's what happened. We left the Methodists usual time. Got splashed by the bus which messed up your trousers, we had a look in Ron's and then went to buy chips. I only had enough for one bag so we shared them. Then I came home your way because we thought Stan and Emm would still be up, but then remembered I had to get up for work this morning so I didn't come in."

"Why aren't you at work, then?"

"Too much snow. They sent us all home. Got the day off."

"Stan saw you last night on your way home. He knows I wasn't with you."

"Alright, then, here's what we say. After we bought the

chips we had an argument. I went home. You can say you were a bit upset so went for a walk around to calm down. That way you don't even have to remember which way you walked."

"Stan knew there was something wrong as soon as I came in last night. He asked if we'd fallen out. He said if we'd been together he'd have given us both a lift home, but he only saw you."

"There you are, then. When he gets home today tell him I came round to make up."

Hot water gurgled in the tank. The clock on the mantlepiece ticked loudly then whirred as a preliminary to striking the hour. The sounds inside the room were sharpened by the silence of the snowy world outside.

Russ opened the doors of the fire with his boot, flicked in the cigarette butt and reclosed them. Jack waited for him to say something: to sympathise, or condemn, or ask some question. But his friend remained silent, staring out at the little back garden. Jack followed his gaze. Snow was still falling.

Russ spoke without turning his head.

"Funny, ain't it, Boyo, how the snow can balance on a washing line without falling off? Like you on that slippery old roof, eh?"

He moved away from the window and grinned.

"Tell you what, though, Boyo, they've got *Dam Busters* at the Odeon tonight. I'll call for you after tea. It's got Richard Todd and I'm payin'." He buttoned up his coat and went into the hall. "Don't forget to take Stan's slacks to the cleaners, or he'll have a fit. Do as I say, Boyo, and nobody need ever know."

Nine

Jack woke early after a better night than he'd expected.

He filled and switched on the kettle and dressed while it came to the boil. A shower could wait until he returned. He needed to walk, to stride out, to think. He went over the arguments again. If it was Ma Vinney's son stirring things up, why would he send a private eye to Brittany, especially one based in Frankfurt? He could have asked Russ, who still lived less than a mile from the old shop, and whose success in business was the stuff of local legend. Or he could simply have typed Jack Boyer into his search engine.

The kettle boiled and he poured water into the teapot. He put a splash of milk into his favourite mug – *I'd rather be sailing* – which Katie had given him at Christmas. He laid out breakfast on the saloon table.

The first shaft of sunlight pierced the forward porthole, forming a golden triangle on the old wood, next to his branflakes.

"Too bright too early," he muttered to himself, "so let's make the most of it."

After a couple of sips of tea, still too hot to enjoy, he pulled on his boots and coat and climbed the steps into the wheelhouse. He checked the battery levels. More than enough power to start the engines, but not today. Not a ripple disturbed the last of the ebb slipping slowly past. A flight of ducks passed noisily overhead. Should he take the Beretta? Conditions were near perfect. But he hadn't prepared. You can't just grab a gun out of a locker, point it in the air and start firing. Everything needs to be checked. Prepared. But he would give it another try, one day. Soon. Not today, though. He drank the remainder of his tea and stepped out onto the damp deck.

Along the tideline, wildfowl pecked at the mud. They'd been up long before him. He turned downriver, walking quickly. Two miles distant he could see the white sail lofts picking up the near horizontal rays of the early morning sun. So what had that detective wanted?

If it was not about what happened in Manor Park that freezing night, could it be about what had happened in Cyprus? An uncle, or brother, seeking him out to take revenge. He passed the sailing school where excited youngsters were rigging their little Optimists while they waited for enough water to sail them.

By the time he reached the lofts the tide had begun to flow. Soon the river would be busy. Brown frothy water crept towards the sea wall along little gullies fringed with the first shoots of the samphire that would soon cover the mudflats. He glanced at his watch. Eight fifteen. Nine fifteen in St Pabu. He turned around to head back towards *Duchesse Anne* and pulled out his mobile. Yann answered immediately.

Jack's French was rusty, but easily good enough to understand from Yann that the private eye had spent a day in St Pabu asking a lot of questions. Yann said he had told him nothing, but you never know. Things can just slip out, sometimes.

Halfway back, he saw Alison coming in the opposite direction. She let Millie off the lead and she raced towards him. Jack stood to the side of the path, expecting to be showered with water, or worse, from the nearest gully. But, unusually, she was still dry.

"You're up early, Monsieur Boyer," Alison said as she approached.

Jack remained at the side of the path, not sure whether to peck her on the cheek, or to leave his hands in his pockets, or whether to turn and walk with her, back the way he had just come, or just have a brief conversation and then head back to the boat. Alison made the decision for him.

"I think I've walked far enough this morning," she said. "You heading back to the village?"

"Yes… I went as far as the lofts. They looked fabulous this morning."

"I bet. What are you up to today?"

"I've nothing much planned. I may have to book a flight."

"A flight? Well, let me guess. France? Something to do with a letter you received yesterday?"

"France, yes. To do with the letter. You've got it in one." He paused. "When I saw the letter I thought some old aunt or uncle that I didn't know might have died. But it was from Yann, that's my cousin, and he suggested I pop out and see them. It's been years since I last went there, and I keep meaning to go. But you know what I'm like. So this time I thought, well, I have a couple of weeks free before I need to get started on my column. And there's not much going on at the yard, so I thought I'd get something booked before I change my mind."

They turned back towards the village. Millie ran on further, determined to have more walk before returning. They watched her for a moment.

"She'll probably jump into the mud just to spite us," Alison said. "Can I take your arm? The path's a bit slippery."

She slid her arm into his. The unexpected movement towards intimacy seemed to make it easier to talk. To be open.

"Well, Yann's letter wasn't just about a visit, but apparently somebody was out there asking all sorts of questions about me. So I thought I might go and see what's up."

"Really? What sort of questions?"

"Seems somebody wants to find me. A private detective."

He felt Alison pull closer to him.

"So, Monsieur Boyer, what have you been up to in your past, eh?"

"Nothing much. And in any case, my life's an open book."

If only.

*

Two days later, at the end of a long day involving trains, a flight and a hire car, Jack found himself in the upstairs dining room of a little restaurant in Aber Wrac'h, idly watching the man at the next table as he removed, one by one, his mussels from their shells, lowering each one back into the creamy sauce in the black enamel casserole. The empty mussel shells he graded into three sizes and piled them neatly, one on top of the other, on the upside down casserole lid. Only when every mollusc had been removed did the man start eating, a task he accomplished with astonishing speed.

God, Jack thought, *could that be me? Am I getting as odd as that, from spending too much time on my own?*

He finished his plate of langoustine, dipped the last *frite* into the little dish of mayonnaise and ordered a coffee.

When he paid the bill and stepped out into the road, he felt a chill in the air. He pulled out his mobile and called Yann's number.

"Yann, it's Jack. I'm in Aber Wrac'h. Is it convenient to call in to see you tomorrow?"

"Aber Wrac'h? What are you doing there? Come tonight."

"I've just drunk an entire bottle of Muscadet."

"So have I. Well, white Burgundy actually. You have a car? Come tomorrow, early. Where are you staying?"

"The Baie des Anges."

"Check out in the morning. You'll stay with us."

*

The view of St Pabu from the crest of the hill was just as Jack remembered. The ugly little grey church and, stretching out behind, up the other side of the shallow valley, the regimented rows of tombstones. He shuddered. Maybe that was why he hadn't been back in years. He slowed for the crossroads as a few drops of rain hit the windscreen. More than fifty years may have passed since he first came to St Pabu, but he could still picture the crowd of strangers, standing in the middle of the road, that he later learned were his only family, their anxious faces peering into the car for a glimpse of the child about which they knew nothing until his mother was killed on a shabby street in East London. This time there was just Yann sitting at a table outside the bar, waiting for him.

Jack parked the little car and climbed out, stretching his back. Driving was becoming less enjoyable and more uncomfortable year by year. Soon he would be too old to hire cars, and that would be that. A warm hug and a black coffee later, they were both in the car heading up the hill to the house where his mother had been born, and where she had lived until moving to London. Now it was Yann's home.

They pulled up on the gravel beside the porch. Below them, the muddy river ebbed and flowed between green, wooded banks. But now it was lined with trots of moorings, at which white sailing yachts swung with the tide. Sometime between then and now, St Pabu had turned itself from a poor fishing village, just about sustained by seaweed and crustacea, into a sailing resort.

"You still catching crabs yourself, Yann?" Jack asked. His French was coming back to him, little by little. It felt good.

"Of course," he replied, smiling, "but not under sail. We now have engines, Jack. Now, what would you like to do first? Do you want to visit Nicole's grave? We put flowers on at *la Toussaint*, of course."

Did he want to do that first, or at all? To stand once again in that miserable place under a heavy sky, feeling anger rather than sorrow? But it was expected of him. He nodded, and they set off to walk the short distance back down the hill to the cemetery gates.

The two men paused before entering. Perhaps Yann was as reluctant as Jack to tread between the black stones.

"Nothing much changes here, Jacques, as you can see," he said, finally pushing the gate open. "Year by year the cemetery fills up. Most of the young people move away, but they come home to bury their parents. The village houses get bought up by Parisians as holiday homes.

"I still remember that first time we went out on my little old sailing boat. Believe it or not, that boat is still in the family. My great-nephews and nieces use it all the time. I can still picture your face when you realised we'd left the jetty.

"The river is not so easy to sail these days, with all

the moorings. But it's good business, Jack, good business. Looking after the yachts. Remember the old shed where we used to keep the oilskins? Well, you should see it now. Maybe we'll eat there later. Their oysters are superb. Gaston runs it. Remember him?"

Jack had forgotten how loquacious Yann could be.

"Don't he ever stop talking?" Emm had asked. Emm. Where was she now? According to Stan, back in Ireland. Maybe he should plan another trip after France, and visit her. Maybe he could persuade Alison to go with him. But he didn't have Emm's address, and he would probably have to ask Russ for it.

They reached the rather grand vault of the Boyer family. Several new names had been chiselled into the dark stone after Nicole's.

"There's still room for us, Jacques, but after that, I think the family will have to start again."

The next name after Nicole was Claudine, Yann's wife. Jack never met her. They had married while Jack was doing his National Service in the Canal Zone, and she had been killed in a car accident less than a year later. Yann had never remarried. The two cousins had never talked about it.

"Both taken too early, both killed on the roads. It is good they are together. Claudine would have loved Nicole, I know it," Yann said, turning away to hide his face. "Shall we head back to the house for lunch?"

They were silent until they were back on the lane. The rain had come to nothing and the sun was trying to get past the thinning layer of cloud. Jack had forgotten how quickly weather moves in Brittany. Yann paused to get his breath. He, too, was getting older. They leaned on a rusting metal gate, watching the river below them.

"When we get back to the house, I must remember to

give you a photo of Nicole we found when we were clearing the shed. Remind me later. There's lots of photos in the albums, of course, but this one seems rather special. It was kind of hidden in the shed." They started walking again. "First, we'll collect your bags from the car. We've put you in the same room as last time."

Last time he stayed at the house? It was donkey's years ago. That was when he realised that the Boyers were the dominant family in the village. They owned the boats, the land, and the oyster beds. And it was when he knew, without anybody telling him, why his mother had left the village so suddenly. It was because of him.

After lunch Yann announced that he had some business tasks he needed to attend to, so would Jack be OK on his own? A chance to get some exercise, collect his thoughts and maybe take a short nap.

At six thirty, Jack went down to the sitting room to find a bright fire burning in the grate and a bottle of Champagne in an ice bucket on the little table in the window that overlooked the garden.

He loved this room. The fine mahogany furniture polished to a deep shine, the worn parquet floor, the family photographs in silver frames – the history of the Boyer family was written into its very fabric. Yann appeared from the kitchen, a striped apron over his day clothes and a broad grin on his face.

"If you don't mind, Jacques," he said, wiping his hands on the apron, "I thought it might be nicer to stay and eat here tonight. We can go to the oyster shed tomorrow."

Music to Jack's ears. It had been a long day and the rain had set in as though it meant it. A warm sitting room in front of an open fire, fresh flowers in the vases and the table already set for two, with candles and a bottle of white

Burgundy beside the Champagne in the ice bucket, was exactly what Jack realised he had been hoping for since taking the decision to travel out to see Yann.

A young girl, late teens, followed Yann from the kitchen.

"Jacques, you won't remember Mathilde, one of my lovely nieces. She was just a toddler when you came for our grandmother's funeral. She has offered to serve us our dinner and, more importantly, to wash up. And I have to tell you, despite her delicate looks she is the best sailor in the family."

Should Jack kiss her, or shake hands, or what? Mathilde solved the dilemma for him by stepping forward and offering first one cheek and then the other.

"You are the uncle who lives on a boat?" she said in near perfect English. "You are so lucky. I would love to live on a boat on my own, like you, but I'll have to wait until after I graduate." She turned to Yann. "Tell me when you want to start eating."

"I don't think your harp would be happy on a boat, Mathilde. The cold, the damp would ruin it," said Yann. "Mathilde has a place at the Conservatoire de Rennes, Jacques."

Jack was clearly expected to say something, but what? It had been a long time since he'd been required to make pleasant conversation with people he didn't really know.

"Fantastic, Mathilde," was the best he could manage, followed by, "When are you hoping to start?"

She gave them a sweet smile.

"Next year, Uncle."

The two men watched her return to the kitchen. Yann opened the Champagne.

"I feel that we should celebrate you coming to see us, so I pulled this from the cellar. A nice one from 2002. The year you came for Grandmother's funeral."

They took their glasses and sat one each side of the fire. Everything seemed so settled, so unchanging. It was as if the house, and the land, and the oyster beds owned the family, not the other way round. And in a way, that was the case. Assets like those, nurtured and valued over generations, provided the living, and so they called the tune. They came first, before any individual.

"Young Mathilde reminds me so much of your mother, Jacques, with her musical talent and her dreams."

Jack took a sip of the Champagne. It was, indeed, delicious, but more importantly, the action gave him time to think.

"Musical talent? I didn't know Maman was musical."

Yann leaned forward and poked the fire.

"Really? She had been offered a place at Rennes. Violin. But then she left, leaving both the violin and her future behind, here, in St Pabu. Once, when she had come home to visit her papa, when he was very ill, I caught her looking at her violin. When I came into the room she quickly put it back in its case. She never played it again here. Are you telling me she never played when she was in London?"

"No. Never. I had no idea."

"That's a tragedy, but they were strange times, Jacques. The war came and changed everything. Lives and dreams shattered, families torn apart. We didn't even know that Nicole had a son until she died, and your dear Emm wrote to us. Years wasted when we could have been friends. How is Emm, by the way?"

A good question, how was Emm?

"She went to live in Ireland with her family. The last I heard she was doing well. She's very old now, of course. You will remember she had this lodger, Stan. Sadly, he's not been well. He had pneumonia, but somehow has pulled through.

He had a good summer." He heard himself parroting the words from Russ's letter, and didn't like it.

Yann stood up and went across to the hi-fi unit, selected a CD and set it to play. The music sounded slightly familiar, as if he'd heard it many years ago.

"Ravel, 'Violin Sonata Number 2'. Our grandmother played it nearly every day, and it regularly brought tears to her eyes. She said it was Nicole's party piece, but that if she lived to be a hundred she would never hear it played as well as Nicole played. Now, what about some food?"

After dinner it was time for the photograph albums. This was a treasure trove. Jack's mother was just a few years older than Yann, and there were many pictures of the two of them having fun on the beach, enjoying the same little boat that had introduced Jack to the pleasures of sailing, working together in the market garden. Yann patiently explained who all the characters were that appeared in the little black and white photos. The two men sipped a fine Armagnac.

Mathilde popped in for a while before going home, and Jack could see the resemblance between the girl in the room and the girl in the photo.

Perhaps it was the effect of the alcohol, or maybe it was simply that he felt unusually secure and comfortable with Yann in that lovely old house, but Jack found the courage to ask the question that had troubled him since childhood.

"Yann," he said, choosing his words with care, "although the albums show Nicole as a child and then well into her teenage years, there are none that show a boyfriend."

Yann shifted in his chair. He put another log on the fire and reached for the bottle of Armagnac. Jack held out his glass. Yann leaned forward to recharge it.

"You can see for yourself, Jacques, Nicole was a very attractive girl. Lots of boys from the village took a tilt at her, but she wasn't really interested. They say she had bigger ambitions. There was one boyfriend for a while, but he wasn't from the village. They got together during the summer before Nicole left us to go to London. He was a bit older than her, a German boy, and there was inevitably talk in the village. Some people said he was in the navy, but I don't know that as a fact. His family had a nice house on the edge of the village, a holiday home. Nobody lived there permanently. Various members of the family came and went. They minded their own business. Nobody used the house at all during the occupation. They came back for a couple of years and then it was put into the hands of an agency that rents properties to holidaymakers.

"A couple of years ago, at the end of the season, the house was closed up and as far as I know, nobody's been there since. A company comes and cuts the grass, keeping the place tidy. I've no idea who owns it now."

They emptied their glasses.

"I'll think I'll go up, Yann, it's been a lovely evening. But talking of Germans, maybe tomorrow we can talk about the mysterious detective who came looking for me?"

"There's not much to tell, but I'll do my best."

Ten

The sun on Jack's arms felt good. The winter may have passed. A hundred metres downriver, at the slip, a Swan 45, one of the best cruising yachts on the market, was being reversed into the water after her winter lay-up. *Duchesse Anne*'s VHF chattered away as leisure sailors, pressed by a lively easterly that had sprung up from nowhere, sought reassurance from each other. Container ships called for pilots.

Jack's mobile chirped into life. Frankie.

"Hello, Frankie."

Silence, then an intake of breath. He knew what would come next.

"Sad news, Jack. Stan passed away during the night. Mrs Charlton went in this morning to make sure he was OK. She found him gone."

What? When Frankie had last called, Stan was getting stronger every day. He said Stan was looking forward to his promised run down to see Jack at East Stone.

"What was it?"

"Heart. The doctor says he wouldn't have known anything about it. Just slipped away. Slipped away. Just like that."

Down at the slipway, the launch pulled the yacht clear of its cradle.

"Does Emm know?"

"We don't think she has a phone. We tried her sister but got no answer. They're both a bit hard of hearing. Russ is writing to her."

"What about the funeral?"

"The undertaker's coming later. We'll know more then."

Neither man spoke for what seemed like half a minute. Perhaps there was nothing more to say.

"You still there, Jack?"

"Yes, I'm here."

"Stan's still at home, in his bed. Russ is hoping the funeral people will leave him be for a day or two. But I don't know if you can do that. But if you wanted to come and see him…"

"I don't know about that… Surely they will take him when they come."

"I don't know, Jack. It's all new to me. I've never had to, well, you know." Another pause. "Well," said Frankie at last, "I've got a bit of running around to do, so I'd better get on. Russ said, if you could call…"

"Just let me know about the funeral. How old was he?"

"We think eighty-eight. You'll be coming, won't you?"

Jack took a deep breath. Of course he would be there. Surely Frankie didn't think otherwise.

"I'll be there," he said and rang off.

The yacht arrived at her mooring and the shipwrights made her fast. The launch headed back towards the jetty, crabbing across the river in the fierce tide. Quite a chop to cope with.

He shouldn't have been surprised at the news. Nor sad. It was for the best. Stan had been released from his troublesome old body. An easy passing, by the sound of things.

Slowly, Jack folded away the charts he had been studying, shut down his computer and stowed them back in the drawer. He switched off the VHF, pulled on his jacket and scarf and went across to the sea wall. Instinctively he headed downstream, towards the sail lofts. The way he always went. He felt the mobile in his pocket. All he had to do was select "Russ" from the list of contacts. Before he had a chance to change his mind, he pressed the green button. A woman answered.

"Russell residence, Mrs Charlton speaking."

Jack tried to suppress his irritation. He should have known he'd first get an intermediary, a secretary or housekeeper. Russ had developed airs, if not graces.

"I'd like to speak with Mr Russell?"

"Who shall I say is calling?"

"Jack Boyer."

"Oh, Mr Boyer, he will be so pleased. He's been saying all morning he hoped you'd call. Hang on, I'll put him on."

A couple of clicks were followed by a snatch of the *Four Seasons*. Jack held his breath.

Even after half a century, Russ's voice was unmistakeable.

"What a sad day for us all, eh, Boyo? Frankie said you'd phone when you heard the news."

"Didn't really have a choice, did I?"

"At least you got to see him in the hospital. He was always talking about you."

"Can't think why."

A pause, and then he answered.

"You were the son he never had, Jack, that's why. Funnily enough, we were talking about you only yesterday, and laughing at some of the old films we saw at the Coronation. He seemed right as rain. And then, wham. He's gone."

Another awkward pause.

"Anyway, Russ, I'm sure you've got a lot on. I just rang to say if there's anything I can do…"

"Just turn up on the day, Jack. I know it will be hard for you, but we owe it to Stan, don't we? Whatever you think of me."

Out on the river, a seal suddenly broke the surface. Barely more than a pup, it had probably been lured upriver by the supply of young sea bass. The next ebb would flush it back to the sandbanks.

"I'll keep you informed about the funeral. And if you want to go and see him, at the funeral parlour, I'll send Frankie for you. I'll be in touch."

Before Jack had time to worry about how to end the conversation, Russ rang off.

He scanned the river, hoping to catch sight of the seal again. A couple of yachts tacked upstream, probably to moor up for lunch at the Old Smack. The launch would be busy ferrying them to and fro. For the next two hours the water would continue to rise silently until it covered all the mud. Then the tide would turn and the whole process would repeat, twice a day, filling and emptying the tiny creeks, while the oystercatchers pecked at the seaweed along the waterline. An egret circled for a moment, then dropped down onto the samphire. Jack turned and headed back towards home.

He walked past *Duchesse Anne*, through the Old Smack's car park, up the lane as far as the gate between the two little bungalows reserved for old people. The massive padlock and heavy chain guarding the gate always made him smile. There was no gold bullion growing there, or even cannabis. Just vegetables. Nevertheless, he locked it shut after him. The pathway led to the village allotments. Alison was already there, digging in the far corner. She didn't notice him arrive.

Jack unlocked his shed and lifted an old sack off a tray of seed potatoes. They had chitted nicely. He spread another old sack on the earth beside the first of half a dozen trenches, and began placing the tubers in the bottom, each one exactly eighteen inches from its neighbour. Some people left only twelve or fifteen inches between them, but they needed room to grow.

His mobile rang as he began drawing the sandy soil over the trenches. The noise attracted Alison's attention. She waved and carried on digging.

"Jack, it's only Frankie. Just thought I'd let you know what's happening."

"So what's the plan?"

"Wednesday week. Eleven o'clock at the City of London. You'll come to the house first?"

"Not sure. Depends."

"Oh."

"Probably. I'll let you know."

"You can go to the chapel of rest any time from Friday. Just let them know you're going."

Jack bent down and tried to pull out a dock seedling. The top broke off, leaving the root behind.

"Not sure it's something I want to do actually, Frankie."

"Nor me, to be honest."

"It's OK not to go, isn't it?"

"It's no one's business but your own, Jack. If you can't face it, that's your choice, isn't it?"

"Thanks, Frankie. Will you be going, though?"

"Depends. I'll talk it over with Russ. I'm going to go and see his plot in the City of London, though, if you fancy it. Be quite like the old days, being in there again. We could have a cup of tea or something. What do you think? One day next week?"

"Let me know when you're going, Frankie. I'll see how things are."

He rang off. Jack slipped the mobile back into his pocket and stared at the river, just visible through the trees. A few people, brought out by the fine weather, walked the sea wall. Another yacht was being towed out to its mooring. Spring was always busy. There was as much work as Jack wanted.

He resumed drawing soil over the tubers, then marked the end of each row with a white-painted stick, like little headstones. Frankie was holding out a hand of friendship, and it was hard to refuse him.

He unfolded his canvas chair from the shed, collected a box of seed packets from the shelf by the window, sat down and began flicking through them. It was almost time to start planting carrots and beetroots if he was going to have anything to sell in the summer. His blackboard brought people down the jetty to see what was in his box. If he liked the look of them, he might come out from the wheelhouse for a chat, but mostly he only put the board out when he went for one of his walks and trusted the visitors to leave the money in his honesty box.

"So, you not talking to me today?" Alison stood before him, gardening gloves in one hand and a winter cabbage in the other. "If you fancy a cup of tea on your way past, I'll leave the door on the latch. Give me five minutes to clean up and get the kettle on."

Jack felt the beginnings of panic. If he stopped for tea, he'd have to tell her, but he hadn't yet worked out the words. Once you say something, once you tell somebody else, it all becomes real. You can't pretend anymore.

He took his time sorting seeds. Most of the packets were past their best before dates but, for heaven's sake, seeds have sprouted when they were hundreds of years old. Sell-by dates on seed packets? I ask you.

He locked the shed, took a last look at his neat rows, and headed off down the path that would have to take him past Alison's cottage.

He stopped outside, pretending he was looking at the garden. Could he tell Alison everything? What Stan and Emm had meant to him, how they had carried him from motherless child to National Service? About Russ's betrayal?

He pushed open the front door shouted a loud "Hello" and walked through to the kitchen, where Alison had set out cups and saucers, a brown teapot and plates and knives. She came in from the garden.

"Sit down, Jack. You make the place look untidy, as my mum used to say."

After tea had been poured and fruit cake sliced onto plates, there was nothing left to do but talk.

Alison took a deep breath, as if she, too, was about to break bad news.

"I see you've got your potatoes in. What are you growing this year?"

Firm ground.

"Well, mostly King Edwards, but I also put in a couple of rows of Rattes. They are second earlies really, but they should be OK. And you?"

Alison put her hand on his.

"Jack, love, what's the matter? If you want to talk about potatoes, that's fine, but I know you well enough to see that, well, something is troubling you."

"Is it that obvious?"

"'Fraid so. But as I said, if you don't want to talk about it, that's fine. We'll just have a nice cup of tea and chat about vegetables."

Jack took a deep breath.

"I had some bad news this morning. I don't know if I've ever mentioned Stan, who was a sort of foster father to me after my mother died."

"Of course. You went and saw him in hospital, didn't you? About a year ago?"

"Yes. Well, I heard this morning that he died last night."

"Jack, I am sorry."

"It's not really sad. He was an old man and died in his sleep. A stroke. Or heart. Something like that. He was a lovely man." Jack sliced a piece off the fruit cake on his plate and took a bite. "Mmm. Did you make this, Ali?"

"Do you know when the funeral is?"

"Wednesday week."

"You'll go?"

He sliced another bite-sized piece off the cake. It really was very good.

"I've no choice, really, have I? Can't say I'm looking forward to it, though."

"You'll have to face your friend, won't you?"

"Yes. But that's not all."

"Do you want to tell me what this is all about?"

Jack shook his head.

"I wouldn't know where to start."

*

In a smart suit, dark tie and spotless white shirt, one hand on the car door ready to swing it open, Frankie appeared every inch the perfect chauffeur when Jack arrived, ten minutes early, at the station. But he seemed to have aged since Jack last saw him, and had a twitch in the corner of his mouth he'd not noticed before. After a rather stiff handshake, Jack slid into the car, where he was met by the smell of leather and the scent of aftershave. He didn't like either.

Frankie started the engine and turned to Jack.

"Shall we go straight there? Unless there's anywhere else you want to go."

"Where else do you suggest?"

"I thought, maybe you'd want to see him?"

"As I said, Frankie, I don't think I'm brave enough for that."

He watched the familiar and the new slide past the window in turn as they drove along roads that as a child Jack had walked and cycled hundreds of times.

"I'm glad it's not a cremation. I don't like to think of... well, you know what."

Frankie concentrated on the road ahead.

They crossed the railway bridge. The air conditioning whisked cool air, laced with a scent he couldn't identify. Frankie continued to stare straight ahead. Jack heard a sniff.

"A proper plot gives you somewhere to go, doesn't it," Frankie said, "a place to visit, if you know what I mean. Russ bought several plots years ago. He said they would only get dearer as the cemetery filled."

"Trust Russ."

"What he didn't know was that Stan had already reserved his own space through some funeral plan or other. He told me, but never told Russ. I still don't know if Russ knows or not. It's not up to me to tell him, is it? If he wants to pay for the whole shebang all over again, well, he's not short of a bob or two, is he?"

"Either way, you're right, Frankie, it's good to have somewhere you can visit."

But he could feel the hypocrisy. How many times had Jack visited his mother's grave in St Pabu? Or his family there, for that matter? Hardly ever, until a few months ago. Frankie drove slowly, as if practising his part in the cortege, and parked close to the gates. Men stood about, stiff in their best suits, worn only for weddings and funerals, smoking and talking about anything but the death of the person who'd brought them there. Young women, glamorous in their black, comforted old ladies, handkerchiefs to their faces. Funeral cars headed in and out, their movements timed to the minute.

Stan's plot was down towards the railway at the bottom of the hill, where ornate monuments gave way to more modest headstones. Fifty years had passed since Jack last walked anywhere beside Frankie. He'd forgotten how he needed to keep his pace slow enough to match Frankie's crooked little steps.

Frankie turned left onto a mown grass track between graves.

"I'll just check on Ma," he said, by way of explanation. Jack followed, expecting to end up beside a humble stone recording the last resting place of Mrs Adams.

They stopped by a simple grave, its dull grey headstone listing to one side like a badly loaded barge. Daffodils rotted in a vase. On the headstone it said, simply, *Louise 'Ma' Vinney taken suddenly on 29 December 1957 — from her many grateful customers.*

Ma Vinney! Fuck! Bile rose to Jack's throat. What the hell was Frankie playing at? Did he know what happened that night? Had Russ blabbed, after all those promises about the secret being safe? But one look at Frankie's face, still as eager to please as when he waited fruitlessly in the school playground to be picked for football, provided the answer.

"Poor old Ma," he said tipping the spent daffodils into a wire mesh waste basket already overflowing with dead flowers and plastic wrappers. "Just dropped dead. Still, I suppose that's the best way. Right as rain one minute, then 'bang', you're gone. Like Stan. Must be something in the air." He pointed to the empty vase. "Should have bought some fresh ones at the flower place as we came in."

Jack leaned against the next grave for support.

"You alright, Jack? You look a bit rough."

Jack pulled himself upright.

"It's OK. I'm fine. Let me walk up and get the flowers. You stay here. I'll be right back."

Frankie reached into a pocket and pulled out his wallet.

Jack waved the offer away.

"No, Frankie, I'll get them."

Frankie began rinsing the vase under a standpipe.

"Right you are. You'll be quicker on your own, the rate I move."

Jack took a couple of steps, and stopped.

"What should I get, do you think?"

Frankie shook the water from the vase, took out a handkerchief, wiped his hands and sat down on a bench.

"It's up to you. But don't be too big-hearted. They put the pot on a bit up there."

Jack turned away and headed up the gentle hill, his pace quickening until he was almost running, as desperate now to get away from Ma Vinney as on the snowy night he'd left her for dead at the bottom of her stairs. It was the same fear he felt as when, home from Pargeter's during school holidays, helping Russ with his paper round in return for a share of his wages, he would cycle through the cemetery in early morning mist, ears straining for ghostly noises, to deliver the *Daily Express* and the *Radio Times* to the keeper's lodge.

He took his time choosing the flowers, delaying the moment when he would have to return to Ma's listing headstone. But why go back at all? In ten minutes he could be at the station. In an hour, the estuary's salty air could be soothing all his fears.

But Frankie was waiting. It was not a time to run.

When he returned Frankie was gone, but there was fresh water in the vase. Jack knelt on the grass, unwrapped the flowers and arranged them as best he could. "The Day Thou Gavest" played over and over in his head. *The darkness falls at Thy behest.* He felt a hand on his shoulder, and jumped.

"They're nice, Jack. Lovely."

"It's only a bunch of daffs."

"All the same, it makes poor old Ma look less neglected. Shows somebody cares, if you know what I mean."

So the man responsible for her death was recast as somebody who cares. Was this the time to return to her graveside, go down on his knees and beg forgiveness?

The odd couple, Jack, tall, upright, still light on his feet, and Frankie, small, twisted, shuffling beside him, resumed their walk downhill between the horse chestnut trees until they came to an area that looked different, more natural. Frankie pointed to a spot among the trees.

"There. This is the natural burial bit. No headstone. Some sort of wicker coffin. Russ isn't happy, but it's what Stan wanted. No headstone, nothing like that. A little wooden marker that rots away in a couple of years."

For a few moments they stood side by side, staring at a patch of grass already marked out with string and pegs for the gravediggers. A long train loaded with cars rattled past, just beyond the railings.

Frankie pointed towards a bench.

"Let's take the weight off our feet."

"Good idea. Then maybe we'll go and get a cup of tea."

They sat side by side, facing the railway.

"We drove down to your place once, me and Stan," said Frankie.

"What do you mean, Frankie?"

"We used to talk about you a lot. About what happened. Then one day Stan said, why didn't we just run down to see you, unannounced as it were. As far as we knew you had no quarrel with us. Just with Russ. And Bel, of course."

"How did you know where to come?"

"Russ had found out somehow. Anyway, we got as far as the pub, parked up."

"Then what did you do? I would have loved to see you."

"As I said, we parked up, got ourselves up onto the sea wall and went along as far as the boatyard. We walked right past your boat, but couldn't see nobody on board.

"So Stan walks into the office, bold as brass, and asks if they knew you. The bloke says to follow him, so we go back to the sea wall, where he points to a motorboat out in the river and says, 'There's Jack. I can call him on the radio if you like.'"

Frankie's voice was starting to break again.

"And did he?"

"No. Stan said not to bother you. I think he'd lost his bottle all of a sudden. Instead, we just stood and watched as you buzzed about out there. Stopping at one boat after another, doing God knows what. Then it looked like you were heading for the jetty so we made a break for it back to the car."

"Why didn't you stay and say hello? As I said, I'd have loved to see you."

"The thing was, Jack, when he saw you out on the river, Stan didn't want to upset the apple cart. You'd moved on, he said. Got another life. We were no longer part of it. Let sleeping dogs lie, he said."

Frankie made a pattern in the dust with his shiny black shoe.

"Stan never blamed you for keeping your distance afterwards. He felt it was his fault. When you were away in the air force, Stan would take them on little outings in the Bond. They would take me an' all if Emm didn't want to go. I thought there might be something going on between Russ and Bel, but then I thought, well, Russ was your best friend. So when they upped and said they were getting married, you could have knocked me down with a feather. Stan said it was his doing, by pushing them together." He took out a handkerchief and wiped the dust from his shoe. "Russ had to beg Stan and Emm to go to the wedding."

Jack stood up.

"But they went, didn't they. Let's go and get a cuppa."

"But I didn't go, Jack, if that's what you're wondering. I'll get started walking back up the hill. It'll take me a while. You come when you're ready."

East London, 1954

James Cagney walks around a wood-panelled room, lecturing a group of men relaxing in armchairs and leather sofas. Behind him is a roaring log fire.

"Everything you learn, everything you do," he says, "is secret. Even your closest relative cannot know you are an agent."

Russ dug Jack in the ribs.

"That your dad, then, is it?" Stan shot him a warning glance. Frankie just stared at the screen, pretending he hadn't heard. Jack pushed Russ away. Of course that wasn't his dad, it was James Cagney. But it was like where his dad was, behind enemy lines.

"This war is no game," Cagney says. "You're going to be taught to kill, to cheat, to rob, to lie. Everything you learn is moving you to one objective, the success of your mission."

It all made sense. Why nobody would tell him anything. Cagney had explained it. He repeated it to himself. "Even your closest relative cannot know you are an agent." He and Maman were his closest relatives, weren't they? So it was obvious.

His dad knew secrets. He'd learned things he could never tell, and done things which meant he could never reveal his identity. There were agents and spies everywhere.

On the screen the agent network has been infiltrated by a German spy. Stan lit a cigarette, his face briefly illuminated by the flare of the lighter.

The scene changes to the inside of an aircraft. Somewhere over Holland, it is time for the agents to parachute in. There's the spy, a real agent and a woman communicator whose job it is to keep in touch with London. Russ again nudged Jack.

"That your mum, then, is it?" he sniggered. Jack ignored him. Stan glared. Frankie said nothing.

When the agents jump, one parachute doesn't open. The spy has cut the agent's rip cord.

*

Frankie wasn't there when Jack reached the cafe. He found him outside the cemetery gates chatting to a couple of the funeral car drivers.

"OK, Jack?" he asked. The cars gleamed in the sunshine. Jack and Frankie climbed into the Jaguar. This time, Frankie didn't hold the door open.

The car murmured into life. Frankie engaged reverse. One hand on the wheel, he turned in his seat, looking back over his shoulder, his face hidden.

"Now, what about coming back?"

Jack didn't reply.

Frankie reversed between a new Mercedes and an ancient Daimler.

"We thought it might be a bit easier than meeting at the funeral, if you know what I mean."

Jack sighed.

"Maybe." He took a deep breath. "OK, let's get it over with."

Frankie seemed to relax for the first time since they met at the station earlier. The task assigned to him by Russ was accomplished: Jack was belted up in the front seat of Russ's car being driven to Russ's house by Russ's driver. The electric door locks clicked as they gathered speed. The car slid into the stream of traffic. Frankie slowed to let a van edge into the main road.

"They were saying, the drivers, that if I was ever interested in making a bit of pocket money, they were always on the lookout for extra cars. They get some big jobs. Some big Asian families want up to a dozen cars, and it's always short notice with them. Well, it has to be. The Coronation is a banqueting place now, and there's a lot of big weddings there."

Frankie stopped to allow a mother to push her pram across a zebra crossing. He stared straight ahead through the windscreen.

"There's no harm in him, you know. Russ, I mean."

"Is he expecting me?"

Frankie turned towards Jack.

"Yes, and no. Do you want me to give him a ring?"

As the woman reached the kerb, an ancient man, stick

in hand, started to cross. He shuffled slowly across in front of them, turning to wave his stick in thanks. Frankie waited until the man was safely on the pavement before accelerating away. The car behind hooted.

"I always think, when I see an old geezer like him, that'll be me one day," he said. "Shall I?"

"I'm sorry, Frankie. What was that?"

"Give him a ring."

"No. I'd rather turn up unannounced."

The gates parted before the front wheels even touched the drive. The car crunched on the gravel, passed down the side of the house and stopped outside the garage Jack had seen months before. Frankie put a hand on Jack's arm.

"Come on, then, let's go and find him."

Jack followed him along a York-stoned path towards the open doors of a conservatory. Someone sat behind a huge desk, facing out over the garden. A man wearing Russ's mask. A bright pink camellia in a fancy pot propped open the door. Jack could neither go in, nor turn back. Russ made no move. Frankie had melted away somewhere.

The scene had been rehearsed so many times in Jack's imagination, but it wasn't as it should have been. He should have been angry. Shouting. But he just stood there, saying nothing.

Eventually, Russ waved an arm towards a cane sofa piled high with soft cream-coloured cushions.

"Come on in, Jack. Have a perch. I knew if anyone could get you here it would be Frankie, bless him."

Jack's feet would not move.

"No thanks. I've been sitting most of the day. I'd sooner stand."

"Know what you mean, Jack."

Beyond the silence of the conservatory, birds fussed in

the trees, a police siren wailed somewhere and the universal sound of children at play drifted across from the school. The two men stared at each other, like heavyweights waiting for the bell. After what seemed like several minutes, Russ spoke again.

"Fancy a wander around the estate before lunch?"

Jack turned to look at the garden, as if seeing it for the first time. Lunch? Who said he was staying for lunch? And was that when Bel was going to put in an appearance? Talk about rub his nose in it.

"That would be nice, if you're not too busy?"

Russ smiled, but the smile that could once open any door seemed faded, false.

"Too busy, Jack? I've waited donkey's years for this moment." Russ still made no move; how much longer was Jack expected to stand at the door waiting?

"Let's go, then. At least if you're walking beside me you won't have to look at my ugly mug." He touched the arm of his chair and glided out from behind the desk in an electric wheelchair.

"God, Russ, I had no idea. What happened?"

Russ guided the chair to the door.

"Nothing happened, Jack. I've just got a touch of the Stephen Hawking about me. Can't do anything about it, but it's a bit of a bugger sometimes."

"Why didn't Frankie tell me?"

Russ stared out into the garden. On a little terrace, a woman was setting a table. It wasn't Bel. Too young.

"Told him not to. Didn't want you feeling sorry for me. Even made him take down the disabled badge from the car if he was meeting you." He chuckled, and at last Jack had something that matched up with his memory. "Complained like stink he did," Russ continued, "'cos it meant he'd have

to pay for parking. Anyway, you look in good nick, mate."
He paused. "It's been a long time."

Jack glanced down at his friend, shrunken in his
wheelchair. And then at the immaculate garden, the shining
Jaguar, the woman laying up a table for lunch, under the
shade of an ancient tree. Somewhere he should have been
able to find an emotion: sympathy for his one-time friend,
envy of his wealth. But he felt nothing. He just shrugged his
shoulders.

"Yes, I'm fine. All in all."

The air felt still, heavy, as if full of rain that hadn't yet
fallen. Deep in the house a telephone rang.

Russ swung the chair, and for an instant Jack again
glimpsed the old seductive grin. But it clung to a face that
had already begun to fall in on itself.

"That's what I like to hear, Boyo. Too much death and
misery around for my liking. You know what, the world
started to go to pot when the Big Bopper fell out of the sky
and it's been downhill non-stop ever since."

He whirred back behind the desk.

"Here, Boyo, get a load of this. It'll crease you up. Stan
loved it." He touched a few keys on his computer and moved
sideways so there was enough room for Jack to stand beside
him. On the screen a man with a microphone is crouched
beside a girl in the studio audience, giving her a telescope
to look through. "What can you see?" he asks. "The Eiffel
Tower," she answers. The compere points towards a stage
and says, "That's right. It's Paris. And there's Chantilly Lace
and the Big Bopper." And there is the Big Bopper, telephone
in hand, drape jacket, crew-cut hair. "Hello, baby," he says.
And then the piano starts belting out the rhythm. The
audience of mostly young teenage girls begins clapping,
more or less in time with the on-beat.

Jack could feel the stirrings of a smile, but it would take more than a couple of minutes from YouTube to erase the righteous pain and grievance he had nursed over so many decades.

Two minutes and forty-four seconds later, the Big Bopper finished his act to thunderous applause from an audience dressed as if going to a wedding in their mothers' best outfits. Russ continued to stare at the now motionless grey figures in the centre of the screen.

"Stan loved that clip," he said again, pulling a box of tissues towards him. His shoulders began to shake. His head went down. All Jack could hear was the whirring hard drive of the computer.

Russ blew his nose.

"Sorry about that. But you know what, I'm going to miss him like buggery. Thank God for Frankie." He looked up, eyes rimmed with red. "And you, of course."

Jack touched his shoulder and gently tightened his grip.

Russ briefly rested his hand on Jack's, and then quickly withdrew it.

"Come on. Let me show you the garden and we can have lunch under the horse chestnut." The wheelchair buzzed across the wooden floor, down a gentle ramp and out into the air. Jack followed, unsure whether he should touch the chair. The garden smelled of freshly cut grass and wallflowers. A whiff of smoke drifted up from behind the hedge where Jack had lain in wait on his ridiculous visit months ago.

The wheelchair paused at a bend in the path, near the bottom of the garden. Russ waved his arm, indicating the extent of the property.

"So this is home, Jack. Has been ever since I bought it from Bel's uncle." He paused, as if he'd already said words he'd wanted to keep inside. "You do know about Bel, don't you?"

"Know what?"

"Me and her. It didn't last, Jack. How could it, when it started on the wrong foot? We needed it pretty quickly."

Russ started forward again, and after a few yards stopped beside a rose bush. He picked off a few dead blooms, pulled each faded petal from the carpel and threw them, one by one, onto the ground.

"We still see a lot of each other, but I wasn't the marrying kind, if you know what I mean. We should never have got hitched in the first place."

Jack watched a heron land on the thin branches of a treetop in the park.

"So why the hell did you, Russ? Why? What had I done to deserve that?"

"You don't know how many times we asked ourselves that same question. Particularly towards the end. And honestly, Jack, if I live to be a hundred, God forbid, I'll never know the answer. As I said, it was a mistake from beginning to end. One long, slow motion disaster."

Russ went to start the wheelchair forward, but Jack stepped in front.

"You don't expect me to be sympathetic, do you?"

"No, I'm not asking for sympathy. I'm just saying I don't know why we did what we did."

"That's just not good enough, Russ. Just not good enough."

"It's like I said, mate. I know it sounds pathetic, but I just don't know."

"It is pathetic! You ruin my life, Bel's life and by the sound of it your own, and you don't know why. What kind of a moron are you? And I'm not your mate. I might have been once, but not after all you've put me through."

Jack walked slowly away, shoulders hunched, up the

garden towards the gravel drive and the elaborate sliding gates through which he'd arrived. He heard the whirr of the wheelchair behind him. He stopped.

Russ's voice was quiet.

"Don't go, Jack. Please don't. If only for Stan's sake, don't run off. We can't afford to lose you again."

Jack sat down on a bench. In front of him water from a little fountain spun rainbows before dropping into a pond to refresh the goldfish. He should never have come.

"Then, however hard it is, however pathetic, at least try to explain. Do me that honour at least."

Russ moved the wheelchair closer to the bench, spun it around so the two men were face to face, at the same level, for the first time in forty years. Russ looked directly into Jack's eyes.

"We loved you, Jack," he whispered. He looked away.

"Strange way of showing it."

"You just don't get it, do you, Boyo? You have no idea what it did to us when you joined up. You were the centre of our lives. Not just Bel and me, but Stan and Emm as well. That first summer you were away, we would all crowd into the Bond for a run out somewhere, and always we ended up talking about the same thing: Jack flippin' Boyer. Why did he go? Why did he leave us?"

"I didn't have any choice. The money stopped when I was eighteen."

"That's bollocks, Boyo, and you know it. You could have gone to college. Got a grant. You didn't have to join up."

Jack swallowed hard. He really didn't need this.

"What difference does it make now, anyway? What's done is done and we are where we are. I'd better go. Get Frankie to let me know the details of the funeral." He stood up.

"No, Jack, bloody sit down and listen for once. Let me

give it to you straight. We were in love with you, both of us, all of us, probably. When you went off in your uniform you broke our hearts."

"And you think that gave you the right to betray me? Steal Bel from behind my back?"

"Betray you? That's rich. You didn't need us, not then. You were away with your aeroplanes and your posh mates and what were we? Four bloody nobodies from the East End. A builder's labourer, a little girl from a prefab, a baker and a part-time shop assistant. What did you need us for? You didn't even bother to write. What else could we do but cling together for comfort? Had you made any commitment to Bel? What was she supposed to do? Sit and do embroidery in case one day you might think of marrying her?"

"It wasn't like that, Russ. I never said I didn't need you."

"You didn't have to."

"And I did write."

"Oh, I'm sorry, yes, you did write. You really did. You wrote, OK, Boyo. A scribbled postcard saying how much you were enjoying yourself. What a great time you were having in the sunshine."

"And I came home to see you."

"Once in a blue moon, when you weren't too busy visiting one of your chums at their country estate."

East London, 1957

Stan carried the tray out from the kitchen into the yard. In the three weeks since Jack had last been home, Stan had built a sturdy bench and painted up an old table from the bakery. The evening was theirs. They had finished the washing up, and it was time to take a breather and enjoy the gentle warmth before it became chilly. Emm had gone out to her Young Wives meeting, where she was taking a course in basket-making.

"Not seeing Russ tonight?" Stan asked as he put the tray down. He hadn't spilled a drop of the two large cups of tea, which he had filled to the brim.

"No, not tonight."

"Any particular reason?"

Before Jack was obliged to answer, they heard the front door close. Moments later, Emm bustled into the garden, with her latest creation, a small basket lined with a jolly patterned cloth.

"What do you think?" she asked, putting it down in front of them.

"Very nice," said Stan, picking it up and turning it over. "What's it for?"

"What do you think it's for? You of all people should know. It's a bread basket. For rolls."

"It's lovely, Auntie."

"There's a cuppa in the pot if you want one, Emm," said Stan.

She started towards the kitchen door and then stopped.

"You know what I would really like, Stanley Gibson? A pale ale. Shall we run over to the George and sit in the garden?"

"My garden furniture not good enough for you, then? I'll go and start up the Bond. You coming, Jack?"

"Sure thing." He paused. "Shall I run round and see if Russ wants to come?"

"No," said Emm. There was something in her tone that suggested that was her final word.

Stan picked up the tray.

"Not tonight, son. So, Emm, shall we just go to the George or shall we run out to Chigwell for the King's Head?"

"The George. They'll be calling last orders by the time we get to Chigwell."

*

Emm insisted on getting the drinks while Stan and Jack found a table. While they were still alone, Jack ventured the question that had been on his mind for the past half-hour.

"What's the problem with Russ, Stan? Why didn't Emm want Russ to come?"

"It's a bit complicated, I think we've seen a bit too much of him while you've been away. He knows you're not here but he still keeps coming round. Seems a bit lost without you, if you know what I mean."

"A bit lost? I wish he would get lost sometimes." Emm was back. "He's trouble, that Russ, ain't he, Stan?"

Stan nodded and raised his glass to his lips. But Emm had not finished.

"People take one look at him with his neat clothes and nice hair and think butter wouldn't melt in his mouth. But he don't fool us, does he, Stan? You were saying the other day, weren't you, that he could charm the birds from the trees, but you can't trust him?"

She paused long enough to sit down.

"Anyway, surely there's some nice boys at Pargeter's you could spend your time with, instead of always hanging about with him."

Emm was right. There were plenty of nice boys at Pargeter's, but they didn't live in the East End in tiny terraced houses backing onto railway lines. He'd been invited to one boy's house for the weekend. Harry, his name was. His mother had picked them up one Friday afternoon in the family's Armstrong Siddeley Sapphire. Their house stood at the end of a long drive through dark woods. The garden ran down to a river. There was a lake and a tennis court. The sitting room had a big log fire and little tables on which stood photographs of smiling young men in uniform posed in front of their Spitfires. A lady came to do the cooking while Harry's mum sat sewing on the biggest sofa Jack had ever seen. Even bigger than those at the Odeon. Harry's father arrived home at six thirty and everyone gathered for drinks. The cooking lady brought ice cubes.

How could he ask Harry back to Emm's little house to share a room with him and Stan? At school, nobody could tell. In his air cadet's uniform, Jack was every bit as smart as Harry. But once outside the yellow brick wall around Pargeter's, it was all too obvious. Jack was not one of them.

He was never asked back, and anyway, it was easier to be at home with Stan and Emm. But that weekend at Harry's house was when he decided that he would sign up to the RAF for five years when he reached eighteen, a decision he'd not shared with anyone.

Eleven

Meeting up with Russ after all that had happened, after all those years of self-righteous anger, was never going to be easy. But he never thought he would be forced to defend himself. He was the one who had been wronged and who carried the wounds. Not Russ.

But here was his one-time friend, now a pathetic old man sick in his wheelchair, on the attack. It was time to go. To return to the sanctuary of his river, his pub, the people whom he had grown to love.

Russ reversed and spun the wheelchair.

"Anyway," he said, "all that was yesterday. What's done is done. Arguing the toss about whose fault it was will get us nowhere. All I ask is that out of respect for Stan and for the sake of Frankie we at least pretend we can get along."

He spun the chair again.

"So, if we've done, there's something I've got to show you." However much Jack just wanted to go home, he obediently followed Russ alongside a long hedge, around a corner until they stopped outside an extension to the house. Would he always have to do as Russ wanted? Russ stopped beside the door.

"Stan's little flat. He used to get so mad, me calling it his granny annexe, but he knew I was just winding him up. I've offered it to Frankie now. Go on in. It's not locked."

Jack pushed open the door and stepped inside. Russ didn't follow. The room could only have been Stan's. One wall was fitted with shelves, home to dozens of cases containing cine film, each one carefully labelled and arranged in date order. *Day out at Margate August 1954*, *Visit to Emm in Ireland 1974*, *Bond owners Rally 1985* – year after year, Stan's life meticulously chronicled on evolving technologies. Jack must have made a few appearances on Cine 8, his moods and movements captured by the wind-up camera held securely in Stan's steady hand. But he was gone before Stan shot his first reel of Super 8, let alone onto VHS tapes or mini cassettes. Jack had left the stage well before the digital age was born. Somewhere there would be *Russ and Bel's Wedding 1962*, but it wasn't there.

He ran his fingers over the boxes of early titles. Some of them he had seen, years before, when the postman delivered back the film Stan had sent for processing. Frame by frame, he could still picture them, so clearly he no longer knew whether the memories he carried were of the events themselves or the images cast on the narrow strips of celluloid.

He turned away from the shelves and, from a coffee table, picked up a silver-framed photograph: Emm, astride the Royal Enfield, a small boy sitting in the sidecar.

More photos covered the tops of the sideboard and the windowsill. There was Jack, in his RAF uniform, outside Emm's house, another of him in his Pargeter's blazer standing by her front gate. A small boy holding a cricket bat on the beach, Maman in the background relaxing in a deck chair. There was Bel, her hair streaming across her face, holding down her skirt against the wind. On the back: *Bel, Southend Pier, June 1961*. A year after Jack joined up. When he was being shot at in Cyprus.

He was searching for the pictures he didn't want to find. He opened a sideboard drawer. Finding nothing more incriminating than cutlery, he slid it shut. He tried the next one, which seemed full of bits and pieces such as matches and fuses. He found it in the third drawer. Face down, a photo in the cardboard frame in which it had been delivered. Slowly he turned it over. A small group of guests standing outside St Mary's church. Bel, as beautiful as Jack remembered, stood there in her flowing white dress, bouquet in hand, smiling into the eyes of her new husband.

Jack gasped. A rush of cold air sank down through his chest to his guts, where it turned to ice. He slumped down into Stan's old armchair, the picture hanging in his hand. Of course Stan and Emm would have been there. How could they not? He studied the picture again. Stan was neither looking into the camera nor at the happy couple, but away to the left, as if something had taken his attention or he was looking for somewhere to run. As if he knew that sometime later Jack would look at the photograph and that he would be unable to meet his gaze. Emm held a handkerchief to her eyes.

But Russ, grinning into the camera lens, was as pleased with himself as a dog with two tails. Sorry, mate, but while you were away I took everything from you. Your girl, Stan, Emm, the lot.

Jack pulled himself up, looked in the mirror above the sideboard, and took a few deep breaths, hoping to calm the churning inside him. When he felt more steady, he strode to the door, the photo still in his hand. Russ hadn't moved: he sat motionless, his face turned towards the sun, eyes closed, manicured hands resting in his lap. Jack stood in front of the wheelchair, casting a shadow across his friend's face. Russ stirred and looked up, blinking as if waking from a deep sleep.

Jack jabbed the photo with a finger.

"Was he best man?"

"What's that, Boyo?"

"You heard. Was he your best man?"

"Who?"

"You know damn well who I mean. Stan."

"He refused. Had to beg him even to come to the wedding. I didn't have a best man. And before you ask, Bel's uncle gave her away."

"So you asked him?"

Russ reversed the wheelchair a yard or so.

"What difference does it make, Jack? What bloody difference? I asked him. He said 'no'. End of story. I've already told you, the whole marriage thing was a balls-up, from start to bloody finish. Alright? Does that make you feel better?"

Jack didn't answer. There was nothing to say. He looked again at the apparently happy photograph, shook his head and returned to the flat. He left the photograph as he had found it, face down in the drawer. When he went back outside, after splashing his face with cold water in Stan's little bathroom, Russ had gone. Jack scanned the garden. In the far corner, half hidden by a rhododendron, he could see the back of the wheelchair. And even from where he stood, the shake of Russ's shoulders was unmistakeable.

Slowly, silently, Jack made his way to the table and sat facing away from Russ, towards the house. He heard the whirr of the chair.

"Hideous, isn't it?" said Russ, nodding towards a wooden building that resembled a Swiss cuckoo clock. "But it's a right little sun trap here. Now, I've got something else to show you."

Again, Jack found himself following Russ around the twisting paths until they entered a door at the rear of the garage. Just inside stood a little red three-wheeled car, its paintwork shining like new.

"Stan's pride and joy," said Russ. "We got it for him for his seventieth. Not been used for a while now, but Frankie starts it up and runs it out of the garage every so often."

Jack touched the bonnet of the tiny car. It really was Stan's Bond, or one just like it. Typical. That was how Russ operated. Prepared to use anything to get his own way. He gave Stan a job. He gave him a home. Even a bloody car. Now it's Frankie's turn. He's already got the job. He's about to get the flat.

When he was a kid, Russ used that smile and an easy charm to get grown-ups eating out of his hand. But not Stan. Stan and Emm could see right through him. But it seems even Stan gave in eventually.

No wonder, then, that Stan was so keen to see everything patched up, papered over. Water under the bridge, he'd called it. Jack wanted to kick the tiny car. Put a great dent in its stupid little doors. He screwed up his eyes and clenched his fists. No. He wasn't going to give Russ the bloody satisfaction. Not this time.

"Frankie was the only one ever went with Stan when he took it out. There's no way I could get myself in it."

"And, guess what, I wasn't around. You may as well say it, Russ, because I know that's what you're thinking." He heard the whir of the wheelchair as Russ spun it round.

"It wasn't what I was thinking at all, Jack. But if that's what you want to imagine, well, it's up to you. Come on. Let's go and find a drink. I think we both need it."

By the time Jack emerged from the garage, Russ was already at the table, which was set with plates, glasses, napkins, shiny cutlery. A bottle of white wine sat in its ice bucket.

"Can you do the honours, Jack?" said Russ, indicating the wine. "I'll just slop it all over the place." And so Jack poured Russ's wine, an elegant Sancerre, into his crystal glasses. Like a bloody butler. He knew it would be like this. Russ in charge.

"Isn't Frankie invited?"

"No. He reckoned we'd be fighting like cat and dog by now, so he said he'd walk up to the Forest Arms for a bowl of soup. I told him not to be too long and to stay off the beer because you'll need a lift back home."

"I can walk to the station from here."

Russ flicked his napkin at a wasp showing undue interest in the wine glasses. It fell to the table. He crushed it with the back of a teaspoon, then picked it up by a wing and dropped it onto the ground.

The woman Jack had seen earlier approached the table, carrying a large tray.

"Oh, Mrs Charlton, this is my old friend Jack Boyer."

She put the tray down. Jack stood to shake hands.

"Lovely to meet you at last, Mr Boyer. I've heard so much about you from Mr Russell, and of course Mr Gibson and Mr Adams. We spoke the other day, didn't we?"

She unloaded the tray. A basket of fresh bread. Butter. A platter of seafood: smoked salmon, prawns, and crab claws, lemon wedges and a pink-coloured seafood sauce.

"You certainly live well, Russ."

Russ thanked Mrs Charlton and gestured for Jack to help himself.

"Life's been good to me. Now, did you go and see Stan's spot under the trees?"

Jack handed the serving forks to Russ.

"Yes. Frankie showed me." He took a sip of Sancerre and stared at an aeroplane leaving vapour trails in the clear blue sky. He cleared his throat. "Frankie also took me to Ma Vinney's grave."

Russ wiped his lips and put down the napkin.

"He didn't, did he? Why did he do that?"

"I don't know, but it turned my stomach over. I thought maybe it was your idea. Soften me up a bit."

"For Christ's sake, Jack. Why would I want to do that to you? I'll have a word with him when he gets back. But I'm sure he didn't mean anything by it."

"You've never told him about that night?"

"What do you take me for?" He looked around as if to be sure they were not overheard. "You're still beating yourself up about it, aren't you? But there's a couple of things you should understand, that only I can tell you. The first is that you only went 'cos you were still pissed off with me about what happened at the party. Right?"

Jack nodded.

"Second, it wasn't your fault she died."

"No? It was me that disturbed her and saw her fall down the bloody stairs, Russ. I didn't even ring for an ambulance. I did a runner. And it's not my fault?"

Russ picked up the napkin and put it in his lap.

"I've seen the police report."

"How's that?"

Russ backed away from the table and guided his wheelchair to the edge of the terrace, not looking at Jack but down the garden to where two magpies chased each other around the grass.

"Never mind how. Let's just say it was through the friend of a friend. All you need to know is she would have been

149

dead that morning, whether she'd got out of bed or not. Her falling downstairs had nothing to do with it."

"You sure?"

Russ rotated his chair to face Jack.

"I've just told you, Boyo. Natural causes. A massive stroke, as it happens. No suspicious circumstances, the report said. You read the *Stratford Express*. Same as me. Natural causes, they said. Where do you think they got that from? Now pour us another glass of wine."

But Jack could sit no longer. He walked down the garden to look at a sculpture that stood on a raised terrace. He heard the wheelchair behind him and turned.

"Why did you never tell me this?"

"I only found out years after. Came about when I went to a do for some police charity or other. You'd gone. It was all history. And, frankly, I didn't know if you cared a monkey's arse."

"But you should have."

"Probably. But your life was a closed book, Jack. A closed book. Let's go and eat."

Twelve

The pavement outside Russ's house was completely taken up with wreaths and flowers. People stood about in groups, while a man wearing a florescent yellow jacket guarded the middle of the road, directing cars into neighbours' parking spaces. Ali touched Jack's arm.

"Why have they left all the flowers on the street?"

"It's traditional in the East End. So the neighbours can see them, read the cards and so on."

"There are so many."

"Everyone loved Stan."

"You certainly did." She squeezed his arm and let go.

"But I never even…"

Before he could go on, she cut across him.

"Jack, love. You are here today, that's all that matters. You're going to stand up in front of a huge congregation, mostly people you don't know, and give the eulogy, which you have spent hours perfecting. If that's not an act of love, I don't know what is."

A van was stopped outside the house, blocking Jack's way. The driver climbed out, wreath in hand. A frockcoated undertaker stepped forward, nodded acceptance, read the card and carefully put the wreath to join the others. On the far side of the road, in the bright sunshine outside a new block of low-rise flats, a knot of people watched the comings and goings.

Somebody in a hi-vis came to the car window, asked Jack's name, consulted his clipboard and directed him towards Russ's drive. When the gates swung open, there was Frankie stepping up to greet them.

"Morning, Jack. Can you pull round and park behind the Jag? Russ is over by the conservatory. Mrs Charlton has coffee on the go." He glanced at Ali, and lowered his voice. "Bel's already here."

As they stepped from the car, a stiff breeze robbed the sun of its warmth. Ali pulled her jacket around her.

"What a beautiful garden," she said. But her eyes were fixed on Russ speeding towards them around the path, smiling broadly. He stopped in front of them.

"Jack," he said, looking Ali up and down. "And you must be Alison. He's a dark horse, isn't he? I didn't know a thing about you until Frankie told me this morning you were coming. Let me show you round the garden. Jack's already had the tour. There's coffee in the conservatory, Boyo."

Ali gave Jack's hand a little squeeze and obediently followed Russ's whirring chair. Jack watched until they reached the first of the fishponds, where Russ stopped beside a bench and indicated to Ali she should sit. He'd never change: always ready to move in on somebody else's girl, even from an electric wheelchair. Fifteen to twenty people had gathered around the doors to the conservatory, drinking coffee and chatting. Men in dark glasses and sharp-cut suits, tailored women showing gold jewellery. Jack's gaze flitted from one to the next. He knew none of them, but Bel was not among the group.

Down the garden, beside the fountain, Russ was waving his arms at the fishpond, no doubt boasting to Ali about his collection of Koi carp and complaining about the herons that ate them. As usual, Russ had planned everything out. He intended to keep Ali occupied while Jack and Bel came face to face with each other. No wonder Russ had made money. Always a step ahead. Every detail thought out ahead of time.

A tall woman wove her way through the coffee drinkers towards him. The breeze blew her hair across her face, and even if her features had been entirely hidden, he would have known he was looking at Bel. He tried to compose his face, but didn't know what expression he wanted to wear.

She stepped beyond the group. Whispers and raised eyebrows replaced the buzz of conversation. Some people stopped and stared, probably the ones who knew the sad story of Russ, Bel and Jack.

Without a pause, she walked right up to Jack and offered a cheek. He brushed his cheek against hers and stepped back.

"Jack," she said, taking his hand, "you look terrific. Hardly changed. How are you?"

Should he try to return the compliment? Say how glamorous she looked? He didn't know how.

"Nervous, actually, Bel. And sad."

She squeezed his fingers.

"We're all sad, Jack. But there's no need for nerves. You'll do just fine, I'm sure."

Jack looked past her face, over her shoulder to where he noticed Ali turn her head towards him and give a smile. He gently pulled his hand free.

"But so many people."

"You'll be great, I know. There's nobody better."

Jack didn't know the patronising, self-assured woman

standing in front of him in her immaculate black suit and high heels. He could recognise the way she moved, how she pushed her hair away when it blew across her face. Her walk hadn't changed, with the same sway in the hips that drew whistles from building sites. But the girl who told him in a letter she was marrying his best friend? She had gone.

"So, Bel, what do we do now?" He nodded in the direction of the conservatory. "We have an audience."

"I suppose we just chat to each other like old friends do when they meet up at a funeral. Catch up on each other's news."

Jack tried to smile, but his skin seemed too tight, as if bound up with brown parcel tape.

"So is that what we are, then? Two old friends?"

She took both his hands and looked him full in the face. Her breath smelled of Parma Violets. Some things one could never forget.

"I hope so, Jack. Whatever you may be feeling, and I don't blame you, for the sake of Stan and Russ, can we be just that? For today, at least? Just old friends. Shall we walk?"

Jack could feel the muscles in his eyelids twitching. Emm would have said it was new blood running in.

"So you want to lead me up the garden path again?"

High above their heads, swallows swooped and dived in their endless quest for enough insects to feed the nest.

"Shall I pretend that was a joke?"

"It's up to you."

They walked in silence for a while, Jack taking care to avoid any accidental touches. They stopped in a little rose garden. Jack sniffed a rose, but it had no scent.

"You asked earlier how I was. I'm fine actually. Much to my surprise, I'm fine."

"So you are not still angry with me?"

"No, not angry. Liberated, actually."

Bel stopped to snap fading heads off a basket of geraniums hanging from a fake Victorian lamp-post.

"Liberated? Oh, I think I get it. I'm not the innocent girl you remember? You are a funny one, Jack. But then, you always were."

She crushed the faded blooms in her hand and tossed them onto the earth.

"Should I say sorry?"

"Only if you mean it."

"Russ told me about your visit last week. When you said he'd ruined all our lives it cut him deep, Jack."

"Then, he shouldn't have..." He stopped, the words dry as dust in his throat. He picked an imaginary piece of fluff from the sleeve of his jacket. Ali and Russ were still beside the goldfish pond, both laughing. That was the future. The wealthy, sophisticated woman in her heels and Chanel was somebody he'd met for the first time at the funeral of a mutual friend. The hurt and anger that he'd stoked and nourished over half a century was ebbing away faster than a spring tide.

Bel reached for his hand.

"I think maybe you should go and rescue your pretty friend. And I could murder a coffee. And there's probably people you'd rather talk to than me."

He felt he should deny it out of politeness, but remained silent.

She kissed him lightly on the cheek and sauntered off in the direction of the house.

Jack followed at a distance and edged inside the crowded conservatory. Ali and Russ had stopped to admire one of Russ's nymph statues on the other side of the garden. A coffee filter bubbled away on a trolley, a plate of biscuits next to it. He squeezed past into the house, following signs for the cloakroom. As he emerged, feeling fresher and finally ready to face the congregation of mourners, he came face to face with Bel in the hall. He searched for something innocuous to say.

"It must have been hard to leave this house."

"Russ never really wanted a wife, just a trophy. And the business, of course. You know what he's like. He can't help it, Jack."

*

Beyond the open front door, the carpet of flowers received another wreath. Bel followed Jack's gaze.

"Reminds me of the gates of Kensington Palace when Diana died," she said, before turning and heading back from whence she came. Jack watched her climb the stairs until her black stockings and shiny high heels disappeared round the bend in the staircase. She didn't look back.

When Jack returned to the conservatory, he found Russ alone, sitting at his desk. The guests had moved into the garden. Russ glanced up, but his thoughts were obviously far away.

"All OK, Boyo?" he said.

"Fine."

"Good. I think your lovely lady is powdering her nose. Grab a coffee. Put something in it. The cars will be here any moment." He went back to whatever was claiming his attention, then looked up again. "You're a lucky man, Jack. Alison, I mean."

Jack poured a coffee and considered the whisky. Single malt. To put in coffee? Typical Russ.

"Yes, I am. Not that Alison and me are..."

"Doesn't matter, Boyo. Time and a place for everything. Get it wrong and it all goes to pot."

"I'm not planning to get it wrong."

Russ's eyes flicked towards the door. Jack felt a hand on his shoulder and caught a whiff of Ali's perfume.

"What's that you were saying? What aren't you going to get wrong?" she asked.

"Oh, nothing. The eulogy, you know. Things."

Russ's face broke into the wicked little grin that Jack had last seen half a century earlier.

"You know, Ali, this man's too good to lie. That's why we love him. I was just saying he was a lucky man, to have you as a friend." A ping from the computer announced the arrival of an email. Russ returned to his keyboard, still grinning.

Ali touched Jack's hand.

"Anyway, did it go alright? She's so elegant and beautiful, isn't she?"

"I suppose she is. It was all a bit odd, really." He caught a reflection of them both in a mirror. "But I'm better than alright. Much better. What about you?"

Russ looked up and winked.

"We're getting along like a house on fire, aren't we, Alison?"

A snatch of somebody whistling "Colonel Bogey" sounded from Russ's desk. Russ picked up his mobile, said, "Thanks," and snapped it shut. "They're on their way. Be here in five minutes. We'd better be going. Stick close."

Russ sped out from behind his desk, swinging the wheelchair this way and that as if he were once again riding the dodgems at the end of the pier. Ali slipped her arm into Jack's as they followed around the garden and out into the street, the crowd parting to let them hurry through. The undertaker, head bowed but eyes watchful, murmured, "Good morning,

Mr Russell," as they passed. In the middle of the road Frankie faced the top of the street, while in the other direction the man in the yellow jerkin persuaded the driver of a Tesco van to turn around and go back the way he'd come.

Out on the main road, Jack could see a police motorcycle, blue lights flashing, blocking the traffic. The rider, hands on his hips, stood beside his machine. Around the corner walked an undertaker, top hat in one hand, silver cane in the other, followed by six other frockcoated pallbearers. A pair of bay horses appeared, then a second pair and finally the hearse itself.

Russ looked up from his chair.

"Same people who did Ronnie Kray, Boyo." He wiped his eyes. "I'd have had the royal gun carriage for Stan, if they'd let me. And the band of the Grenadier Guards."

The crowd parted to make room for the cortege. The black-plumed horses, their brass gleaming, stopped, their heads lifting and shaking, enjoying the moment. A movie camera made from black roses stood on top of the hearse, while on each side, pressed up against the windows, the word *Stan* was fashioned in white daisies.

Four black limousines lined up behind the hearse, the driver of each one, hand on door, waiting for his passengers. Frankie, clipboard in hand, moved about the crowd, directing the mourners to their assigned cars, while the undertaker's men loaded the flowers onto the roof of the hearse.

The undertaker walked to the front of the cortege. He lifted his hat just a fraction and the whole show began to inch towards the park. Russ was unusually quiet.

"Where's Bel?" Jack asked. "We've not left her behind?"

"She's in the second car. Didn't know how things would work out between you two. Never could, never will. But we couldn't have an atmosphere in the car. Not at this time."

He pulled out a gold pocket watch, opened the case, closed it again and dropped it back into his waistcoat pocket. "Stan always blamed her, you know. They never got close after that. I think he forgave me, but not her. Not fair, I know, but there it is."

What could he respond to that? They reached the bottom of the road and stopped. Frankie climbed out.

Jack looked up.

"What's going on?"

"Look over there, Boyo."

From behind a row of garages emerged a tiny car, not much bigger than a wheelbarrow, with just one wheel at the front, two at the back and its roof open to the sun. Black ribbons hung from the corners of the windscreen.

Jack leaned forward to get a better view.

"A Bond. Look, Ali, a bloody Bond Minicar, just like Stan's. I wouldn't have believed it."

Russ seemed to be bouncing with excitement.

"Just you wait, Boyo, just watch and wait."

As the little car left the gap between the garages, another appeared, and then another, each one wearing bunches of black ribbons and moving so slowly the drivers might have been pedalling them along. One after another, the cars bumped across the pavement and down into the road, until there were five of them lined up behind the horses, their ribbons fluttering in the ghost of a breeze. Frankie went over to the driver of the first minicar. He looked up and down the procession, gave a thumbs-up, and returned to the Rolls-Royce.

Jack leaned forward and spoke softly into Russ's ear, as if too much sound would make everything disappear.

"How in God's name, Russ? How did you manage to organise that? Where did you find them all?"

Russ glanced up into the mirror.

"Wasn't me, Boyo. It was Frankie here."

The cortege moved off again, the undertaker swinging aboard the hearse to sit beside the driver. They turned the corner and slowly made their way towards the main road.

Ali turned to Frankie and covered his hand with hers.

"It's wonderful."

Frankie looked away, trying to hide from the praise.

"Stan was a member, you see," he said. "They thought it was a great idea. First time for them. They've never done one before. A funeral, that is."

Frankie stared out of the window.

"I tell you, Stan would've bloody burst into song. He loved his little Bond. But you know what, what would've really bucked him up is seeing you and Russ together again. Ain't that right, Russ?"

Thirteen

The solicitors had gone up in the world since Jack visited with Emm after his mother had died. Not only did it have a couple more names in the title – it was now Bernard, Smithers and Grant LLP – but also it was located in a fine Georgian town house in Laurence Pountney Hill, a little street in the City close to the Thames. He climbed the half-dozen steps to the elegant grey-painted front door and pushed the brass bell button.

A woman's voice answered immediately.

"Ah, Mr Boyer. Please come in."

The lock clicked. Jack pushed open the door. Two girls in smart black suits sat behind an antique desk on which stood a clear glass vase of fresh flowers. The room smelled of polish and the girls' perfume. They both looked up from their screens and smiled their polished professional smiles.

"I'll tell Mr Bernard you're here," said the dark-haired one. "Please take a seat. Would you like a drink? Tea, coffee?"

Two black leather sofas faced each other across a coffee table on which lay the *Financial Times* and *Harpers & Queen*. A smiling young man entered the room, hand outstretched.

"Mr Boyer, good of you to come all the way up to town. My name is Mark Bernard. Please come through."

This was not the man Jack had expected. Without thinking he had imagined meeting the same Bernard who'd told him he could stay at school and live with Emm and Stan. But of course, that would have been ridiculous. The Bernard with the brown teeth and a liking for huge mugs of coffee must have died years ago, given his taste for Capstan Full Strength.

Mark Bernard stood back for Jack to go through the oak-panelled door that led into the interior of the building and then, as if reading his thoughts, said, "I told my father I was seeing you today and he asked to be remembered. He's quite frail but still as sharp as a pin. He's determined to make it to a hundred. And they say smoking's not good for you."

"He's not still on Capstan Full Strength?"

"You've a very good memory, Mr Boyer, but, no, I'm glad to say he gave up smoking at the age of seventy-eight, after his brother died."

Jack muttered something about sending his regards and they went into a meeting room. A long polished table was set up with pads and pens. A plate of biscuits and a bowl of fruit stood one each end of a mat in the centre of the table. Shiny chrome jugs sat on a trolley. Bernard laid a beige file, marked *Confidential*, on the table and invited Jack to sit.

"Now, Mr Boyer, would you mind if I called you Jack?"

"By all means."

After setting down the cups and sliding the biscuits to where they could both reach them, Bernard twirled off his jacket as a matador might spin his cape. Jack caught a flash of red as the jacket was flung carelessly over an empty chair. He sat back and stirred his coffee, looking at Jack as if assessing his suitability for a job. He opened the file and closed it again. Finally he spoke.

"Well, Jack, firstly thank you for coming to see us today. I hope you don't mind, but there are just a couple of formalities we need to go through so that, should any complications or challenges arise, we can say without doubt we are talking to the right person."

Jack felt in his briefcase, pulled out the passport which they asked him to bring and placed it on the table. Bernard spoke into a telephone, and one of the receptionists, the blonde one, appeared. He handed her the passport.

"Do you mind, Julie," he said, "just the one copy for our files.

"I'm sorry about all this, Jack, but it's the way things are these days. Would you mind just answering a couple of establishing questions?"

Jack sat back as if considering a weighty matter.

"Of course not. Fire away." He picked up a biscuit. White chocolate chip. It tasted as good as it looked.

"Would you mind telling me your date and place of birth?"

"18 April 1942. London."

"And where you went to university?"

"I didn't. I was in the ATC at school and went into the Royal Air Force at the age of eighteen. I was sent to Cyprus after basic training."

The girl reappeared and handed Jack his passport, smiling as if she was giving her child the best Christmas present ever. He smiled back.

"Thank you, Jack. Now, I expect you are wondering what all this is about." He put on a more serious expression. "It is my sad duty to tell you that your father passed away in March. I believe you never knew your father, or even his identity."

Jack sat forward in his chair.

"That's right."

Bernard put his hand on top of the file. Perhaps he thought Jack might try to grab it. He kept his eyes downcast for a moment and then looked Jack full in the face, clearly preparing to break bad news. Jack knew what was coming next.

"I'm sorry to say, Mr Boyer, that it was the express wish of the deceased that his identity should remain confidential. I hope you understand that this is not our decision."

A door had opened a fraction, and through it Jack had caught a glimpse of sunlight. And then it slammed shut again. He took some deep breaths, trying to hide his disappointment. Of course he understood Bernard's position. He was merely doing what he was paid to do. But Bernard had information to which Jack had much more right than him.

What was to stop him leaning across the table, grabbing Bernard by the throat and demanding the information? Or wresting the file from him? The secret would be in there, alright.

Jack remembered the stories he used to tell Russ about the great war hero who was still working behind enemy lines. Was he in there, hidden away? Bernard was not going to tell him, that much was sure.

"Of course I understand your position, Mr Bernard. I expected nothing else. But I have to say I am very disappointed."

Bernard got up from the table and collected the coffee jug from the tray. Jack pushed his cup an inch in Bernard's direction and it was refilled. Bernard replaced the jug and sat down again, opening the file.

"Your father did, however, leave you a letter. I have not

seen the contents." He handed Jack a small cream envelope, marked *To be given to Jacques Boyer after my death.*

Jack took the envelope, laid it down on the table and continued to stare at Bernard, wondering what would come next.

"Would you like to have a minute or two to yourself to read the letter, Mr Boyer?" Bernard made as if to stand.

Jack picked up the letter and slid it into his briefcase.

"No, it's alright. I'll read it later, when I get home."

Bernard smiled. He clearly thought the worst bit was over.

"Now, on a more positive note, I am pleased to tell you that you have been treated *pari passu* with any other children there may have been when it comes to…" He paused. "When it comes to my client's will. He left a not inconsiderable estate."

At that moment, Jack would have exchanged all the money, no matter how much it amounted to, for a father. He didn't need money, but he also had to remind himself that until the letter had arrived from the solicitor, he'd managed quite well all his adult life without his father. He had imagined into being his own version of a dad, and was quite happy with it. It didn't seem to matter very much that he would never know even the name of the man from whom he was made. And there was certainly nobody alive who was going to tell him. Maman was dead, Emm may have known, but would never tell. Stan had gone.

Bright sunlight streamed through the long windows of the room, which had probably been the dining room when the building was still a house. On the other side of the table, Bernard wittered on about valuations and inheritance tax and a whole lot of things that Jack could not be bothered to take in. He realised Bernard had stopped talking.

"I said, Mr Boyer, that in fact it might be better and help your understanding of the situation if you were to read the letter. In a note attached to the will itself, that is what my client suggested. As I said, I have no knowledge of the contents of the letter, and have no wish to know."

Jack was back at school in front of the headmaster, when "I suggest" meant "you will, if you know what's good for you". This young man, scarcely half Jack's age, was calling the shots.

"Well, then," said Jack, trying to smile but knowing he sounded sarcastic, "we'd better do as he says. He was my father, after all." He leaned down and reached into his briefcase, pulled out the envelope and ostentatiously slit it open with his finger, Bernard watching every move.

"I'll leave you in peace," said Bernard. "Just poke your head around the door when you're ready." He hurried from the room.

Still holding the letter, Jack stood up and went to the window. Outside a brown UPS van pulled up, entirely blocking the seventeenth-century cobbled street. The driver got out, selected a package from the back of the van and disappeared into the building opposite. A taxi pulled up behind the van and hooted. Men in shirtsleeves and girls in dresses hurried up and down, some carrying little brown paper bags from one of the many cafes in the area. It was a day for sandwiches in one of the City's many shady squares.

Jack sat down in a chair by the window and pulled out the typewritten letter.

My dear Jacques,

You may well wonder why you never heard from me until now. The reasons are my own lack of moral courage, family pressures and money. From the feedback I received via your school, it seems that your childhood was happy and that life has treated you well. My eternal gratitude is due to Mrs Donovan and Mr Gibson, and I have remembered them both in my will.

My London solicitor will explain in detail what I have left you, but I wanted to tell you why it includes my house in France. It is close to your mother's family home in St Pabu and it was there, in France, that your mother and I met and fell in love. I hope you will be able to enjoy using it, as your maman and I did on a few precious occasions, and that you may find some comfort there.

In due course you may discover my identity. All I ask is that when you do, you will respect my wishes and not try to contact other members of the family. They do not know of your existence, and should not do so. I realise I am asking much of you, but please do this for me and for the sake of your dear mother, Nicole, whom I loved till the day I died.

Wishing you every continued success.

And then, handwritten, had been added:

PS Marie-Louise was your grandmother.

The letter was unsigned. Jack reached into his briefcase and from the back pocket pulled a small envelope. Inside was the picture of his *maman* that he'd asked to keep when he and Yann had been going through the family albums. He looked at the young girl smiling at the camera, clearly blowing a kiss to the photographer. On the back it said *Nicole, St Pabu, 1938.* The writing was clearly from the same hand as the PS to the letter he'd just read.

Jack read the letter over and then again. A house? Good God. Who could this man have possibly been? This father who loved his mother, but not enough to marry her. He had been concerned for Jack, to the point of financing his upkeep and education. But not concerned enough to ever know him. Stan and Emm had been included in the will. Even if it was too late for Stan.

He sat watching the non-stop activity in the street and then re-reading the letter. A clock on the mantlepiece of what was probably a genuine Adam fireplace struck midday. Finally, Jack went to the door.

"Can you tell Mr Bernard I'm ready."

By the time Bernard returned, all smiles, the file in his hand, Jack had slipped the letter back into its envelope and replaced it in his bag. Bernard stood with his back to the fireplace, and looked uncomfortable. Was he trying to guess what might be in Jack's mind?

"Do you have any questions, Mr Boyer? As I said, I have not seen the letter myself." He seemed to have forgotten that he had been given permission to use Jack's given name.

Bernard's voice seemed to drift off, and then returned, with just a hint of irritation.

"Are you alright, Mr Boyer? Would you like a drink of water?"

Jack pulled himself back to the present.

"I'm fine, thank you, Mr Bernard. A drink of water would be good."

Bernard placed the folder on the table and went to the sideboard. One of the cupboard doors concealed a small fridge, rather like a hotel minibar. Bernard pulled out a small bottle of water, took a glass from the sideboard and put them in front of Jack. Only then did he resume his seat.

"As I was saying, Mr Boyer, Jack, if it is OK with you I will outline the scope of your inheritance, run through a few formalities and then if you've time, I hope you will be able to join me for a spot of lunch. How does that sound?"

Without waiting for an answer, Bernard leaned back in his chair. This was obviously the moment to which he'd looked forward. He adopted a warm and reassuring smile, signalling to the client he was about to get some good news.

"Your inheritance consists of two main items, cash and property. By value, the cash portion is the greater and amounts to just over half a million euros."

He paused for effect. Jack could feel himself being closely watched. He couldn't think of anything to say, and finally came out with what seemed, even to himself, a somewhat inadequate, "Are you sure? Could there be some mistake?"

"No mistake, Jack, I can assure you. I am the sole executor in the UK of the deceased's…" Leaving the sentence hanging in mid-air, he looked anxiously at Jack before continuing. "I mean, your late father's, estate. It is also most unlikely there will be any challenge, for reasons that need not concern us at the moment. My client absolutely insisted the will be watertight."

Bernard reached out for a biscuit, but then changed his mind and pushed the plate away.

"An occupational hazard, Mr Boyer, hand-made biscuits in the meeting rooms. Anyway, I expect you'd like a few more details of your inheritance?" He didn't wait for an answer. "In terms of cash, the sum is, as I said, just over half a million euros." He looked down at his notes. "Five hundred and twenty-three thousand, six hundred and eighty-one to be precise." He paused. "After payment of all taxes and legal and other fees.

"As for the property, I haven't visited it myself, but I understand that it is a rather fine village house located on the banks of a river not far from Roscoff. I am pleased to tell you that our Paris office advises that transfer of ownership can take place almost immediately. It will be legally yours once you have signed certain papers, which I can give you, and lodged them with a *notaire français*."

Bernard went on. "As I said, I haven't seen the house, but according to the information I have been given it consists of a detached family house of around 150 square metres, located just outside St Pabu, where I believe you have family connections. It has been valued locally for tax purposes at 325,000 euros."

This was serious money, and it could change everything. Was that what he wanted, to be responsible for sums of money and property? He tried to keep a smile on his face, attempting to show the pleasure he ought to have been feeling. But he had spent his life trying to avoid being committed to property. And people, for that matter. Bernard continued talking about the technicalities of transferring the title of the house, and then stopped, looking at Jack expectantly. Had he asked Jack a question?

After a rather uncomfortable pause, he resumed.

"Obviously, if you would like to think about it, or you already have another solicitor, I quite understand…"

"I'm sorry," said Jack, trying to remember what Bernard had just been talking about. He'd offered to act for Jack, that was it. "Of course, Mr Bernard, I would be very happy for you to act for me. After all, you are our family solicitor."

Jack hadn't meant to sound sarcastic and a shadow crossed Bernard's face. Then he seemed to relax.

"Excellent. Thank you very much." He opened a second file, which already had Jack's name on it and was marked

Client File – strictly confidential, and pulled out a letter of engagement which he asked Jack to sign. There were a number of other papers that needed signing.

Just before one o'clock, Bernard announced that all the immediate business was concluded, and asked if Jack was ready for lunch. From one of the files, he produced several photographs, which he slid across the table.

"This is the property, Mr Boyer. If you'll just excuse me while I pop these files back to my desk we'll walk around the corner for something to eat."

He left the room and Jack turned to the photographs. The first showed a traditional stone house. It had to be the house that Yann told him about. So the village gossips weren't wrong. The front door was at first-floor level, stone steps leading up to a landing which gave access to the arched doorway. Ivy clung to one end of the building. The front door was wide open. The house looked cared-for. In the garden, hydrangea bushes were in full bloom. On the back, in faded black ink, was confirmation, not that any was needed. *Villa Marie-Louise.* The second photograph was a view of a wide river. A handful of craft, fishing boats, flat-bottomed oyster barges and a couple of yachts, were moored in line, while beyond it was possible to see the sea, waves crashing on the rocks. He knew the river instantly.

The third picture was a tiny creased and faded print showing a group of young girls in traditional Breton dress standing around an ancient stone cross. The back showed where it had been repeatedly stuck in and removed from various photograph albums. The same handwriting, very faded, said: *Nicole dritte von links.*

He stared hard at one of the girls. It was Maman. No doubt. So his father was the young German. No wonder they kept it from him.

*

Jack sat on the train at Liverpool Street, waiting for it to pull out. He looked at the *Evening Standard* headline. Brexit, always Brexit. What had the Eton boys done to us? Maybe he'd just bugger off to France and live in his stone house, the house his father had left him. Invest his half-million in the stock market and watch himself get richer and richer, just like them.

Why had he told Ali he'd been summoned to the solicitor's? She was bound to ask how he got on. What could he say? That he'd inherited a bit of money, and leave it at that. She was too polite to ask how much, of that he was sure. But she would know he wasn't telling her the whole truth, and that could be the beginning of the end of something that hadn't even really started.

What had he said to Russ at the funeral? "I'm not planning to get it wrong this time." Something like that. If he had told Bel that he was going to have to sign up for extended National Service, rather than keeping it secret until the last minute, might have things turned out differently? Might she not have been so angry? Or hurt? Might she have waited? It didn't matter now, anyhow. Water under the bridge, as Stan insisted.

He had to learn to open up. Alison had the right to know. And was it so bad, having cash to spare even if that did mean he had to make decisions? Didn't he want *Duchesse Anne* overhauled from stem to stern? No problem. He even had somewhere to live while she was in dock.

He loved his old boat, his life among the salt marshes, his trips to the pub, his allotment. Yes, there were sadnesses. He would have liked to have been a father, for by now he could have had grandchildren. He could have taught them to sail the way Yann had taught his nephews and nieces.

The carriage filled. More and more *Evening Standard*s stared at him. The doors hissed closed. The destination and the intermediate stations were listed over the loudspeaker.

After Romford more people were getting off than getting on. He pulled out his mobile phone and called Alison. He wasn't going to get it wrong this time. That much he'd promised himself.

"Hi, Ali. Look, I wondered if you were free for supper at the Smack tonight. I had some interesting news at that solicitor's today I'd like to share with you."

"It's going to be very busy there tonight, Jack, love. Katie was saying before she went out there's a crowd coming in. How about you come here instead?"

"Love to, if you're sure that's OK. Do you want me to bring anything?"

"What about a bottle of that lovely *pinot noir* you were talking about? I have just put a nice chicken pie in the oven, so there's plenty to eat. Can you come about seven thirty?"

At seven twenty-five, having hung his suit back in the closet and put on his favourite cords, Jack slid the wheelhouse door closed, turned the key in the lock and headed across the sea wall. Katie had been right. There was a hell of a racket coming from the Old Smack. The door was wide open and a number of young people sat outside, enjoying the spring sunshine. Inside was heaving.

In addition to the *pinot noir*, his carrier bag contained a bottle of Taittinger Champagne. Alison's front door was open. He rang the bell and went inside.

"Come on through, I'm in the garden."

Jack put the red wine on the table, which was already laid for two, and went into the back garden.

"Hello, Ali. Now, do you have a couple of glasses

suitable for this stuff?" He put the Champagne down on the cast iron garden table.

"I certainly do. But they are in the top cupboard, first on the left, and I can only get them if I climb up on the steps. Can you be a dear…?"

Most of the way home, and while he was changing and finding the wine to bring, and all the way up the lane to Alison's cottage, he had tried to work out what he would say to her. He didn't want to hide anything, it wasn't that. But how do you tell somebody that you've just inherited a lovely house and half a million? He still didn't know, so he concentrated on pouring the drinks.

"Goodness, Champagne. So, Jack, I can take it it wasn't bad news."

Jack handed her the first glass and poured another for himself.

"Well, in a way, it was bad news. You see, the father I've never met and know nothing whatsoever about, has died." He took a sip of Champagne, and for the first time since Mr Bernard gave him the news, felt more than a pang of guilt.

"But I do know a bit more. He was a young German who holidayed in the village before the occupation."

Ali smiled and touched his arm.

"So that's why you're so tall and handsome!"

"If you say so. Look, this may sound sentimental, Ali, but would you mind if we just raised our glass to him, whoever he was, because without him, well, you know…"

"You wouldn't be here?"

"Something like that. So, here's to my dad. May he rest in peace. Whoever he bloody well was."

Jack felt into his pocket. His fingers found the letter. He left it there.

"You know we were talking the other day about taking a trip to Ireland to see Emm?"

"Yes."

"How about we go first to France to see my house and then take a ferry from Roscoff to Cork on our way home?"

"Jack Boyer, are you being serious?"

He pulled out the envelope containing the photographs and spread them out on the table.

"What do you think? Of the house?"

"There's one thing that your friend Russ said that I do agree with, and it's that you can be a dark horse. Is that really your house?"

"Once some papers are lodged with the authorities."

Alison picked up the photographs one by one.

"It looks really lovely, Jack. I'd love to come and see it with you. So that's what the call to the solicitor's was all about?"

"Yes, my dear Alison, my inheritance. Well, part of it anyway. As I say, it won't be technically mine until I go to France and sign some papers but, yup, that's mine. A village house of about 150 square metres, the solicitor said."

"And where is it?"

"Just outside St Pabu, the village where my cousin Yann and the rest of them live. It's where my mother is buried."

Alison continued to examine the photographs.

"Villa Marie-Louise."

"Apparently, my grandmother was called Marie-Louise."

"You said the house was just part of your inheritance?"

"There was a bit of money, too."

"Well, what a turn up for the books, eh? Now, if you'd like to put your photos away for a moment and tidy up the table, we can have some supper."

By the time Jack left Alison's cottage just before midnight, an exhausted Katie was home from the Old Smack, and they had set some tentative dates for their trip.

Fourteen

The warmth dropped from the evening as a cool breeze developed. Jack was glad to get into the Mocha, and perch on a tall stool. The Gaggia machine stretched almost the entire length of the bar, its four handles showing above the chrome shelf piled high with glass cups and saucers. Beside it stood a gleaming coffee grinder, the rich brown beans contained in a transparent hopper.

There were no other customers. Jack ordered three cappuccini, correctly tensing the Italian, and produced a ten shilling note to pay.

"Where did that come from, Boyo?" Russ demanded.

"What? The Italian or the money?"

Russ sneezed violently.

"Hay fever. Too much grass out there for me. I meant the dosh, Boyo, not your froggy lingo. Everyone knows you're only half English."

Handing the note over to the girl behind the counter, Jack sighed.

"You're such a nosy bugger, Russ, you know that? As

177

it happens, Stan slipped it to me on the way home from school. Said he's had a bit of luck on the horses."

Russ reached for a paper napkin from the counter and blew his nose.

"Well, when we saw him Wednesday he was saying he was done with the 'orses and would put everything on West Ham to win on Saturday. Didn't he, Bel?"

"I wasn't listening, Russ, so I don't know."

The coffee grinder growled. The girl behind the counter put Jack's change on the counter and banged used coffee from the filters. Jack could feel a familiar knot in his stomach. He tried to sound casual.

"So where did you go to on Wednesday? With Stan, I mean." His voice was croaky.

Russ slid off the stool.

"You tell 'im, Bel. I'm gonna see what's on the jukebox. This place needs livening up a bit."

Bel kept her face turned towards the window.

"You know it was Stan's birthday so we all went out, Emm as well, to the King's Head in Chigwell. It was nice."

"A nice neat foursome. Touching, I'm sure."

Bel put her hand on Jack's.

"It's nothing to get upset about. Stan wanted a little celebration."

"You could have picked me up on the way."

"It was all last minute. Emm said Stan suddenly got up from his chair after tea and said he wasn't going to just sit there on his birthday. So the first I knew was when they all turned up on my doorstep. I couldn't say no, could I?"

"No. I just, well, I miss you during the week. I'll be glad when I leave stupid school and join up."

Frankie Lymon and the Teenagers began belting out "Why Do Fools Fall in Love". Russ climbed back onto his stool.

"This one's for you, Boyo."

Bel stared at Jack.

"What did you say, Jack? About joining up. What did you say?"

"It's called National Service."

"I thought you'd go on to college, or something."

Russ looked at each of them in turn, slipped off the stool and returned to the jukebox. Three steaming coffees arrived on the jet black Formica counter. Jack added a spoonful of sugar and slid the glass sugar pot to Bel. Everything seemed to be happening in slow motion, as if there was about to be an accident. He drew a deep breath.

"I'll have to do it sooner or later, so I may as well get it over with."

Bel added sugar to her cup and began spooning the froth into her mouth.

"Russ is going for a deferment because he's doing an apprenticeship. Couldn't you do something like that?"

Russ came back and took a sip of coffee.

"Three plays for a bob. Nine for half a crown. I've put the lot in," he said. "You'd better stay till they're all played, though. I'm going to drink this and get home. Early start tomorrow."

Bel smiled at Russ and patted Jack's hand.

"We might need another cup of coffee, then."

A few clicks and whirrs came from the jukebox. Then came the deep-voiced introduction to "I'm Not a Juvenile Delinquent", followed by the doo-wop and then Frankie himself, his voice still to break, picking up the refrain and belting it out as if there were no tomorrow.

Russ downed his coffee.

"Not like our Frankie, eh?"

"What about him?"

"Don't tell me you didn't know. Wednesday night he

only nicked his uncle's car and smacked it into a lamp-post. He'll get at least a month inside, poor little sod. They'll make his life hell."

Bel scraped the last of the froth from her coffee and examined her lips in the Gaggia's mirrored front.

"Well, he deserves it, if you ask me."

"No, he don't. He's just a poor little bugger trying to look big, like his brothers."

Jack took another sip. Still too hot.

"Well, it was a stupid thing to do, wasn't it?"

"Can't deny it, Boyo. Stupid." With that, Russ sniffed. As he passed, Russ gave Jack a light pat on the back. "Don't do anything I wouldn't on the way home, then. Watch him, Bel. He's a tiger."

As the glass door closed, Jack cleared his throat.

"Look, Bel. It's not that I want to do National Service, but I can't afford to live on my own."

"But you live with Emm when you're home."

"Yes, but... Well, I have to leave school next June. I can't afford to go to college. I'll need a job and somewhere to live, and if I sign up I'll get both."

"I don't understand. Why can't you stay with Emm and Stan?"

"Because... Look, this is a secret, but Emm's going home to Ireland to look after her mother. Someone pays her to give me a home at the moment, but that will stop when I'm eighteen. Like school will stop."

"Who pays for you?"

"I don't know."

"You mean you won't tell me."

"No. I mean I don't know."

*

Jack sat in the wheelhouse studying advertisements for cars on his laptop. Did he really want one? Should he allow that money to change his life? Why not simply put Villa Marie-Louise on the market and give away the proceeds to some charity or other? Lifeboats, maybe. Or the people who ran the lightship at Tollesbury – youngsters learning to sail? Surely better than yet another car to pollute the planet.

He liked the look of the Volkswagen Golf. Good quality, everyone says. Unostentatious. Grey, perhaps. Or silver. Alison would know. Katie? She'd say bright red. He smiled at the thought of driving around in a bright red car. Village tongues would wag.

The mobile vibrated and then rang. A number he didn't recognise. Probably about claiming compensation for the accident he'd never had. One to ignore. He shut down the computer and went on deck, the warmth of the sun on one cheek and the chill of the breeze on the other. But for early May, it was a pretty good morning.

He felt the mobile vibrate again. OK, fraudsters, you asked for it.

"Hello," he said, his voice deliberately sharp.

A woman's voice. Warm. Startled.

"Jack?"

"Yes. Who's that?" But even as the words fell from his lips, he knew.

"Jack, it's Bel. Frankie gave me your number. He said you wouldn't mind. Do you?"

Yes, he wanted to say, yes, I do bloody mind. But different words came out.

"Of course not. What can I do for you?"

"Jack, we didn't really get a chance to talk properly at the funeral. It went well, didn't it? I loved your eulogy, just the right touch. You described the Stan that I knew.

The Stan we all loved, especially you and I. Always full of enthusiasm. Never downcast. An example to us all, Jack. And you captured that beautifully. Thank you."

Jack stared downriver. He could just make out the bulk of the nuclear power station. The mist would soon lift completely.

"Nice of you to say so, Bel. But that's not why you're ringing. What do you want to talk about?"

"Jack, I don't even know where to start. Could we meet sometime soon? Have lunch, perhaps?"

Down at the stone jetty, a group of anglers began boarding the launch that was taking them out to the sandbanks. They would probably get to see some seals on the way. They would bring out their cameras and snap away like nobody's business. But the seals ate the fish the anglers wanted to catch. For some reason, Jack found that amusing.

"I'm not sure, Bel. What's done is done and I really don't want to rake over the past anymore. I don't see the point."

"I know that, Jack, and of course I understand. But there are some things I need to say face to face, with nobody looking on. Is that OK?"

"I'm not sure, Bel. Can I think about it?"

"Of course. Can I call you tomorrow?"

"Yes, call me tomorrow." The anglers' launch left the jetty. He felt a pang of envy. "Hang on. Yes, OK, then. But can it be soon? I don't want this hanging over me for weeks."

"How about tomorrow?"

"What? Tomorrow? OK. Tomorrow."

"They're forecasting another lovely day. Shall I come your way? Supposing I make up a picnic? Where shall we meet, or can I pick you up?"

This was all moving too fast. Where could they meet? He didn't want her coming to East Stone.

"Do you think you can find your way to a village called Tollesbury?"

"My satnav can."

"OK, then. Meet me outside the church."

"What time?"

"How about twelve thirty? We can walk out on the sea wall and find a bench. Watch the kids learning to sail."

"Sounds perfect."

"You can find the way?"

"Don't worry. I'll be there."

He closed the connection. Why had he agreed to it? The phone was still in his hand. All he had to do was press the button and say he'd changed his mind. He slid back the wheelhouse door and stepped into its warmth, put the phone into the chart drawer and woke his laptop from its short sleep. But the pictures of brand new cars no longer interested him. He slipped it into the drawer with the phone and went below to put on his walking boots.

Unusually, he chose to walk upstream, towards the lock. He didn't want to meet anybody, especially Alison.

East London, May 1960

Stan sat down on the low wall that separated the little patch of grass from where Emm kept her mangle and where the dustbin lived. He took a swig from the glass of water he'd carried into the neat garden from the scullery.

Jack looked up from his book.

"You OK, Stan?"

"A bit hot and bothered to be honest. You don't want to work in a bakery this weather. It was only a half-day, but I'll tell you what, it was half a day too much. I'm knackered."

Jack put down his book.

"So, do you want to give this afternoon a miss, then?"

"Course not. I tell you something for nothing, I can't wait to get up the top of that hill and feel the wind on my face." He finished the water and stood up. "I suppose you're used to the heat by now, where you are."

Jack got up from the deck chair, conscious that he was several inches taller than Stan.

"You know, Stan, you never quite get used to it. It was up in the nineties when I left, and it won't cool down until the end of September."

Stan sat back down on the wall.

"Funny, isn't it. All winter we long for the warm days, and then when they come, we end up moaning about the heat."

Jack returned to his book, but it was obvious Stan wanted to talk.

"What are you reading, son?"

"Something you might enjoy, actually, Stan. *Once There Was a War*, by John Steinbeck. About his time as a reporter. Probably stuff that you would remember."

"Blimey, Jack. Why would I want to read that? I had enough of it at the time." He stood up. "Right, I'm going up for a quick bath and then we'll be going. I thought Bel would be here by now. There's a bag of fresh rolls in the kitchen to make up. I think Emm said there was some cheese we could use."

"I can make up the rolls."

Stan hovered by the back door.

"I didn't ask Russ. I thought you might like some time with Bel without him always around."

"You're right, Stan. Not sure I can cope with Russ right now."

Stan took one step, then stopped again. He reached out to put a hand on Jack's shoulder.

"You OK, son? You've seemed a bit on edge since you came back this time. Isn't it working out for you, the RAF? I know you were hoping to get a bit more flying."

"No. It's fine. Maybe I'll get more if they move me."

But he wasn't going to get more flying, he knew that. Just one training flight since they'd sent him to that godforsaken hole. Just one. Ninety minutes, and it was all over. He hadn't signed up for five years to lug a bloody great heavy rifle round some dusty village waiting to get a bullet in his back, with a bunch of moaning National Service blokes trailing behind him. But that's what he'd got. And it was no use complaining.

Stan resumed his seat on the wall.

"I didn't know you're on the move again. Where are they sending you?"

"It was supposed to be a base just outside Baghdad, but luckily that got kiboshed by the revolution. Now it's almost certain to be Aden. But I doubt I'll see much flying there, either."

"Aden. Blimey. But once you've done your stint on foot patrol, then it will be your turn up among the clouds, won't it?"

Why couldn't Stan shut up? He didn't know what he was talking about. Why didn't he just go up and have his bath, and stop going on about things he didn't understand? But the strange thing was, Jack knew that if he could just learn to trust him, Stan, of all people, would understand how things happen, and how easily they can go wrong in an instant. In the D-Day landings he dropped from a lumbering C-47 into searchlights and tracer fire. He'd won a medal, but he would be the first to say he didn't always stick by the rules.

Jack wasn't going to win any medals. Not now. He tried to smile.

"Maybe, Stan, maybe. You go up and have your bath. I'll do the rolls. Is there any pickle?"

Stan stood up, stretched his back and shook his head.

"I used the last of the pickle yesterday. There's a bottle of salad cream, though." He paused before continuing. "Just so long as you're not in any sort of trouble. Life in the forces is no bloody picnic. You don't need me to tell you that."

Jack slid back the patterned glass doors of the new kitchen cabinet and took out the cheese. He found the tin cheese grater in one of the lower drawers. He pulled down the flap in the centre section of the cabinet to provide the working surface. After cutting the cheese to size, he gripped the grater hard and turned the little handle as fast as he could. He could feel the pressure behind his eyes. Dare he tell Stan? Maybe tonight, when they would both be secure in their little shared bedroom. He grated the hard cheese into a basin and opened the salad cream, half of which went into it with the cheese. As he chopped an onion he allowed his eyes to stream with tears he'd been holding back since he came home. He would tell Stan later on. The onion went into the basin. He sliced up a cucumber, halved the eight warm rolls Stan had brought home and spread the cheese mixture inside, adding a couple of thin slices of cucumber to each.

He heard the front door slam.

"Hey, Boyo, you finished making them sandwiches yet? Bel said you was going on a picnic. I'll buy the ice creams."

"Bugger," said Jack under his breath, as Russ barged into the little scullery closely followed by Bel. Jack pulled out a handkerchief and wiped his eyes. "It's Stan's onions. Why he grows them so strong I'll never know."

He looked from Bel to Russ, and back to Bel again. Why had they arrived together? Where had they been?

"You'll have to ask Stan if you want to come. It's his picnic, not mine." He turned to the sink and ran some warm water into the bowl.

"Is he upstairs? I'll pop up and ask him," Russ said.

"He's in the bath."

Russ gave Jack a wink.

"He won't mind. I won't see nothing I haven't seen before."

When Russ left the room, Bel grabbed Jack's hand and gave him a peck on the cheek.

"You don't mind if he comes? I bumped into him on the Romford Road and he asked what we were doing today."

"You didn't have to tell him, though, did you?"

"What's the matter? I thought he was your friend."

"He is, but that doesn't mean I want to spend all my leave with him. I need some peace and quiet."

"Jack, what's the matter?"

"Why does everyone keep asking me what's the matter? Nothing's the matter, alright. We're all going on a picnic and I couldn't be happier. Maybe Russ can hold one of your hands and me the other, then you'll both be as happy as me."

Bel put her arms around Jack's waist and pulled herself tight into his back.

"Jack Boyer, I do believe you're jealous."

At that moment, Russ reappeared at the door. Jack caught sight of his own reflection in the back window, and hated what he saw.

Russ picked up a crumb of cheese from the breadboard.

"Stan says it's fine by him, but it's up to you two."

So Russ was coming, and that was that. Why couldn't anybody ever say no to him?

Stan, in a beautifully ironed white shirt and khaki trousers, came down the stairs and rattled his keys.

"Right, we all ready, then? You'll have to go in the back, Russ, if you're coming. Jack will sit up front because of his long legs. Do you mind squeezing in the back with Russ, Bel?"

"Do I have to?" she replied.

"I'll just sling me hook if that's how you feel," Russ responded, turning as if to leave.

If only. If only Russ would stop his senseless chatter and stupid jokes for a while. If only Bel hadn't met him on the Romford Road, if that was what really happened. If only it was going to be himself squashed in the back of the tiny car with her, and not Russ.

Stan held the door open while first Bel and then Russ climbed into the small space behind the front seats. Bel turned sideways and put her legs across Russ's lap. Jack got into the front seat, trying to see where Russ's hands might be, for they were not visible amongst the froth of white net petticoat peeping from under Bel's bright red skirt.

And if only Stylianos Karalis hadn't chosen, seven months earlier, to take a walk in a dusty orange grove patrolled by jumpy British Forces.

*

After a surprisingly good night, Jack shaved and dressed with care. He checked his nose and ears for wayward hairs. He put on a new pair of cords that he'd bought last time he'd been in Woodbridge, his favourite Viyella shirt and a cotton mix jumper from Marks & Spencer. He polished his walking boots. It was two hours to Tollesbury along the river, but the alternative was to take the bus, which meant passing Alison's cottage to get to the bus stop. And besides, it was another one of those spring days to remember.

Shortly after a quarter past twelve, Jack arrived at the village. As he walked up Church Street, he could see the back of a small white sports car parked outside the church. A woman, wearing a pale blue headscarf sat in the driving seat. When he was about fifty yards behind the car the door opened and Bel, elegant in white linen trousers and pale blue jacket, and of course film star sunglasses, climbed out, arms spread as wide as her smile.

What was she thinking about? This wasn't a date. Or was it? He'd not told Alison, he'd dressed up for the occasion. And when he'd woken that morning and saw the sun streaming through the starboard porthole, he realised he was looking forward to a picnic on the sea wall with an attractive woman. He should have brought a bottle of wine.

Bel stepped forward and briefly pulled him close before taking a step back, her hands still gripping Jack's arms hanging limply by his sides.

"Jack, you do look terrific, I must say. This sea air must really agree with you." She let go. "Or maybe it's Alison. So pretty and, Russ tells me, such fun to talk to. Or maybe a bit of both? Now, I have a confession. I didn't bring a picnic."

Jack stepped back, out of reach.

"No matter. We can eat at the pub."

Bel took his hand and led him around the back of the car to the passenger side.

"No way, Jack Boyer. We can do better than that. I had Mrs Charlton book at Le Vieux Manoir in Dedham. A table in the garden. It's very sheltered. Out of the wind. Hop in. Unless you'd like to drive my new toy?"

Jack obediently opened the door. What was he playing at? He'd fallen in love with her once, lost her to his best friend, and just when he thought it didn't matter anymore, she appears from nowhere, as if none of that had ever happened. But he said nothing. Did silence amount to acquiescence? Probably. After all, he was in her car, being driven by her to the lunch she, or maybe Russ, had planned. And he was more than willing to go along for the ride.

Bel was known at the restaurant.

"Good afternoon, Mrs Russell. How nice to see you again. I've put you in the garden." The *maître d'hôtel* led the way to a table in a sheltered corner of the terrace. Below them, a little electric launch was moored against the riverbank. Everything perfectly manicured. The scent of newly cut grass in the air. The *maître d'* fussed about, pulling chairs in and out, smoothing non-existent creases from the immaculate white tablecloth.

"How is Mr Russell keeping?"

Bel smiled a smile perfected to be graced on people paid to serve her.

"Oh, he's as well as can be expected, thank you, Henri. I'll tell him you asked."

"Will you be warm enough here, Mrs Russell? I have reserved Mr Russell's usual table inside just in case. Or I can bring you a heater. Can I get you an aperitif?"

They had been at the restaurant for a good five minutes, but this was the first opportunity Jack had been given to speak. He was about to say no, he didn't want anything other than water, when he checked himself. He had nothing to prove. He didn't need to hold back. Having agreed to the meeting, there was no point in being difficult. And the idea of a well-made Americano, with its tinkling ice cubes and slice of orange, had taken root.

They ordered the drinks. She took off her sunglasses, folded them carefully and laid them beside her plate.

"So, Jack, how are you? Honestly?"

"Honestly? I'm fine. I live out my days by the river,

which I love. I have good health and enough money. I look forward to every single day. I have time to potter about on the water for the boatyard and earn money at the same time. What about you? I notice you still use your married name."

She smiled that smile again.

"The name Russell opens doors, Jack, so why change a winning ticket? You never married?"

It was Jack's turn to smile.

"I might have, once. A long time ago. But you know all that."

The drinks arrived. The Americano hit the spot. Bel had sparkling water.

She sipped the water and then held her glass so that it half covered her face. She looked at him with one eye. Even in a woman of past seventy years, it was successfully flirtatious.

"Ouch," she said, "I asked for that, didn't I? Shall we order? And just so there's no doubt, it's my treat."

Jack looked at the prices on the *à la carte* menu and decided he'd better opt for the fixed price lunch. Terrine followed by skate. A good choice, the *maître d'* observed. Bel ignored the menu and ordered a Caesar salad. This woman had travelled a long way from her little prefab.

"Is your mother still with you, Bel?" It seemed the right time for polite conversation. To stay on safe ground. Before she could answer they were asked about wine. Jack went for a Viognier; Bel declined.

"She is, I'm glad to say. She's ninety-eight this year, and in good spirits. She's in a home, of course, but still has all her marbles."

"Is it a nice place?"

"Jack, it's lovely. If I end up there, I'll have no complaints. It's not cheap, but not all old folks' homes beat up their residents and half starve them, no matter what the papers might say. Russ helps out with the fees, obviously."

Obviously! He would.

"Maybe I should get the name from you, for when my time comes."

"Then I'll book myself in too. Then we can at least go into our dotage together."

This was not the direction he wanted to take. He had to change the subject.

"I should know this, but where do you live, Bel?"

"Wanstead. Where else? Just a stone's throw from Russ, as it happens, opposite the park."

It felt OK again. Perhaps they could be nothing more than two old friends catching up on each other's news. Maybe that's all Bel wanted, after all.

A waiter came and removed Jack's empty tumbler. He thought about ordering a second, but it wasn't offered. Instead, the waiter set down a decent-sized glass of Viognier. Bel reached across and picked it up.

"What a lovely colour. Do you mind if I just have a sip?"

"Go ahead."

She took the tiniest of sips, leaving a smudge of lipstick on the glass.

"Mmm, you know your wines, Jack. That is truly lovely. What is it?"

He explained what he knew about the Viognier, which wasn't much, and felt relieved when his terrine arrived.

*

After an hour of surprisingly easy chatter and fine food, they ordered coffee and *petits fours.*

"Shall we take our coffee inside?" Bel said. "It's getting a bit chilly out here."

The waiter led the way inside where they settled into armchairs, face to face across a small coffee table. Jack sensed something more than the air temperature lay behind the move.

"So, Bel, it was good to chat and the meal was delicious, but am I right that there is something you want to say to me?"

"You always were perceptive, Jack, I should have remembered that. So, what I wanted to say is this. Russ needs you."

"What do you mean, needs me?"

"He needs your friendship."

"But he's got loads of friends. What about all those people at Stan's funeral?"

Bel reached across the table and laid her hand on his. He had expected it to be warm, but it was cool. She put her head on one side and smiled.

"Jack, you know, one of the things I've always loved about you is your innocence. You saw Russ's so-called friends for yourself, the sort of people they were."

"So? I'm not sure what you mean."

"Let's just say they were… let's be polite and call them business associates. They were there because they need to keep in with Russ, not because they like him. Or cared about Stan. He needs somebody he can trust."

Jack withdrew his hand and turned his face away from the table, looking instead down the garden to the river.

"Why me? I think he needs to look elsewhere."

He felt Bel touch his arm.

"Jack, please. Listen. Russ is suffering, you saw that. He needs you, desperately. Otherwise I wouldn't be here, down on my knees pleading with you."

Jack sighed and sunk his espresso in a single gulp. He picked up a *petit four*. He didn't much like marzipan, but needed the sweetness.

"You know, Bel, I don't care. I've got a good life, and I've a lot to look forward to. Now, if you don't mind, I would like to be getting home."

"Before we rush off, can I tell you something?"

"If you must."

"The simple fact is, Jack, it was you that Russ was in love with. Not me."

"So why did you end up married? What was wrong with him? And you for that matter?"

The bill arrived. She scribbled on it and the waiter took it away.

"Russ has an account here, in case you're wondering. I'll try to explain. While you were away we became great friends. We got on like a house on fire. He was interested in me the way not many boys were. He noticed what I wore. He liked to come shopping for clothes with me. He noticed what scent I was using. He knew at once if I changed my shampoo. I could tell him anything and he seemed to understand. But it wasn't only that. There was the business. He was practically running the whole thing. Uncle relied on him absolutely. It made sense for him to become part of the family."

"So you married for money. I think I've heard it all now. Well, it was certainly a good move. Congratulations. When it comes to cash, Russ is your man. I think it's time I was getting back."

She reached across to take his hand. He pulled it away.

"Jack, please try to understand. It wasn't just the business. Everything seemed to point in the same direction. You seemed to have lost interest in me. It's so hard to explain. The way I think of it is that we three were locked into a sort of eternal love triangle, but when you went away one side of the triangle was missing. The other two collapsed in on each other."

Jack eased himself out of the chair. A waiter came to pull back Bel's chair as she stood. She looked away.

"Jack," she said, "can you just think about what I said? Russ is in a very bad place right now and you, and probably only you, can make it better for him. It's up to you."

Jack took a deep breath and stood up. "Only You" by the Platters was playing at the back of his mind. He spoke quietly.

"I don't see that as my responsibility, I'm afraid. Why don't you just go off now in your cute little sports car and report back to Russ. I'll get a taxi to the nearest station. Thanks for lunch. Or should I say, thank Russ for my lunch."

"Jack, please, don't be like that. I'll run you home, or just back to the station if that's what you'd prefer." She tried a smile. "I'll leave the hood down. It's so noisy you won't have to talk to me."

Jack stared down the garden, watching two gulls squawking at each other, and managed to smile back.

"OK," he said. "If that's a promise perhaps you could just take me back to where you found me."

Bel was as good as her promise. She left the top down on the car. She drove fast, but with confidence. The noise of the wind did, as she said it would, make conversation impossible. Jack had to admit to himself that he was enjoying the idea of being driven by an attractive, sophisticated woman, the wind in his hair and the sun on his face. Maybe he should buy a car like Bel's? Katie would love that, he was sure. A different colour, though.

Too soon, they drew to a halt outside Tollesbury church in the shade of a huge horse chestnut tree. Bel turned off the engine. The silence seemed absolute. What now? Was she waiting for him to lean across the car and kiss her? Should he just say, "Thank you," and get out? Were they meant to continue their conversation? Make arrangements to meet again?

The fun of the drive over, he just wanted to get away. But he had to say something. What came out was, "I love your car. How much was it?"

It was such an off-the-wall question it caught both of them by surprise. Bel chuckled, a deep throaty chuckle that would commonly be said to be sexy.

"I don't know, actually, Jack. Russ bought it for my birthday."

He might have guessed it. Can you really take seriously a divorce when one party still buys the other birthday presents costing God knows what. OK, Russ could obviously afford it, but a car for God's sake. So typical of him. Not a bunch of flowers or even a nice necklace, but a bloody sports car. He reached for the door handle.

Bel put her hand on his sleeve.

"Are you still mad with me?"

"No, not mad. Just a bit confused."

She took off her sunglasses, and Jack noticed again how green her eyes were.

"What about? There's no mystery. Things that shouldn't have gone wrong did go wrong all those years ago. The fact is, Jack, we miss you. And seeing you again made us realise how lovely it would be to have you back in our lives. First love can be very hard to forget."

He took off his seat belt and opened the door.

"Thanks for lunch. It was good to see you again. Say hello to Russ for me."

He walked off down Church Street towards the pub, expecting to hear the car engine start and for Bel to come speeding past. But all he heard were the birds in the trees and the voices of excited children at the end of their school day. When he looked back over his shoulder, Bel was still sitting there, head down, with her sunglasses back on. He turned away and quickened his step, cutting through the churchyard where dirty confetti still lay where it had been thrown the previous Saturday.

Out on the river wall, he walked for half an hour and then sat down to watch the boats coming up with the tide. He recognised several as vessels on which he had worked, and waved if their skippers happened to be looking his way.

When did it all go so wrong? Did his friendship with Russ start to unravel with that kiss on the bed? Why did he and Bel do what they did, when neither of them gained any benefit from the hurt they inflicted on him? And what was really going on now? Why were the very people who had betrayed him now trying to inveigle him back?

He got back on his feet and continued upriver, walking fast. Did they really think him so stupid that all Bel had to do was crook her little finger, buy him lunch and take him for a ride in her car and he'd come running back? That's what it felt like. He tried to think of other things. Of his house, yet to be entered, in France. The money he'd inherited. The potential of his relationship with Ali, who was worth half a dozen Bels. Of Katie and the new little car he planned to buy and then give to her. Just like Russ did for Bel. He smiled at the irony.

There was no point in being angry with them. What was done couldn't be undone. There was no compensation they could offer that would take away the hurt. He could simply ignore them both. Turn his back, the way they'd all turned their backs on him. Until, that is, they wanted something. What did he owe Russ? Nothing, nothing at all. Or Bel, for that matter. Frankie. Well. You had to feel for Frankie, but even he knew which side his bread was buttered. It was up to him.

The next turn in the river brought *Duchesse Anne* into view. He was safely back on his own ground. Russ could bombard him with all the letters he liked, but he didn't need to respond. Not anymore.

East London, Easter 1956

As the cinema lights went down, Jack felt a jab in the ribs.

"Bet you wish you were here with Bel, eh, Boyo?" said Russ, loud enough to be sure that Stan heard too. "Instead of with me and Stan. Up in the back row. Now you know what to do. Fiddling with her buttons, getting your hand inside her shirt?"

Why couldn't Russ just leave it? What they'd done that morning was disgusting. If he didn't shut up, Stan might start asking awkward questions.

"Shhh," Jack said. "The film's starting."

"Give it a rest, you two, can't you?" said Stan. "Otherwise go and sit somewhere else." Russ sank down in his seat. Jack wanted to hit him. Punch him until his pretty mouth was bleeding.

Blue cigarette smoke wafted through the beam. Jack looked up, watching the smoke twist and turn. He found it calmed him. *Island in the Sky* began with a curious monologue from a DC3 aeroplane. A few minutes later, John Wayne is wrestling with the controls as the plane bucks and tosses its way through a high-altitude storm somewhere over the wastes of Northern Canada. Ice coats the wings. They are in big trouble. Jack felt another nudge.

"Old Wayne should have stayed on his horse. What's a blinking cowboy doin' flyin' a plane? Askin' for trouble."

Stan glared at Russ. The engines start to cough and

splutter. The propellers almost come to a standstill. They are out of fuel. Spotting a frozen lake, Wayne and his crew glide the plane down to a bumpy landing in a white wilderness.

At the end of the film they stood for the National Anthem and then made their way out into the chilly night. Stan turned up his collar and stuck his hands deep into his raincoat pockets.

"Wasn't bad," he said, "but I'm waiting for *Cockleshell Heroes* to come out, which I reckon will be better."

Jack wound his scarf around his neck.

"The thing with *Cockleshell Heroes*, it really happened."

"So did *Island in the Sky*," said Russ. "It said it was based on the true story."

"Based on doesn't mean it's true. Just means bits of it are."

"Learn that at Pargeter's, did you?"

Stan grabbed Russ by the arm.

"No need for that, just 'cos Jack goes to a decent school. Wouldn't do you any harm, either, if you ask me."

Russ moved out of reach and they walked in silence for a minute or two.

"Anyway, would you do that? Like in *Cockleshell Heroes*? Get in a tiny little boat and go and attack a battleship?"

"What's that you're saying?" said Stan, clearly still irritated.

"And like that American bloke did in the floods. Get in a little rubber raft to rescue people. Would you? And what about you, lover boy, would you jump in the water to rescue Bel?"

Stan lit a half-smoked cigarette.

"Impossible to say."

"Well, I would," said Russ. "Like a shot. And I'd climb blinking Everest as well, given half a chance. And run a four-minute mile."

They stopped to look in the window of the army surplus store.

"Do you remember," Russ went on, "that film where one squaddie says to the other, 'If you ever get hit and are on your last legs, do you want me to finish you off'?'"

Jack sighed. They'd had enough of Russ for one day.

"Course I do."

"Would you do that, then?"

Another sigh.

"Course I would."

"What about you, Stan the Man, would you pull the trigger to put your oppo out of his misery?"

Stan flicked his cigarette end into the gutter.

"It's a stupid question, Russ. If you'd ever had to fight for your country you'd know that already. Fact is, we all said that sort of thing to each other, son. In the war. It doesn't mean anything."

Russ skipped in front of Stan, walking backwards.

"If I said it, I'd mean it. Otherwise I wouldn't say it. What about you, Jack? Would you promise me? And mean it?"

"Why should I?"

"What if I promised to keep all our little secrets? Would you, then?"

"I suppose so."

"So, I promise to keep our little secrets. Every one of them. Now it's your turn. Say you promise to finish me off if I ask you."

Would he never shut up and just go home?

"OK, I promise you."

Russ turned and ran off without another word.

Stan and Jack trudged on in silence until they reached the window of Ken's Bargain Store.

"Didn't they really mean it?" asked Jack, addressing Stan's reflection.

"Mean what?"

200

"About finishing each other off. Didn't they? Even if the other one's screaming in agony?"

"You've never looked down the sights of a gun, have you, son? You have to tell yourself you're just looking at a target, not a person. Otherwise you'd never be able to pull the trigger."

"But what if your mate is begging you?"

Stan sniffed.

"He's still your mate, isn't he? And it's still you what's got to see his head blown to bits, and know that you did it. Let's get home. I've had enough stupid questions for one night, and Emm will be wondering where we've got to."

They quickened their pace a little, with Stan always a few yards ahead. He suddenly stopped.

"You OK, son? You seem a bit off colour tonight." Without waiting for an answer, he looped his arm around Jack's shoulders.

"Come on. Let's just get home."

*

After the lunch with Bel, a week went by, and then another week. Russ had sent him the local newspaper report on Stan's funeral. *War hero baker given Bond send-off.* Russ was quoted extensively in the story, as Jack would have guessed. Russ said he'd sent a copy to Emm in Ireland.

He'd said nothing to Ali about the lunch. It wasn't that it was a secret, but what was there to say, after all? That Bel had asked him to lunch at a fancy restaurant and asked him to be nice to Russ? Trouble is, Ali would probably agree with Bel. He could imagine what she'd say: "It costs nothing to be nice to someone."

Well, maybe. If it could be just an occasional visit. But

with Russ it would be the thin end of the wedge. And he couldn't risk that.

The money left him by his father was in his bank account. Half a million on deposit, with still enough in the current account to buy that car with a swipe of his debit card. The keys to Villa Marie-Louise hung on a hook in the wheelhouse. He spotted Ali returning along the sea wall from her evening walk with Millie. She often passed by about that time, which was one of the reasons he was sitting on deck. He waved. She waved back. He pulled himself up and went to meet her at the head of the jetty. By that time, Millie was already aboard.

"There's a nice white Burgundy in the fridge," Jack said, extending a hand to steady Ali as she came down the jetty.

"I'd hoped you would say something like that."

Jack went below to fetch the wine and slipped *Buddy Holly's Love Songs* into the CD player, turning the volume just high enough to hear out on deck, but not so loud as to disturb the tranquillity. The harbour master creamed past in his launch and waved. It was one of those beautiful early summer evenings where everything seems to be falling into place. Swallows swooped low over the water, collecting insects for their first clutch of chicks.

Ali took a sip of the wine and smiled.

"Now, Monsieur Boyer, I have a bone to pick with you. I was just chatting to George Sunnocks, down by the basin, and he said he'd seen you at Le Vieux Manoir a couple of weeks ago." She raised her eyebrows and put her head on one side.

Who'd live in a village? You can't blow your nose without somebody seeing you and telling somebody else. Only one way – forward.

"I didn't see him there. Anyway, before you ask, Bel bought me lunch there."

"Jack, love, I wasn't going to ask. It's none of my business."

"I should have mentioned it but, honestly, I wasn't trying to hide anything from you. It's just that I didn't know how to tell you about it without sounding like a miserable, bitter old bugger."

"What do you mean?"

"Let's just say it wasn't a very enjoyable occasion. Essentially she was trying to convince me that I should patch things up with Russ."

"Would that be so terrible?"

"I knew you'd say that, and maybe you're right. But you saw him at the funeral. How he was. He just has to be in charge of everything. Bel said she'd bring a picnic for our lunch but we ended up at Le Vieux Manoir where, guess what, Russ only has a bloody account. All she had to do was sign the bill." They watched the Swan 45 return to her moorings. "See what I mean, Ali, I'm already sounding off like some sad old sod, which I am not. It's just the effect that talking about them has on me. I can't help it."

"You don't have to explain, Jack. As I said, it's none of my business."

Jack topped up her glass.

"How's the Burgundy?"

"Delicious. But then I've never known you serve me a duff glass of anything. Now, shall we talk about that trip?"

*

"Do you know, it's the anniversary of D-Day? Seventy-two years."

Ali ceased hoeing between the beans and wiped her forehead, leaving a trace of mud just above her right eye.

"Is it, Jack? That's interesting," her voice betraying that she found the fact of no interest whatsoever.

Jack continued to pull at the weeds which seemed to have sprung up overnight among the lettuces.

"As I said, in the eulogy, Stan was there. Dropped by parachute behind the German lines. You've got mud on your forehead, by the way."

"And under my fingernails. That was quite something, wasn't it? I don't suppose many people knew that until you mentioned it?"

She put down the hoe and went to sit in the shade of the shed.

Jack rubbed his hands down his dungarees and went to join her.

"I booked the tickets this morning. The dates we agreed. First week in September, after the schools go back. I left the return from Roscoff to Plymouth open. We can stay at the house as long as we like."

"I'm really looking forward to it, but I'll miss Katie, you know."

"They do have telephones in France. And the email. And ferries every day."

"Is there internet at your house?"

Jack nodded.

"How do you know? If I know anything about the French everything will have been disconnected. No electricity, no phone, no water."

"You forget, I have family there. Yann has all that in hand. By the time we get there, all the services will be on, the grass will be mowed and the beds made. How about that?"

"I think I'm going to like your cousin Yann. Is he married, I wonder? Come on, let's get our weeding finished and go back to the cottage for a cup of tea."

Neither of them heard the squeak of the gate to the allotments, but looked up at the sound of a voice.

"I thought I'd find you two here, when you weren't at either the pub or the boat." Frankie painstakingly picked his way towards them along the earth paths between the plots. Jack stretched his back. Weeding on his hands and knees was beginning to become something to which his muscles objected.

Ali dropped the hoe and hurried across to meet Frankie, who seemed to be having trouble finding his way through the maze. She gave him a big hug. Why was it that, when he prompted such tenderness in women, Frankie had never married nor, so far as Jack was aware, ever had a serious relationship?

She led Frankie by the hand, just the way Bel's friend Keelin had led him to the dance floor all those years ago. But this time, Frankie was not in good shape. His normally bright little eyes were dull and bloodshot. He was dragging his foot more than usual. Deep lines marked the face that, until then, had largely kept its boyishness.

"What's up, Frankie? You look whacked, mate."

Ali gave Jack a look which suggested he'd been too blunt. But there was no point in beating about the bush. Something was wrong.

Frankie slumped down into one of Jack's once white plastic garden chairs.

"Tell you the truth, Jack, I am a bit wrung out."

"What's the problem?"

"It's just Russ. He gets so angry with his illness. I know he's done a lot for me, but to be honest, Jack, me and Mrs Charlton are just about at the end of our tether. We don't know what to do."

Ali passed Frankie a bottle of water from her cool box. "What do the doctors say?"

Frankie took a mouthful of water.

"That's the thing, we've no bloody idea. He won't talk about it. How are we supposed to help him when he's shut up like a clam?"

Jack watched the colour drain from Ali's face.

"But it's not much more than a month from when we saw him," she said. "He seemed OK at the funeral."

Frankie looked up and managed an unconvincing grin.

"You know what he's like. He can rise to the occasion when there's an audience, people to impress. It may have been poor Stan's funeral, but I tell you, Alison, it was Russ's show and no mistake. The old house full of people, arrangements to make, you two there as well. Tables full of food. Plenty of drink. Lots of chat about old times. That's Russ for you."

Jack found himself nodding agreement. Yes, that was the Russ that he knew, or used to know. Always in charge through the sheer force of his personality. Setting things up so people could have a good time. Like when he asked Keelin to have that last dance with Frankie. He would always rise to the occasion, no matter what the cost.

"But since the funeral, it's been downhill all the way. I don't want to put any pressure on you, Jack, and I know where you're coming from, so to speak. But he'd been hoping you'd pop in and see him again. I told him, Jack can't just pop in when he lives forty miles away, so do you know what he had the cheek to say to me?"

Jack shook his head.

"He says, 'Go and bloody fetch him, then.' As if you will drop everything and come running when he snaps his fingers."

206

Ali touched Frankie's arm. He looked away, out over the river below.

"Sorry," he said. "But I thought I'd better let you know. Hope you don't mind."

What could he say? It was just so typical.

"Frankie, listen. Of course I don't mind and it's lovely to see you anyway. But I'm not sure what I can do to help." For probably a full minute they all sat, side by side on their grubby plastic chairs, watching the activity on the river, listening to a cheerful bird song.

Frankie broke the silence.

"It's beautiful down here, isn't it? What bird was that singing?"

Jack smiled and put out his hand to touch Frankie's shoulder.

"I'm pretty sure it was a willow warbler. And I'll tell you the funny thing about it. What he's actually doing with that song is warning other birds off his territory. He wants all my worms for himself. Now, I bet you could do with a cuppa."

Ali put the hoe back in the shed.

"I'll go ahead and put the kettle on. You two come when you're ready. Can you remember to bring the cool box back with you?"

The two men watched her walk away.

"Now, Frankie. We're on our own. What's this all about? I thought you and he got on like a house on fire."

"We did, right up until Stan died. But now... Well, to be honest I'm thinking of telling him to stuff his job and get himself a new driver. I've just about had enough of it. I know he doesn't sleep and all the rest of it, and it might be the pills, but as I said, there's no pleasing him."

Jack rinsed his hands under the cold-water tap. Out on

the river, two yachts tacked upstream, making slow progress against the wind and tide.

"Not sure that me going to see him will help, but I'll give it a go if you like."

"Really, Jack? It would mean so much to him. Just let me know when. I'll pick you up at the station."

"No, don't do that. I'll just turn up. Catch him unawares."

*

The next day Jack took the train. The line ran right past the cemetery. Jack pulled out his phone.

"Russ?"

"Who else, Boyo?"

"How did you know it was me?"

"Recognised the voice. That, and the fact that your name's on the screen."

"I was going to pop in for an hour or so, if that's alright?"

"Delighted. To what do I owe the pleasure?"

"Bloody awful day. Too wet to do anything useful, so I thought I could while away a couple of hours with you. If you're not doing anything?"

"I'm just sitting here staring at the rain. Where are you? I'll send Frankie." He sounded OK.

"We're just pulling into Manor Park. But don't bother Frankie. I'd sooner walk from the station."

"But it's pissing down."

"Honest. I need the exercise, and I've got my brolly."

"You always were an obstinate little sod, Boyo."

"And you were always a bossy one. So I'll walk and see you in half an hour or so."

This was not the Russ Frankie had described the previous day. Perhaps he sounded more tired than before, but it was hard to tell. He turned out of the station entrance and his step lightened. It might not be that bad after all. The rain beat ever harder on the umbrella.

Too soon, he was past the cemetery gates and turning into Russ's road. Opposite his house a banner declared a new development of low-rise flats *60% sold*. A board, mounted on springs to allow it to bend with the wind, told passers-by, *Russell Homes. Show Flat Open*. The front garden was waterlogged. A cement mixer stood dripping on the drive, beside a pile of turfs from which mud ran across the tarmac.

He started up Russ's front path. The housekeeper was at the door before he reached the porch. She, too, looked drawn.

"Monsieur Boyer. How nice to see you. You'll find Mr Russell in his usual place, in the conservatory. I'll bring you some coffee. Or would you prefer tea?"

She took his coat and umbrella. From the hall, he could see Russ at his window, staring out at the rain. He suddenly backed the chair, spun around and moved forward.

"Jack," he said. "Good to see you." He was, as ever, immaculately turned out, a soft check shirt showing above a cashmere sweater. But the clothes hung off him, his neck lost in the shirt collar, his shoulders barely half as wide as the sweater, his eyes sunk deep into their sockets. Jack's shock must have shown on his face.

"It's the bloody medicines they give me, Boyo. They're killing me." He waved Jack to a cane armchair set close beside the wheelchair.

He reached out and grabbed Jack's hand.

"Thanks for coming. It's so good to see you," he said again. "You'll stay to lunch? Mrs Charlton can whistle up a famous cauliflower cheese with bacon if that's still your fancy. It was one of Emm's specialities. I know you and Stan both loved it."

Was there nothing this man didn't remember? No detail too insignificant that it shouldn't be anticipated and planned. It all fitted. Mr Big, his fingers in every pie, shrunk to half his size in a wheelchair but still in command. Jack nodded.

"Cauliflower cheese and bacon. What could be better when it's pouring down outside."

Russ stared out of the window, where little rivers of rain chased each other at an angle of forty-five degrees as gravity and the wind joined equal forces to propel the droplets.

"So, how have you been? Busy this time of the year, I suppose, with that old tub of yours."

"Yes. Plenty of work at the yard. Spend most of my days on the river, running people in and out to their boats."

"And the market garden? How's that?"

"Not exactly a market garden. Just an allotment."

"Well, whatever it is, it's made a big impression on Frankie. But then, he always did worship the ground you walked on."

"That's bollocks, Russ, and you know it."

"I'm serious. He can't wait for any excuse to run down to East Stone."

"You should come with him sometime. But more important, how are you?"

"Getting by."

The two men sat in silence, watching the rain. The grandfather clock struck once – half past. Russ spoke first, still not looking at Jack.

"I'm glad you came, Boyo. We didn't quite finish our little chat the other day, did we?"

"Didn't we? I thought we'd said more than enough."

"Not quite, not quite."

Why couldn't Russ just leave things where they were? There was no point in raking it all up again. Jack was about to say all that when Mrs Charlton arrived with the coffee.

"Just put it down on the coffee table, if you don't mind. Jack here can pour. And it will be lunch for two. Cauliflower cheese, with a few rashers, if that's OK?"

Jack stood up and went to the window. He wanted to leave.

"What about Frankie?" he said. "Isn't he invited?"

"Good thought, Boyo. Can you ask him, Mrs C?"

She hurried from the room, closing the door behind her. Russ reversed the chair and stopped at the coffee table, opposite the cane settee. Jack sat down and poured coffee.

"To answer your question, Russ, I've said all I wanted to say. What's done is done, and that's it."

"You didn't like her, did you, when you saw her at the funeral?"

"What makes you say that?"

"It was obvious. You avoided her when we came back here and she said you left without saying goodbye."

"There didn't seem anything more to say."

"Funny, that's what she said."

"It wasn't a question of like or dislike. We weren't the same people."

Russ didn't seem to know about the lunch at Le Vieux Manoir. Odd, since he seemed to have paid for it.

Jack picked up his coffee and took a sip. He really did not want to talk about all this. He meant it when he said he was done. He could cope with a harmless discussion about old times, the good times, the mischief. About climbing over the baker's wall and pinching buns from the back of the van, or the time they managed to lose control of the soap box running down the sandhills and ended up in the lake.

"She knew from the start it was a mistake, marrying me. But she was carrying and there was no way a little 'un could be pinned on you when you were a thousand miles away."

Jack felt a sudden, heavy weight in his stomach, as if he'd just eaten a huge suet pudding that was refusing all his body's attempts to digest it. He said nothing.

For almost the first time that morning, Russ looked directly into his eyes.

"Why else did you think it was all so sudden? You saw the photo the other day. It was obvious."

Jack leaned back and closed his eyes. Why hadn't Bel told him? He tried to keep his voice calm, cool, quiet.

"Why tell me this now, Russ? What the fuck are you and Bel playing at? What are you trying to do to me? You can stuff your bloody cauliflower cheese and all the rest of it. And I'll tell you something else before I go. Don't send me any more of your letters, and by the way you can also tell her not to get in touch again. Am I making myself clear? And now I think I'll go."

"Calm down, Jack, for God's sake. There's no game, as you put it. But we thought you should know everything. Once it's all on the table we can move on."

Move on? What the hell was Russ on about? Move on to where?

"Or we can go our separate ways. That's up to you. But not until you know everything there is to know."

"So what happened to your baby?"

"She lost it. At about twelve weeks. Only a bloody month after the wedding, would you believe? And it wasn't my baby."

Jack took a deep breath, exhaled and took another. What did it matter anyway? Russ was right, he didn't even like the woman.

"So whose baby was it, then, if it wasn't yours?"

"I've no idea."

"Really. What kind of a fool do you take me for? You're telling me that you married my girlfriend because she was up the spout but it wasn't yours. And it wasn't mine. Honestly, Russ, you've got to do better than that."

"If you are asking why we got married, I'll tell you, if you can listen without flying off the handle. When she told me she was late and thought she might be expecting, I knew it couldn't be yours because you'd been away for months. She was so ashamed, Jack, and was talking about getting rid of it. Or even getting rid of herself. I couldn't allow that."

Rain hammered down on the conservatory roof. Somewhere far away in the house a telephone rang.

"So, whose was it?"

"As I told you, I didn't know. She's never said, and I've never asked."

Jack stood up, pushed past the wheelchair and went to the window. He saw Frankie come out of the back door. He waved and disappeared into the garage. Could it be Frankie, or even Stan? But surely neither of them would have betrayed him in that way. He turned back to Russ.

"And you've no idea? I don't believe you."

Russ shrugged his shoulders, and whirred up beside him.

"It's up to you what you believe. But at the time, it didn't really matter to me. And don't cast me as some sort of knight in shining armour, rescuing a damsel in distress. The fact was, I knew that one day I would want a little 'un. I would want to be somebody's dad. To be the father I never had. I also knew I would never get married in the ordinary way. Bel and I were great mates, and still are for that matter. But that's all either of us wanted. What's more, I was more or less running the business that one day would be hers. And then our kid's. It was a neat and tidy solution. The only complication was you, but you'd moved on, Jack. You hardly ever came home. You didn't write. You didn't give a toss about us."

"I would have married her."

"Would you, Jack? Really? In the circumstances? I'm not so sure."

Jack opened the conservatory door and walked out. The rain had subsided into a warm drizzle. He thought he'd put all that hurt behind him – the years when just hearing the words "Manor Park", or even just the mention of "the sixties", brought pain, when listening to Buddy Holly, or Jerry Lee Lewis, or Muddy Waters brought a tear to his eye.

It was always Russ, wearing his little boy lost expression.

But now? If it wasn't Russ, who was it? He walked as far as the fountain and turned back. Russ hadn't moved. He sat there, still as a rock, stranded in his chair. Jack walked on, and turned again. Russ was gone. Jack returned to the conservatory and sat on the cane sofa. Out in the hall, the grandfather clock struck twelve. And then Russ whirred back into the room, his face flushed.

"You can't turn back the clock, Jack, but you'll never know how many times I've wished I could. We should have been honest with you from the start, but Bel couldn't face you."

"So then you got divorced. Why was that?"

Russ looked up from his chair. Some of the twinkle had returned to his eyes.

"Didn't have to get divorced, Boyo. The marriage was defective, or voidable as my solicitor said. First off, it was never consummated. Second off, she was pregnant with another man's child. In law, two watertight reasons why the marriage never happened."

"So why did you decide not to be a couple?"

"I wanted her to be free to meet somebody else, to start over without the complication of being a divorcee. She was single again, officially, if you know what I mean. A spinster of this parish."

Russ repositioned his chair and reached out his hand, resting it on the arm of the sofa where Jack was still sitting. Was Jack supposed to take it, give it a squeeze and say everything's alright? After a moment he withdrew it and they sat in silence. The rain had stopped and a pair of magpies stomped about the lawn. Steam rose off the paving stones drying rapidly in the sunshine. Frankie had brought the Bond out of the garage and was checking the tyres. Mrs Charlton fussed about, laying a table outside the summer house. Frankie saw Jack at the window and waved. Jack took a deep breath and put his hand on Russ's shoulder. He could feel every bone.

*

Despite his illness, Russ could still eat.

"I've got an idea," he said, wiping his mouth on a starched linen napkin. "Let's run through some of Stan's old films. Could you get them, Frankie, after lunch, and pop them downstairs?"

The film show was set up in the basement. Red plush cinema seats formed an arc around the screen. A deep freeze with a sliding glass lid hummed quietly in the corner, while numerous bottles shined and glinted behind a bar, which looked like it might have been a prop from *La Dolce Vita*. One wall was lined entirely with videos and DVDs. Frankie concentrated on threading Super 8 into a vintage projector.

Russ sped into a space in the centre of the row.

"Put on that one that Emm took, the jerky one where all three of us are piled into the Bond and Stan's so busy waving he nearly crashes into the coal lorry."

Frankie grinned.

"What do you think I'm setting up at the moment? You always want that one first."

The symbiosis between the two of them was not something that Jack had noticed before. It was certainly not there when they were youngsters, when Russ usually bullied them both. But then, we can all change. Maybe the baby was Frankie's, after all. But then Frankie would surely have been the groom. He wasn't going to get the answer watching old films. But did he really care a damn who Bel slept with nearly fifty years ago? Yes, he did.

Frankie dimmed the lights. A succession of numbers on the screen counted down. Jack saw the outside of Emm's house. The Bond is parked in the kerb, leaning into the steep camber. One by one three boys come out of the front door, wave to the camera and climb into the car. Then out comes Stan, a straw hat on his head, which he lifts to the camera. Slowly he walks around the car and climbs in. Frankie is in the front, beside Stan. The other two boys sit on the back, only their legs and feet actually in the car.

Russ was already chuckling.

"None of that seat belt nonsense then, eh?" he said to neither of them in particular. "Now just watch."

The Bond pulls away from the kerb, the camera following it down the street until it turns the corner. Then the camera pans jerkily around and focuses on the other end of the street. Somewhere from the depths of his memory, Jack began to recall the scene.

"I remember now, Stan said we could sit on the back only while we went round the block."

"Now watch," said Russ again, spluttering with laughter. Frankie, too, began to chuckle. The little car comes speeding around the corner, and as they pass the camera, Stan lifts his hat and everybody waves. Just before the next corner a coal lorry appears, belching smoke. There is then a view of some out-of-focus chimney pots and the film comes to a sudden end.

Russ could barely speak.

"Emm only dropped the bloody camera. Poor old Stan, nearly gets flattened by a coal lorry and then finds out Emm's dropped his beloved camera. But you have to hand it to Stan, he could always see the funny side of it."

More films followed. Russ had obviously seen them all before, and took care to ask mostly for films that included Frankie, as if he really had been one of three and not an often-shunned outsider. None had included Bel. The apparently random selection had been carefully edited for Jack's benefit. Nothing left to chance. No wonder Russ was such a success in business.

Without warning, around four o'clock, Russ fell into a deep sleep. Frankie and Jack watched a couple more films, but it was not the same. The fun had gone out of the afternoon.

"Let's call it a day, shall we, Frankie?"

"Do you want me to drop you back home? I fancy a run out. Russ doesn't want to go far these days and it would make a change."

Mrs Charlton poked her head around the door.

"Would you like some tea? And are you staying for dinner, Monsieur Boyer? I know Mr Russell would like you to."

Jack nodded at the sleeping figure in the wheelchair.

"I think Mr Russell may have had enough excitement for one day, thanks, but I'd love a cup of tea before I go."

"He'll sleep like that for about half an hour. I'll wake him up before you leave."

Frankie turned off the projector, and began gathering up the films.

"I'll pop these back," he said. "And put the Bond away." The room was strangely quiet, except for the hum of the refrigerator and the sound of gentle breathing from the wheelchair.

217

"You got the letters, then, Boyo?"

Jack was not sure whether or not he had himself dozed off, lulled by Russ's regular breathing and the comfortable feeling in his stomach.

"You know I got them, but I still don't know what they were all about."

Russ spread out his arms and looked down.

"This is what they were about. Me. My condition. I need your help."

"What are you talking about? If the doctors can't help, what can I do?"

The refrigerator clicked off, and the room fell silent.

"You don't understand. I've had enough of this. I want out, before it gets any worse."

"Don't be dramatic. You're just depressed because you've lost Stan."

"Think about it, Boyo. I started to write to you a year before we lost Stan. I've got it all worked out. All I need is for you to say you'll do it."

"You mean Switzerland? That clinic?"

Jack heard the soft click as Russ engaged the motor on the chair. Russ inched forward, his back to Jack, and then spun around. He turned on the grin, playing the little innocent again.

"No, I don't mean Switzerland. You've seen my garden, my roses, the fountain, even the hideous summer house. I mean here, not in some miserable little room which looks like a youth hostel."

"You're serious, aren't you? You really mean it."

"Never more so."

"But where do I come in?"

"I want you to pull the trigger."

"You must be out of your mind. Why the hell should I risk everything for you, even if I could?"

218

"You've killed before."

"What do you mean? Killed before? I didn't touch Ma Vinney if that's what you mean? You said…"

"No, I don't mean Ma Vinney. You know what I'm talking about: Cyprus. I've read your service record. I know what happened. And I'll tell you something else while we're about it. I know who your father was. I know why your mother left home. I know more about you than you know yourself. You don't do anything, you don't go anywhere, without me knowing. What do you think of that?"

Russ's come hither smile had turned into a malevolent grin, but he hadn't finished.

"Now, what do you say about finishing me off? I bet you'd love to. The tales I could tell. Silence me for ever. Think of that, Jack Boyer, and then give me your answer."

Russ propelled himself out of the basement. Jack heard the lift doors open and then close again. He stared at the dark screen. The fridge clicked on again. What was he doing even listening to that man? Why on earth had he allowed himself to be lured back into their lives? Russ had to be exaggerating. How could he have found out about what happened in Cyprus? It was never public. The RAF made sure it was all hushed up.

He needn't do anything. He could just call Russ's bluff. He was exonerated over Cyprus. Ma Vinney died of natural causes. Russ had nothing on him. Why not just take the train back to the coast and not open any more letters? Change his telephone number? And if none of that worked, he would simply go to France and live in the house he'd not yet seen. He emerged into the sunshine. Frankie was over by the Jaguar, giving the spotless car yet another polish.

Russ sat at the table by the fountain. He waved.

"Come and have a cup of tea, Boyo. Mrs Charlton has

baked some Chelsea buns. I know how you love them."

Did the last ten minutes down in the video room not actually happen? Had he dreamed it all? How had Russ managed to remember over decades that he had a weakness for Chelsea buns? And did he have to sit with Russ over a cup of tea? Why couldn't he just walk straight past the table and out the gates?

He stood by the door, undecided. Russ beckoned him over. He went and sat down, and without thinking picked up one of the buns. It was still warm, and the big sugar crystals stuck to his fingers. He began to unroll the spiral of dough, took a bite, and licked his fingers.

Russ grinned. The winning face was back, unchanged. Untainted.

"There's some butter there, Jack. I'll tell you what, this doesn't half bring back memories, watching you unroll that bun. Can you pour? I'll slop tea all over the cloth and be in trouble with Mrs C."

Jack pulled the teapot towards him and put a silver tea strainer on top of Russ's cup. Russ took his hand.

"It's not that big a deal, Jack. I'm on my way out anyway, even you can see that. I just want to speed things up a bit."

"Don't be so stupid. It's a huge deal. There's no way, Russ. No way. Sorry, but the answer's no."

Russ dropped the grin. Was another threat coming?

"Do you remember the night we went to see that terrible film, *Island in the Sky* with John Wayne trying to fly a DC3 and Stan got yet another brush-off from the usherette, what we said on the way out of the cinema?"

Jack shook his head.

"No, not really."

"I asked you, if I was on my last legs after being hit in some battle, would you finish me off?"

Jack remembered clearly, but he was not going to admit it. He could see Stan's face illuminated by the flare of his lighter as they made their way down the steps after the film.

"What I do remember is Stan saying it was just what people said, that they didn't mean it."

"Well, Jack, my friend, you said you would do that for me, and I said I'd keep all our little secrets. And I meant it. So here we are. The time has come. I need you like I've never needed anything in my life. You don't have to say anything now. I'll write to you in a couple of days."

"That's one hell of an ask, Russ."

Russ looked up, his wet eyes telling their own story.

"I know. I know. Just don't tell Frankie. This is between you and me. OK?"

"So, another little secret to keep, eh?"

After half an hour of pretending, Jack could stand it no longer.

"Well, it's been great seeing you again, but I think I'd better be getting along." As he stood up to leave, Frankie emerged from the garage.

"I'll run you back. The Jag's already out."

"No. It's OK. I'll take the train. I feel like a walk anyway."

Russ touched his arm.

"We won't hear of it, Boyo, will we, Frankie? There's too much to carry anyway."

"What do you mean, too much to carry? There's only my backpack and an umbrella."

"I got Frankie to put a few bottles in the boot for you. I've got far too much, and I'm not supposed to drink it anyway. Getting rid of it now will save on the death duties."

"Honestly, Russ, I'd sooner take the train. I don't need any more wine. I've plenty at home, and it doesn't keep too well on the boat."

Russ seemed not to hear.

"I want you to have it, Jack. And there's plenty more where that came from. Gallons of the bloody stuff. Would you like to see the cellar, while you're here? See if there's anything you fancy?"

This was just like it had always been. Push, push, push until he got his own way. Well, not this time.

"Russ, another time, alright? I really need to be getting along."

Russ turned to Frankie.

"Could you pop inside and tell Mrs C that Jack's off. I know she wanted to say goodbye."

Frankie hurried away towards the house. Russ motioned for Jack to move closer.

"Let him take you back, will you, Jack? It's all he talks about, his little trips down to see you and having a cup of tea with you and Alison. Any excuse, and he says, 'Do you need me to pop down to Jack's?' He's not got much going for him at the moment, poor little sod. I'm a complete pain in the arse and he really misses Stan. So, for Frankie, if not for me, eh?"

Why does this man always have to win?

"OK. But only for Frankie. And I don't want to see your bloody wine cellar, so don't ask again."

"Alright, Boyo, keep your hair on. But I'm going to pick out some more good stuff for you, like it or not."

Fifteen

Russ kicked a stone along the road.

"You going with them to the pictures tonight?"

Jack shrugged his shoulders. It was really too hot to be bothered with Russ's endless questions. Sometimes it would be nice if Russ could just shut up. Mind his own business. But that wasn't the way Russ was.

"Well, are you, or not?"

"My mum wants to go, but she don't like going on her own," Frankie said.

"Well, I'll tell you something, Boyo. I ain't going and that's that. *Singing in the flippin' Rain*. Load of singing and dancing. What's the point of that? I'm goin' to the club."

Jack sighed. Sometimes, when he came home from school on Friday afternoon, he just wanted time on his own. But Russ was always there, waiting for him.

"I don't fancy it either, but I think Stan wants me to go so it doesn't look like Emm is his girlfriend. He's still after that usherette at the Coronation."

Russ gave the stone another big kick.

223

"Then why don't he ask Frankie's mum and you and me can go to the club. Frankie's coming, ain't you, Frankie?"

He put his arm around Frankie's shoulders and wandered off to stare in the window of the army surplus store. Ranged along the back of the window was a selection of full dress uniforms. Admirals and generals rubbing shoulders with wing commanders and humble able seamen and guardsmen. No matter what their rank, all the servicemen had the same pink bodies, painted faces and hair. Their trousers were tied at the bottom with string. In front of them the shop had arranged equipment they would need for the desert, or the Arctic or a battle in mid-Atlantic. Pots, pans, folding sets of cutlery, spirit stoves, primus stoves, tin openers, and canvas bags to put it all in.

"Look at that telescope. Bet you can see the moon through that," said Frankie, pointing.

Jack turned to face him.

"Frankie, you don't need a telescope. You can see the moon anyway."

"Not properly, though. You can't see the rivers," said Russ.

"Except there aren't any rivers on the moon," Jack countered.

"Canals, then."

"They're on Mars. Not the moon."

They stood in silence, side by side, lost in the possibilities offered by all the stuff.

"Bags the telescope," said Russ.

Jack bagged a vicious-looking knife.

"Bags the searchlight," said Frankie.

"We gonna let him 'ave it, Jack? What would Frankie want with a searchlight?"

"I don't know. Ask him."

"So what do you want a searchlight for?"

"Dunno," said Frankie.

"What's that uniform right in the middle, the one that looks a bit like the RAF?" asked Jack to no one in particular.

Russ turned to face him.

"It's not the RAF you cloth-head. Don't you know? Really? It's a German Navy captain. I thought you'd recognise that alright."

"Why should I?"

"Wouldn't you like to know? Eh? Wouldn't you just like to know what I know?"

Cyprus, October 1960

The boy appeared at dusk from between the trees. One moment the track was empty. The next he was standing there, one arm raised with something small and round in his hand. Everyone would swear he was about to throw it. They all said Jack was only trying to protect his patrol.

Sixteen

"How did you find him, then?" asked Frankie as the Jaguar pulled out of the gates and turned towards the A12.

"Not as bad as I expected, actually, Frankie. A bit up and down, maybe."

"That's what I meant the other day. Russ can rise to the occasion, but he sinks again just as fast. Today he was happy as Larry to see you, but tomorrow he'll be right down again."

"Must be tough to live with, day after day."

"That's putting it mildly, Jack. He's a nightmare. But, do you know what, no matter how bloody awkward he is, I can't look at him without... I don't know how to put it. He keeps talking about wanting to end it all. But then he gives that smile of his, and, well, you know..."

So Frankie knew, or maybe not. Had Russ primed him to pile on extra pressure?

"End it all! How does he think he's going to do that?"

"Don't ask me. He plays his cards so close to his chest, but he's got some plan or other. Did he say anything to you about it?"

"Not specifically, Frankie, no."

This conversation had already gone too far for comfort. Time to change the subject.

"Do you know, Frankie, you are a really good driver."

"You can thank the Metropolitan Police for that."

"How come?"

"I did their training course. The one the police drivers have to go on. Russ insisted on it before I was allowed to drive him."

"I didn't know they were open to the public."

Frankie noticed a woman with a pushchair standing on the central reservation and slowed to let her cross.

"They're not. But you know Russ, his connections, contacts. You don't ask him how or why. He'll tell you no more than he wants to, and if you push it he just gets pissed off. And then you really know all about it."

Contacts, connections? It made sense. That was how he'd got his hands on Ma Vinney's post-mortem report. How he'd found out what happened in Cyprus. Why, when he claimed he knew all about Jack, he was so cocksure. There was probably a tracking device fitted to the Jag, so he could keep tabs on Frankie. He might even be listening in to their conversation in the car. Jack imagined him sitting at his computer with a big map up on the screen, watching a blue flashing dot chart their progress to the coast, headphones on, listening to everything they were saying.

He felt in his pocket for his phone. Had he left it out of his sight at any time? They could load tracking software onto a smartphone in seconds, he knew that. But he was being melodramatic. Paranoia was not going to help.

Soon, they were back at East Stone. Jack pulled himself back to the present. The car came to a halt. Frankie cut the engine. Katie was out front of the pub, watering the hanging baskets. She waved to them. Frankie waved back.

What did that mean? Nothing. Only to somebody with a problem.

"That's Katie, Alison's daughter. She works at the pub."

"I met her there when I left that letter for you. But I didn't know she was Alison's daughter. She seems very nice."

"Didn't Russ tell you that, then?"

Frankie appeared confused.

"No... how would he know? He's never been down here."

"But he claims to know everything, doesn't he?"

"That's just his way, Jack. Just what he says to wind people up. Don't read too much into it."

Why was he taking it out on Frankie? Frankie, who'd just driven him all the way home, and seemed not to have a malicious thought in his head? That tongue.

Frankie opened his door.

"I've parked close to the steps, so we won't have to lug the wine too far."

"You can take it back with you for all I care, Frankie. I told Russ I didn't need his wine."

"You know Russ, Jack. Never could take no for an answer. And if I take it back again, there'll be hell to pay. I'll get it in the neck. But you go on, I'll bring it over."

"Don't be daft. There's no need for you to cart it all. Come on, open the boot. I'll take the bloody stuff."

They picked up a box each and climbed the steps up to the river wall. *Duchesse Anne* lay directly in front of them, geraniums in full bloom, her brass glinting and her windows reflecting the last of the late afternoon sun. Jack felt that flush of pride and pleasure, and not least comfort, that returning to his beloved river so often brought about.

The tide was low and the gangway steep.

"Put your box down at the end, Frankie. I'll take it the rest of the way."

A flicker of disappointment showed on Frankie's face. He put down the box.

"I'll go and get the last one," he said, turning away.

"And I'll go aboard and put the kettle on. I'd like to show you over my pride and joy, if you've got the time."

Frankie's expression changed in an instant. That was the thing with Frankie, too easy to please but also too easy to hurt.

"Really?" he said. "I've been itching to see over *Duchesse Anne* ever since that first day I came down here. Sure you don't mind?"

"I wouldn't have invited you if I minded, would I?"

Jack carried his box down the gangway and left it on the foredeck, then went back for the one that Frankie had left by the sea wall. Frankie followed him down to the boat with the third box.

Puffing from the effort, Frankie followed Jack below. While Jack busied himself with the tea, Frankie walked all around the saloon, peering through portholes and running his hands over the smooth woodwork.

"Do the engines still work?"

"What do you think, Frankie? What's the good of a boat with no engines?"

"What are they?"

"Perkins. The best."

"I know this is a real cheek, Jack, but would we be able to start one of them up? I'd love to hear what they sound like."

"Come back up to the wheelhouse, Frankie, and let's turn them both over."

The engines roared into life, one after the other, as soon as the key was turned. Jack pulled back the throttles and they settled to a burble. A gentle vibration could be felt throughout the boat. They sat in the wheelhouse, sipping tea.

"Heard enough, Frankie?" He nodded. Jack pulled the stop levers and the silence was at once heavy. "Frankie, Russ said something to me that I am not sure about. Can I ask you about it?"

Frankie stared out of the windscreen. The tide had been flowing for nearly four hours, and at any moment *Duchesse Anne* would lift off from the mud and be afloat again. A little fleet of Optimists, each one containing a couple of children, drifted past, watched by instructors in orange RIBs. They both waved.

"Do you know everyone on this river, Jack?"

"Well, most of the regulars, as it happens. So, do you? Do you mind if I ask you about what Russ said?"

"If it's all the same to you, Jack, I'd sooner you didn't." He picked up the mug of tea. "I'll just get this down me and be getting back to the Smoke."

After Frankie had left, Jack took out his little rowing dinghy. He rowed across the river and tied up at the jetty on the other side. He wanted to walk, to think, but not to meet anyone. It was a pleasant two miles to the Anchor, where he could enjoy a quiet pint in the garden.

Russ must have been bluffing when he said he knew who his father was. How could he possibly have found out? And, in any case, what was it to Jack now? He'd left him a house and a stack of cash, and asked that Jack didn't try to establish his identity. So, that was that. But it raised the possibility that the detective who'd been snooping about, asking questions at St Pabu, had been sent by Russ. Not to find out where Jack might be, but to find out who might have fathered him.

But if Russ thought he could bribe him or scare him

into ending it all, as he put it, he could think again. In any case, Russ could do what he wanted on his own. He wasn't paralysed, nothing like that. He had the connections to get all the drugs he needed.

He began the walk along the quiet lane which led only to the pub. A couple of aeroplanes came over fairly low, en route for Southend airport. Where did they fly to, he wondered? When he got back on board he would have a look.

*

Thanks to his inheritance, for the first time in his life, Jack had money. Real money. And at that moment, walking up the lane to the Anchor, he made the decision to spend some of it to have *Duchesse Anne* made ready for sea. He'd get the boatyard to lift her out for a full survey, get the bottom plates properly examined and the gearboxes checked. He'd have them fit a decent marine GPS.

If anyone asked, he would say he was preparing her for the next Dunkirk Little Ships Rally. *Duchesse Anne*, albeit under a different name, had been there in May 1940 when the Expeditionary Force had to be evacuated. She had been a working boat until Jack bought her, and she deserved another outing before being consigned for ever to a secure mooring on a quiet river.

And while the work was going on on the boat, he would take a refresher course on navigation. He didn't want to run her onto a sandbank halfway across the Thames Estuary. But could he do it? Not alone, that's for certain, but perhaps John at the boatyard, a navy-trained engineer, might be prepared to act as crew. He had, a number of times, suggested that he and Jack take *Duchesse Anne* for a couple of days' trip around the estuary. And, after all, Jack had brought her single-handed from the Medway when he first bought her.

The thing about living on a boat was that, if he wanted to, or needed to, he could simply cast off and go. One day he'd be there, the next he wouldn't. He'd need to tell nobody where he was going, or why. He'd just disappear. And, one way or another, Russ might just be menace enough to make that happen.

He stayed at the Anchor long enough to down a couple of pints, eat a sausage roll he didn't really want, and start a list of jobs he wanted done. It was the perfect time of year to put *Duchesse Anne* into the yard. The pre-summer rush was over and the weather was good for any external work that needed doing. And the yard would make *Duchesse Anne* a priority.

By the time he got back to the jetty, the tide had dropped again and the light was going. He dragged his dinghy down to the water's edge. Across the river, *Duchesse Anne* lay silhouetted against the glare of lights from the Old Smack. He imagined himself at the wheel as she creamed across the estuary in the moonlight, the diesels humming sweetly beneath his feet, the radar screen dotted with the green outlines of other ships on the move, and the VHF chattering away with reassuring calm as he drew ever closer to Ramsgate harbour, his first stop.

*

Jack slept well and woke only when he heard his mobile commanding attention. It was already morning, much to his surprise. One of the yard's regular customers had lost their steering out in the estuary, been towed to Brightlingsea by the Clacton inshore lifeboat and needed to get his boat back to East Stone for repair. Could Jack possibly take the big launch and collect the yacht and the owner? The yard said they had already fuelled up the launch and made sure it had sufficient ropes and fenders on board to do the job. All they needed was somebody to go and fetch the yacht.

Could he? What a ridiculous question. Just try to stop him.

"Give me half an hour for some breakfast and a cup of tea and I'll be down," he said. He poured muesli into his favourite blue china bowl, added a handful of blueberries from Alison's allotment and a spoonful of yoghurt. He made tea, and while it drew, pulled on the overalls he always wore when working around the yard. Warm sun streamed through the wheelhouse windows. He clicked on the VHF. Each day, it seemed, there was more and more traffic from leisure sailors and sea anglers, and each day they needed to be reminded that Channel 16 is for calling up, not for conversation.

From the wheelhouse he could see the yard's big launch tied up at the jetty, waiting for him, ready to go. Close to the top of the tide. It would be a fast run down, but they would be fighting the ebb all the way home, not that that would be a problem, it would just slow things up a bit. The river seemed unusually peaceful. Was it only a few hours ago that Russ had been threatening him, demanding that he fulfil some stupid childhood pledge? What did it matter? He'd made his mind up. He wasn't going to do it, and Russ could go to hell with his bullying. There was nothing to fear. Nothing to hide.

The trip downriver to Brightlingsea would take less than an hour, but he was nevertheless anxious to get going. He hurried his breakfast and drank the tea while it was still hotter than he wanted, grabbed the lifejacket he always wore on the launch and walked quickly down to the jetty. The yard manager saw him coming and the two met at the landward end.

Jack loved the big launch. Unlike the newer, small launch which had wheel steering amidships, the big launch had a proper heavy wooden tiller, the sort you can lean against to get a tight turn. It had heavy and still beautiful rope fendering, hemp, all the way around and an engine you could easily get at if there was any trouble. The engine, already warm, started with the first turn of the key. As it settled into its familiar burble, Jack cast off, added a few revs and reversed carefully away from the crowded jetty.

What little early mist there had been had largely burned off: downriver the silent nuclear power station stood out clearly as the dominant feature of the skyline. Soon he was clearing the last of the East Stone moorings and shortly afterwards began to feel the gentle swell of the North Sea. This is what it would be like. *Duchesse Anne* powering downriver towards the tricky navigation across the estuary. But he could do it. Didn't he know every buoy, which swatchways he could trust and those he couldn't. He glanced at the echo sounder. Eighteen metres under the keel. By instinct he was bang in the deepest part of the channel. He wouldn't need a chart to get across, although he'd need to be careful around Margate Sand.

He clicked the VHF to channel 68. He knew the lads down at Brightlingsea and they were expecting his call. They told him where the yacht was tied up, and that they'd left an empty berth in front of her so Jack could tuck in if he wished to tow astern, or there would be water enough in the creek if he chose to tow alongside. Much depended on whether the steering on the yacht was jammed to one side, or if the rudder was free to follow the tow. The owner, he learned, had left for London on the morning train. So much the better. Yacht owners just can't relax when anybody else is in charge. He would be the same, wouldn't he, if it was *Duchesse Anne* taking a tow.

Soon he was passing Tollesbury Creek – only twenty minutes to cover the distance that had taken two hours to walk, the day he met Bel. He still didn't know what that had really been all about. And then Frankie turning up at the allotment. Were they all in on the plan to make Jack kill again? Was he being taken for a ride? Somebody to carry the can. But why? He'd done Russ no harm, nor Bel.

Another half-hour and he was alongside the yacht, cleating up the springs that would take the strain as they pushed their way back against the falling tide to East Stone. The owner had left a thank you note and a thermos of coffee ready for him. He saw nobody from the Brightlingsea yard – it felt good to be trusted. He poured the coffee and listened to the big diesel idling quietly, his ears tuned to pick up any skip in the steady rhythm.

Once all was secure he cast off, and began the journey back upriver. The earlier peace of the river had yielded to activity. Half a dozen anglers' boats had anchored off the baffle of the nuclear power station. Although it had been decommissioned and no longer pumped warm water into the river, fish had retained the habit of breeding there. The sandbanks were still too well covered for any seals to spend the morning sun bathing, but a little fleet of Optimists, their young crews watched over by a couple of rescue launches manned by young men with megaphones, tacked upstream.

By the time the first moorings of East Stone came into view, Jack was looking forward to his lunch. He called up the boatyard to ask where they wanted the yacht to be moored, which is something they hadn't seemed to have thought of, so Jack was asked to simply tie up alongside the jetty, leaving the tow attached.

As he closed on the jetty, he was surprised to see Alison standing there. She waved, but even from a distance of thirty yards or so, Jack could sense, maybe from the expression on Alison's face, that this was not a chance encounter. She had been waiting for him and, unusually, didn't have the dog Millie at her side.

Jack pulled alongside and Alison took the ropes.

"Hi, Ali. Where's Millie?" he asked.

"Oh, she's at home. I gave her a long walk this morning and she was quite happy to doze in the sunshine. Good trip?"

One of the shipwrights came down to help with mooring, and as soon as the launch and its tow were secured Alison grabbed Jack's arm and guided him to the sea wall. Looking all around as if to make sure they were not overheard, she said, "I've had a visitor this morning while you were off downriver."

"Really, who was that?"

"Your friend Russ."

They stopped walking.

"Russ? What on earth did he want? Was he looking for me?"

"Probably… I don't know. Well, no, thinking about it, he already knew you'd gone off in the launch. It was really odd. I saw a Jaguar, like the one Frankie drives, in the car park when I came back from my walk, but didn't really take much notice. Then a few minutes later, Russ arrived on my doorstep in that electric chair of his."

"He came to your house?"

"Yes. Millie heard him at the door. I was out the back so didn't hear him knocking."

They walked on a few paces. This was an intrusion into his space, whichever way you looked at it. Being pestered by letters was one thing, but this was something else. Ali continued where she left off.

"I said you weren't here so he should try the boat, but he already knew more than I did, and told me Frankie had seen you leave."

"So where was Frankie while all this was going on?"

"Hang on a minute, Jack, and I'll tell you. Anyway, I asked him in, of course, but his chair was too wide to go through the door, and in any case there's the step. So I made some coffee and we sat in the front garden, him in that chair and me on the old bench. Then he told me Frankie had brought him and was dropping off a few more bottles of wine at the boat, something about forgetting the best stuff yesterday? Then Frankie drove up and parked across the road."

"And he stayed in the car?"

"Yes. I went over and asked him if he wanted to come and join us for coffee, but he just shook his head. There was another bloke in the car as well, in the back. I only got a glimpse of him, but he looked a bit of a bruiser to be honest. Frankie was embarrassed, or frightened, or something. Like he wasn't allowed to talk to me. I don't remember seeing the bloke in the back before, and he didn't say a word. Then Russ came speeding across the road. The other bloke got out and helped him into the car, folded up the wheelchair and they left."

So Russ had arrived with a heavy, probably Glover, who he had sent to the sea wall all those months ago.

"I think I know the bloke you mean. He delivered the first letter I had from Russ. His name is Roy Glover. Another remnant from our childhood."

They had arrived back on the sea wall alongside *Duchesse*

237

Anne where, on the foredeck in front of the wheelhouse, more cases of wine were piled up.

Jack stopped and stared.

"I told him I didn't want any of his bloody wine, let alone all this. I've a good mind to chuck the lot straight in the river."

They stood side by side, looking at the stack of boxes.

He felt Ali squeeze his hand.

"Jack, love, don't be like that. I'm sure he doesn't mean anything by it. Not anything nasty. Can't you just accept it as a gift, and if you really don't want it, put it in the raffle for the village hall campaign? He seemed genuinely sad that he'd missed you. Surely he's not that bad?"

Not that bad? If only she knew. No, he wasn't that bad. He was worse, much worse. Maybe if she'd heard his threats and demands, she might have other ideas. But none of this was for sharing. Not now. Not ever.

"Anyway, after all that, what did he want?"

"You know, I'm really not sure." She paused, deep in thought. "He told me all about you three watching some of Stan's old cine films and falling about laughing. Then he said that Frankie had been going on and on about *Duchesse Anne* so much that he decided that he ought to come and see for himself where it was that you lived."

"So why didn't he let me know he was coming?"

"Jack, love, I don't know, do I? He gave the impression that the visit was all a bit spur of the moment. He asked if I thought you were happy, and enjoying life."

"What did you say? You should have told him I was happy as Larry until he waltzed back into it."

"I said that, yes, you were very content with your life. Which is true, isn't it? Russ can't change that, can he? Not unless you let him."

Jack put his arm around Alison's shoulders and squeezed.

"No, I'm not going to let him. Now, I've had a lovely morning running down to Brightlingsea and earned myself a few pounds into the bargain. How about we take a row across the river and stroll down to the Anchor for some lunch? I went there last night after I got home. They've got a great new menu and I fancy a bit of time with you, if you can bear it, without feeling we're being chaperoned by your lovely daughter."

"He just asked me to make sure you thought really seriously about all that he told you yesterday, whatever that may mean. Now, I just need to pop home for a minute while you get the dinghy ready. I'd love to go across to the Anchor. Is it OK if I bring Millie?"

It wasn't a question that needed an answer.

*

They returned early evening, after enjoying a long walk along the south side of the river and had then spent the best part of an hour on the river rowing up to the canal lock and back.

He thought that would be enough to push Russ out of his mind, but could think of nothing else. He then made the mistake of drinking nearly a whole bottle of red during the evening. So he slept badly, and each time he woke he found himself still mulling over all that Russ had said. How had he found out about Cyprus? And his claim to know who his father was. How much did Russ really know about him? What else could he drag up to threaten him with? And why had he come down to East Stone without warning?

Around 4.30 he did fall into a deep sleep. On waking, later than his usual 7.30, he made his morning tea and carried it up to the wheelhouse. The three boxes of wine that

239

Russ had insisted he take home were just inside the door. The newer arrivals remained piled up on deck.

He pushed the boxes to the top of the companionway, took his tea back to the saloon and then from there grabbed a box and carried it to the table. Using a screwdriver from his toolbox he levered open the lid, throwing the wood into the basket beside the stove he kept for kindling. The top layer of three bottles lay side by side. Margaux 2008. Not bad, not at all bad.

So Russ knows his wines, or at least his wine merchant knows his wines.

He pulled down the second box. It had a big red sticker in Russ's own hand. *Open this box last.* That must have been the box that Frankie carried aboard, for he'd have seen the sticker if he'd carried it himself. Typical Russ, even trying to dictate the bloody order in which to open the boxes. It was wine, for God's sake. He levered off the lid. Inside, lying on top of the bottles, was another of Russ's familiar envelopes. Now what? He slit the envelope open, pulled out the handwritten letter, and read:

My dear Jack,

It was so good to have our little chat. Under the Meursault you will find a toy for you to practise with. It's brand new and clean as a whistle, with decent optics and an effective silencer. I've checked on your gun licence. It doesn't cover this sort of kit, so don't go bragging about it.

Enjoy yourself. Will be in touch soon to let you know what to do next.

Your friend,

Russ

PS Don't worry too much about Cyprus. If it gets

out, Alison will understand, I'm sure. After all, the little bastard deserved it.

Jack backed away from the table and climbed up to the wheelhouse. On the towpath, and on the river, everything was normal. A couple of people from the village, out walking their dogs, appeared to be having an argument, the big launch bobbed up and down up behind the yacht to which it was tethered, the gulls screamed overhead. All as it should be. *Duchesse Anne* lifted off from the mud and sank back, tensioning the warps that kept her on station.

He thought about going ashore, taking a long walk, but knew that when he returned everything would still be as he'd left it. Worse, Russ would have won, wouldn't he?

Back in the saloon, he lifted out the three bottles of Meursault. Underneath he could see several packages. One by one, he removed them, lining them up side by side on the table. They were quite heavy, and smelled of oil. But although each piece was tightly wrapped in engineers' paper, there was no doubt what Russ's "toy" was – a takedown hunting rifle, complete with scope and silencer. At the very bottom of the box was a black padded canvas bag to put it all in and, beside that, enough boxes of rounds for a firefight.

Without unwrapping the parts, he packed them, with the ammunition, into the bag. There was no point in fitting it all together, however satisfying that might be on one level, because he was never going to use it. But what was he going to do? Just leave it to rust in the chain locker? Put it on eBay? Throw the whole lot overboard and forget he'd ever seen it? In the end, he stuffed the bag and its contents into the chain locker with his shotgun.

He read through the letter again. The reference to Cyprus. Where was Russ getting his information? Fifty years ago, in the middle of a terrorist uprising, he had made a mistake, an error of judgement, when exhausted and fearing for his own life and the lives of those around him. Now that mistake was something Russ could hold over him.

And his PS: *The little bastard deserved it.* What did Russ know about it? He wasn't there. But somehow he did know. Somebody has spilled the beans. Who would do that, even for money? He thought about the men who knew, the men who had been with him on patrol. No, none of them would do that.

Stan? Stan never knew, or at least Jack never told him. The press? Google? But the story never found its way into the British papers, so where? Jack hadn't told a soul, not one. Not Bel, or Alison, or Stan and certainly not Russ. But somebody, somewhere, knew, and Russ had found him. And this could change everything.

But that wasn't all, was it? When they first met after Stan died, Russ couldn't resist letting Jack know what he'd found out about Ma Vinney's death. His relationship with the police. Getting that driver training for Frankie. Reminding Jack that he held secrets he could pass on, maybe to Alison, or to Bel.

Russ was tightening the screws turn by careful turn, every step planned, calculated. It was true what he said. He does know more about Jack than he knows himself. Step by step it was becoming clear that getting rid of Russ would seem necessary for Jack's own survival.

Jack picked up his mobile. The devious bastard could go hang, and now was the moment to tell him so. He found Russ in the list of contacts. His finger hovered over the call button.

But he didn't call.

He put down the phone and opened the book of instructions that would tell him how the gun fitted together.

And Jerry Lee Lewis cried out in pain, *"You win again"*.

Seventeen

The gun went together like a charm. Click click, just like in *Day of the Jackal*. It came apart just as pleasingly, each part allocated its own place in the shoulder bag. It would be obvious that the bag contained a gun. But it was a hunting rifle, a firearm, and he had a shotgun licence.

He retrieved his old Beretta, in its bag, from the chain locker. Russ's gun nicely fitted alongside. He could take both but there was no point. He removed them and stowed the Beretta in an overhead locker. He broke down and then reassembled the rifle, just as he'd done with rifles of an earlier vintage when completing his basic training for the RAF. He fitted the sights and suppressor, opened a porthole and lifted the gun to his shoulder. It felt odd, unfamiliar, but the quality of the optics was superb. He lined up a gull on the far bank 200 yards distant. He loved the gun's weight, the way everything was in exactly the right place. His finger rested on the trigger, the safety catch on.

In the crosshairs a boy stood in the middle of the dusty track, one arm raised. In his hand he held something small and round. "*Une grenade*," he shouted. He was all of thirteen years old. As he lay dying, his blood seeping into the dust

243

as they tried to stem the bleeding, somebody replaced the pomegranate he had been holding with a Greek hand grenade confiscated earlier that day at one of the many checkpoints. The boy was buried next day. His family was quietly compensated with enough dollars to open their own taverna. Jack never faced a court martial, but he never got to fly. And he never knew why the boy had chosen to speak French that afternoon, but his choice of language cost him his life.

The gull took off and circled around, as if challenging him to squeeze the trigger. He followed the bird in the sights. He could have brought it down, no problem. But a person? Russ? That was another matter. He laid the rifle on the table.

It was no sniper's rifle. It was a survival weapon designed to pick off the occasional rabbit or fox. But why on earth had Russ chosen a .22? Perhaps with the right ammunition, depending on the accuracy of the shot, it would be possible, just so long as the target was within a hundred metres or so.

Target? Was that possible, to see Russ as a target?

"You've never looked down the sights of a gun, have you, son? You have to tell yourself you're just looking at a target, not a person. Otherwise you'd never be able to pull the trigger."

"But what if your mate is begging you?"

Stan sniffed.

"He's still your mate, isn't he? And it's still you what's got to see his head blown to bits, and know that you did it."

How was Russ planning to set this up? He read the letter again. *Will let you know what to do next.* What did that mean, for God's sake?

He examined the ammunition. None of it was familiar. Technology had moved on since he last handled anything but his Beretta. One box contained hollow point rounds, on which was written, in Russ's unmistakeable hand, *This one will probably be best, but it's up to you.*

Less than a minute on the internet told Jack all he needed to know. With a hollow point round, a .22 was quite enough to kill a deer at 150 metres. So Russ had done his homework, as always. All that was required of Jack was to await the next communication. He put the gun into the overhead locker, alongside his Beretta, pulled on his walking boots and heavy jacket and walked up the steep gangway onto the sea wall.

Was it easier to do what Russ wanted rather than resist? One way or another, Russ would get his wish, because he always did. He got Bel. He got rich. He got Stan, and Emm. Now he had Frankie, too. And Roy Glover. He had won Ali over. He would have Jack, given enough time. And there was only one way to stop him. He'd been given the tools to do the job.

And, no, he hadn't forgotten that conversation on the steps of the cinema. And, yes, since then he had looked down the sights of a gun, many times, and been able to squeeze the trigger. He had killed. Birds, animals, a sniper, a thirteen-year-old boy. So why not Russ? Why not rid himself of a ghost from the past who was alternately begging for help and threatening to unload the secrets that threatened the life he had built for himself. So yes, push had come to shove, and he could do it.

But would he? He had everything he wanted. More money than he'd ever dreamed of. A house in Brittany. His friendship with Ali. Why put all that at risk? Mercy killing was still killing, still a crime.

Russ couldn't do him any real harm. If Russ decided to tell all, if all the history came out, who would be interested? It would be embarrassing, but not terminal. It might test

245

his relationship with Ali. He could live with whatever Russ chose to do. He could simply walk out on everything and go to live far away in France.

But could he? Russ would never let that happen. Russ only ever won. Every time, every situation, Russ came out on top. He always did, and always would. Until Jack did as he was bid, it would never end. He quickened his pace. There was no way out.

Russ had blocked every exit and given Jack the tools and the motive. He knew everything. Jack picked up a stone and hurled it towards a mooring buoy about twenty yards out into the river. Fuck you, Russ. Fuck you, fuck you, fuck you.

He walked on towards the cafe. Out on the sandbanks he could see both common and grey seals. Tomorrow, he would pick one of them out and see how good a shot he really was. And he would imagine Russ in the sights.

He woke early, and in those few precious moments between sleeping and waking, when his limbs were warm and heavy and even the *Today* programme on the radio seemed soothing, he was not troubled by the events of the previous few days. But as he pulled himself up on one elbow to check the time, the full weight of Russ's demands hit him. He dropped back into the soft, warm pillow. Surely Russ would not give him away, not after remaining silent for all these years?

But he could, that was the point. Russ was a danger and Russ didn't want to live. There was no ambiguity or hesitation in what he'd asked. Jack filled the kettle, lit the stove, made tea and carried his mug up to the wheelhouse. The sun was chasing away the few wisps of mist that still hung over the river. It looked like summer, but it already smelled like autumn.

The morning was too good to waste. There would not be

many more like this until the other side of winter. He pulled on old clothes and his walking boots. He downed his tea in one gulp, made sure he had enough cash in his pocket for a bacon sandwich and stepped out onto the damp deck.

Then he turned back, into the wheelhouse and down to the locker. He picked up the bag, checked that the hollow point rounds were there, climbed back up the companionway and onto the deck. Some poor seal was going to stand in for Russ.

It was colder onshore than he expected. He zipped up his coat and began a brisk walk downstream. Half an hour would bring him opposite the second or third sandbank. A falling tide and a bit of sun. Conditions were perfect.

Then half an hour more would bring him to the cafe. Breakfast and a read of the papers. Normal. Nothing unusual.

If he did decide to move to France, it would not be difficult. He would not have to leave *Duchesse Anne*. The yard was not busy and the work could all be done in a month. He could sell the house or let it to somebody who needed a home. Maybe one of his French relatives. He'd walked out when Russ and Bel got married, and he'd managed to avoid them all for forty years. Russ would track him down, of course, but it was too distant for Frankie to come running down on his employer's errands every five minutes.

He owed Russ no favours. Russ could do what others had done, get himself to Switzerland and have an injection. Go to sleep and never wake up. Frankie could drive him to the airport. Mrs Charlton would look after the arrangements. If Russ really did want to end it all, he could do so without Jack's help.

He walked beyond the most upstream of the sandbanks, where he could see a few seals taking advantage of the patch of sand just uncovered by the falling tide. Nobody around. There'd be more seals further downstream. He felt the weight of the rifle on his shoulder.

Another half-mile brought him to the spot. Some seals were already there, most of them just motionless lumps of blubber. Now and again, one would hump itself down to the water. He looked for one of the old ones, one that probably wouldn't survive to see another summer in any case. It would be easier that way, but still not legal. He wasn't a fisherman, and the seals posed no threat to his livelihood. So he wasn't allowed to shoot one with a weapon for which he had no licence. But that was precisely what he intended to do.

And unlike when he took out the Beretta to go to shoot the geese, and flunked it, this time he was going to do it. He would settle himself close to the foot of the sea wall, from where he could see up and down the path to make sure he was on his own. He would take out the gun, load hollow-tipped rounds and wait his moment.

He scanned the sandbank through his binoculars and settled on an old bull nearly 200 metres distant. He reckoned that if he could take the bull with a clean shot to the head, he would have no trouble hitting a closer target. He climbed up to the path and looked up and down the sea wall. Not a soul in sight. Back down at the foot of the wall he brought the gun up to his shoulder and found the animal in the sights. In the crosshairs was a sleek black head, so clear he could not possibly miss.

He lowered the gun and looked around for something else to shoot. A mooring buoy, dirty white and so covered in weed it clearly was not in regular use, lay about a hundred metres away, bobbing in the water. He lined it up and this time he did squeeze the trigger. The buoy burst like a balloon and disappeared beneath the waves, dragged to the bottom by its heavy chain. The gun had kicked a little but was so quiet that even the pink-footed geese carried on grazing.

That's all he needed to know. He could shoot straight. The gun was true. And quiet. He didn't need to kill an old bull seal to prove it. He packed the gun away and set off the final half-mile where he would find a sandwich waiting for him behind those welcoming steamed-up windows. All that remained was to await Russ's instructions.

He found the envelope, tucked in the usual place behind *Duchesse Anne*'s windscreen wiper, when he returned from the allotment the following day.

My dear Jack,

I hear you've been having fun with the little toy I sent. That dirty old buoy you shot didn't stand a chance, did it? Typical of you to let the sea lion enjoy the rest of his days, just don't chicken out when you've got me in your sights. We've both come a long way, haven't we, since we planned how to rob Ma Vinney's shop? But, Jack, my friend, I've come to the end of the road, and I'm relying on you to turn off the lights. I know you can do it, because you've done it before.

There's just one week left in September and I don't want to see October. Each day, the pain gets worse.

So here's the plan, and you know me well enough to know it will work. I don't leave loose ends.

I own the house next door to mine, number 23. It is empty. Arrive and leave by the back gate. It is unlocked. You will not meet anyone on the path as I have already had it cordoned off to the public. In the shed you will find a full SOCO's kit. Put on the SOCO stuff, go in the back door and up to the attic bedroom. There you will find the exact same rifle that I sent you, already assembled, and the self-same ammo. The window is open. Unless it is raining, I will be sitting in my garden with my back towards you between 3pm and 4pm tomorrow, and each day until the end of the month. Nobody else will be in the garden, because that's my siesta time and nobody's allowed. I'll be fast asleep. When you've done the job, leave the gun behind, go back to the shed, put the SOCO stuff in the sports bag. Take it with you and leave by the back gate. Get rid of the bag your own way – you will know best how.

I have laid a careful trail for the police. A particularly nasty piece of work who has killed many people more innocent than me has used that gun before. It has his DNA all over it and he will be quickly traced and arrested. They have been itching to get him for years, and it is well known he hates my guts.

That's all, old friend. Farewell. Remember, I always loved you, and so does Bel.

Russ

*

Jack woke early. Still in his pyjamas, he took his first cup of tea up the five steps to the wheelhouse. The night had been clear and cold, but now the wheelhouse was bright with sun and already toasty-warm. Russ's "instructions" were still on the chart table. He read them again. No, he was not prepared to sacrifice everything for Russ. Not his river, not the tatty office chair on which he sat to plan voyages he knew he would never make – all those trips across the estuary, heading for the rugged and dangerous coasts of Brittany.

Sorry, Russ, but get this: one day soon Jack Boyer intends to drop anchor right alongside his cousin Yann's fishing boats in the deep shelter of another river. Far beyond your reach. He crumpled the note, then made a half-hearted attempt to smooth it out again. He already knew every word. He put it into the drawer, out of sight.

Upstream, he heard the chug of an approaching boat, taking the ebb. He knew the boat and Nick, its young skipper. Jack slid open the wheelhouse window, leaned out and waved as the little boat passed close in. Its engine slowed to a tick-over.

"You busy, Jack, mate? I could do with another pair of hands," Nick shouted.

Nick wasn't kidding, either. Jack counted at least eight anglers on board his little fishing boat. Unless they were already experts – unlikely, given their neatly pressed chinos – they would all need help with baiting their hooks, untangling their lines and, hopefully, getting their fish on board. Not to mention feeding them and supplying them with beers. Nick would have more than enough to handle. And somebody would have to look after the boat.

"Sure. Give me five minutes. Come alongside."

As he threw on some clothes he felt the fishing boat bump gently against *Duchesse Anne*'s massive hull. Wasn't this just what he needed, a day free from Russ? Maybe the last day. Then it could be all over. He put on his boots and climbed the companionway, grabbed his jacket from its hook by the door. He picked up his mobile phone, was about to slip it into his pocket, when he paused.

He had come to dread a sound he once enjoyed – the ping of an incoming text. Before Russ, it would have been Ali inviting him to supper or to suggest a walk, or Katie letting him know that the day's special at the Old Smack was steak and kidney pie. Or the boatyard offering him work. Now, ten to one, it would be Russ to suggest they had another hilarious afternoon watching Stan's old movies, or reminding him about events that took place nearly sixty years ago. And always, behind every message, lurked the threat. The things Russ knew about Jack that the rest of the world didn't know.

Today, Russ would be silenced. He put the phone back onto the chart table. This was a day off. No interruptions.

Ten minutes later he was at the helm of Nick's boat, riding the outgoing tide at some twelve knots over the ground, while Nick was below making sandwiches. The little group of anglers, who all worked for the same City firm, argued about events in the finance world about which Jack knew little and cared less. They were already into their second or third beers.

Nick emerged from the hatch as they rounded the last finger of the East Point sandbank and into the swell of the North Sea. The City guys moved to sit along the benches behind the wheelhouse, out of the wind and within reach of the sandwiches. One of them produced a bottle of Scotch – it was going to be that sort of trip.

Jack left the boat to steer herself for a moment while he went to claim a sandwich.

"Where to, Skipper?" he asked, taking a bite and twitching the wheel a few degrees to starboard, anticipating a course for the Black Knock buoy.

"Steady as you go, Jack. Can you take the Little Gut and then head out towards the forts? I'm told there's some decent bass there at the moment."

Jack edged the throttles forward. The little boat responded.

On the sandbanks to starboard, a few seals had settled to enjoy a day's sunbathing. He tried to see the one he spared the day before, but couldn't pick him out. Nick busied himself with the rods, checking reels and baiting hooks while the paying guests finished off the sandwiches and took pictures of each other.

Out there, away from the confines of land and out of the reach of Russ, Frankie and everybody else, he felt he could breathe again. The boat barged its way through the short, choppy waves. Jack kept one eye on the depth sounder – there was scarcely more than eight feet of water left in the channel at that state of the tide – and the other fixed on the black buoy that marked the northern end.

He could still touch how he felt when, after the first four weeks of initial RAF basic training, he'd been given a weekend off. All through that weekend he knew that Sunday night he had to go back to Wales, to face the bullying obscenities of the barracks and the parade ground. He'd been judged by the men to be too posh to be one of them. But he did go back. He faced them down. He did it.

But this time he would just go away and stay away. He had a house and he had money. There was nothing he needed from Russ. Except his silence. Was it worth it? Worth risking everything because two little boys, who knew nothing of the world, made silly promises to each other on the steps of an East End cinema? Russ could take his own life if he wanted to. But not Jack's. He could do it himself with a dose of diamorphine – he would know where to get it. He didn't even need to go to Switzerland.

Jack could feel the anger returning, and that was not what he needed. He just wanted to stand in the little boat's wheelhouse, his feet apart, weaving through the swatchways between the shoals. This was one day Russ was not going to wreck.

They were through the worst of the shallows with time and water to spare. Jack took his eyes off the echo sounder. The forts, built to support anti-aircraft guns, were no more than a mile off.

Twenty minutes later, they dropped anchor. The fishing party cast their lines. The boat gently rose and fell, each time lifting with it Jack's spirits.

Around about midday, when every one of the fishing party had landed at least one decent sea bass, and the photos had been uploaded to Facebook, Nick brought a cool box up from below. Jack dished out beers while the skipper went back down, emerging moments later with a folding table. Then came plates of smoked fish, salads, bread and butter. Chilled white wine. The boat swung slowly around on her chain: the tide had turned.

After lunch, another hour of rather half-hearted effort produced few more fish. They moved to a different spot with little success, and by three o'clock everyone was ready to go home. The clients were happy, and Nick was keen to get them back to West Stone before their mood changed.

"OK, Jack. Do you want to take us home?"

Jack started the diesel and switched on the depth sounder and radar – not that he really needed either; the tide was half full and running. Visibility was perfect. The bow lifted slightly as the boat got under way. The skipper sat back with the clients, cleaning their fish and sealing them in plastic bags before settling them in ice.

They were about to enter Gofer's Gullet when a porpoise appeared off the starboard bow. Jack slowed the engines as the excited fishing party brought out their phones. Then there was another, and then a third. In the end, Jack counted half a dozen going through their routine, as if they had been trained. The City boys would go home happy – with fish to share, full bellies, videos they could show their loved ones and memories they would hold for years to come.

Nick joined Jack in the wheelhouse.

"They enjoyed that, didn't they, Jack? By the way, what

do I owe you for your help today?"

"Pay me? I've had the best day out for ages. Any time you're short-handed, just give me a shout. Provided I'm not needed at the yard, I'll be happy to help out. Especially if the weather is like today."

"I'd feel happier if I gave you something for your trouble, though."

Jack slowed the engines a touch. They were back in the river. He clicked off the radar and the screen went dark.

"Then give me a bass the right size for two. As I said, I've had a great day. Just what I needed."

An hour later, Nick took the helm and gently eased the little boat alongside *Duchesse Anne*. Jack swung aboard and watched as they turned to motor the last half-mile to the West Stone jetty. For the first time since Russ had said what he wanted, he allowed himself a broad grin.

"That takes some beating," he said to himself. "That sure takes some beating."

That grin dropped as soon as he saw the envelope under the windscreen wiper.

"Oh, for God's sake, Russ. Give me a break," he said, pulling the envelope out. But the handwriting was Ali's.

He ripped open the envelope.

Dear Jack,
    Can you call me when you get back?
    Love,
    Ali

He unlocked the wheelhouse door and switched on his mobile. It bleeped with three messages. He dialled Ali's number and she answered immediately.

"Jack, are you alright?"

"Of course I am. I've just been helping Nick out on a fishing trip. I would have let you know but it was all on the spur of the moment and I went off pretty early this morning. Sorry, I forgot to take my phone, so only just picked up your message."

"I know. I saw your phone on the chart table when I stuck the note on the windscreen. How did it go?"

"I've come back with a ruddy face and a nice sea bass. Why don't you come down to *Duchesse Anne* about six thirty for a drink and to help me eat it? I can give you all the news then."

"Jack, that sounds lovely. I'll bring something for pudding."

Before putting down the phone, Jack deleted three texts from Russ without reading them. He retrieved two bottles of the Meursault, put them in a string bag and lowered them down into the cool water of the river.

After a shower, Jack sat on deck, enjoying the beginnings of evening. The shipwrights who had been working on one of the big yachts out on the moorings motored back towards the jetty, their voices carrying easily across the flat water. A few sailors, tempted out by the prospect of a couple of hours on the river before nightfall, struggled in the light breeze against the fast-ebbing tide.

He saw Ali pass the Old Smack, retrieved a bottle from the net, and by the time her foot hit the gangplank, he'd drawn the cork and poured two glasses. Earlier he'd prepared the fish, added fresh dill, olive oil and a few capers and wrapped it in foil, ready for the oven. He'd scrubbed and steamed some tiny potatoes from the allotment. Now he was ready for the perfect end to a rare and wonderful day.

Millie padded up the gangplank ahead of Ali, did a quick tour of the deck and settled down for a sleep.

"You had me worried, you know," said Ali, as Jack took her hand to help her across the last yard of the gangplank. "I wondered where you were. Then they told me at the yard."

Jack handed her a glass.

"More ill-gotten gains from the personal cellar of Mr Brian Russell. It's good stuff, too."

She took a sip and raised her eyebrows.

"It most certainly is." They sat down side by side on the garden bench that took up most of *Duchesse Anne*'s foredeck. She touched his hand. "So, you had a nice day today, out with Nick?"

He stared downriver, where a pocket cruiser, sails sheeted in tight, appeared to be attempting to make the moorings in one tack.

"He won't do it, not in one, not against this tide." He turned to Ali. "Do you know what, Ali, I had a great day. Just for a while I managed to forget about Russ."

"That's good. He's so persistent, isn't he? Was he always like that?"

"Always. You could never say 'no' to Russ. Nobody could. Not children, not adults. Even the teachers let him get away with murder."

A cool breeze came off the water. Ali gathered a stole around her shoulders.

"And now? Can you refuse him now? If all he wants is your friendship?"

"Do you know, Ali, I'm not sure I can. Let me tell you what happened the other afternoon. We had a weird time watching some of Stan's old films, pretending we were still the best of friends. Needless to say, Mr Brian Bloody Russell has a cinema in his basement. He's even got a freezer full of ice creams. Then, when it was time to go home, I said I would walk to the station. It was a nice evening, and, to be

257

honest, I wanted to walk, as much to be on my own as for any other reason. But Russ wouldn't hear of it, and insisted that Frankie drive me all the way home. It didn't matter how many times I said I would take the train. He wasn't interested. He'd made up his mind."

Ali took a sip of wine.

"So what happened?"

"What do you think? Frankie drove me home, of course. And when we get here he unloads half Russ's bloody wine cellar."

High above their heads, two hot air balloons crossed the river. They watched the balloons' slow progress in silence. Ali turned her gaze from the sky to Jack.

"Aren't they taking a bit of a risk, flying so near to the coast?"

"As long as the wind stays in the east, they'll get blown inland," said Jack. "I'm going to light the oven. Then, do you fancy a stroll as far as the basin, otherwise I'll drink too much before supper."

"So will I. A walk sounds just right." Millie sensed the change in activity, stood up, stretched and went to wait by the gangplank. When they reached the path, Ali slipped her arm into Jack's. Out on the river, the yacht they had noticed earlier barely made any headway. The skipper put in a third or fourth tack, still a good hundred yards from the moorings.

Ali followed Jack's gaze.

"You were right about them not making it in one go, Jack. I'm not sure they'll make it at all at that rate. Why don't they just start their engine?"

"They're enjoying the challenge, Ali, that's why. Mind you, if they are still flaffing around out there when it gets near closing time, I think they'll start their engine and forget all about the challenge."

258

Millie ran down the sea wall, chasing away the oystercatchers and dunlin gathered to harvest whatever minute creatures had been left by the falling tide. Ali whistled and the dog reluctantly returned. She slipped the lead over her head.

"Would you like to tell me about Russ?" she said. "I get the feeling you may have things bottled up inside you that might be better let out."

Jack took a deep breath. Ali deserved more than the evasive stuff he'd so far given her. Unlike Russ, she seemed to understand that friendship was not possession, but the opportunity to share. They reached a narrow section of the path, so Jack stood aside to let Ali go first. It seemed easier, somehow, to talk when they could not see each other's faces.

"Russ and me'd been mates since infant school. We knocked around together all the time. Every afternoon he'd get me to walk home with him after school, even if I didn't want to. Sometimes he'd hold me by the ear and pull me all the way to his house."

Ali stopped and turned around to face Jack.

"The little bully. Why didn't you stop him?"

She let Millie off the lead. They watched her race ahead, and into the salt marsh.

Jack grimaced.

"She's going to get covered in mud. You know, I didn't mind. He was Russ and I was me, and that's how we were. Pretty much inseparable. With hindsight, yes, he was a bully. It never occurred to me at the time, though."

"But there's no doubt about it now, is there, however much he dresses it up as generosity? What is it he wants from you? Really?"

Jack could have confessed. Said, "He wants me to kill

him." Instead, he just shrugged his shoulders and sighed. "God only knows."

The path was now wide enough for them to walk side by side again. Ali slipped her arm back into Jack's.

"It's not so surprising, is it, that he wants to turn back the clock? His life must be miserable, stuck in that wheelchair all the time. He's lost Stan. He's in pain. Who wouldn't want to look back to better times?"

Ali let go Jack's arm, took a step ahead and turned to face him. She took his hand.

"Would it be asking too much, Jack, for you to pop up and see him once or twice a month? You obviously mean a lot to him. It's not like you to set your face against someone who needs you, is it?"

He should have known it. In just a couple of meetings Russ had won her over. The easy charm, the little boy lost routine, the pathos beneath the jokes, the grin – he could switch it all on at will. Ali's question, if that's what it was, remained unanswered. If only she knew.

They turned around, towards home, and put Millie back on the lead. The sun dipped below the trees. The yacht made its moorings. Lights began to flicker on.

After supper, as Jack washed the dishes and Ali wiped, they turned to the subject of Jack's house in France.

"Do you think you'll go and live there?" asked Ali, as she reached up to slip the plates into an overhead cupboard.

"Ali, I haven't even seen inside the place yet. But did I tell you, *Duchesse Anne* is going into the yard next week so I'll be homeless until she's done?"

"No, you didn't tell me, but Katie said you'd reserved a room at the pub so I guessed that was what it was. You've got your family in France, haven't you? Family is important, especially as you get older."

Was this her gentle way to tell him that, if he did go, she wouldn't be going with him? She'd never said, and Jack had never asked. He'd framed sentences that included the word "we", always watching for her reaction, in constant dread of rejection. Over the weeks since he first outlined his plans, she hadn't once corrected him.

He plunged his hands into the warm soapy water. Through the porthole above the sink, he could see the number 8 buoy blinking its green light.

"Does that mean you are not coming with me to see the place?"

She grinned and touched his forearm.

"No, of course it doesn't. I said I would come with you. I said I would stay and help you get it sorted out and I will. I'm really excited about the trip."

"But you wouldn't want to live there?"

She dried her hands on the tea towel.

"Jack, love, how can I answer a question like that?"

"Shall we go a bit earlier than planned? Next week, even? It would be good to go while the weather's still good and *Duchesse Anne* is laid up."

"That's fine by me. I'm pretty free right now and I agree it would be good to go before autumn really sets in."

"That's settled, then. I'll change the travel arrangements and let Yann know. Oh, and I meant to ask, would it be alright to borrow the car one day next week? I need to pop up to London before I go away."

Eighteen

"Bad business, though, Jack, isn't it?" said Frankie, shaking his head.

Jack took a sip of wine and picked up the *Stratford Express* Frankie had brought out from England. *Gangland link to Russell murder* yelled the headline on the lead story.

Jack put down the paper, stood up and put his hands in his trouser pockets.

"You know, Frankie, I just couldn't take it in when Bel phoned me at Stansted and told me what had happened. We were just about to board. Hummed and hawed about whether we should go back. But there was nothing we could do, so we boarded the plane and bought ourselves a stiff drink as soon as we took off.

"Anyway, lovely to see you."

Frankie pushed the paper across the table. Jack resumed his seat.

Frankie jabbed the paper with his finger. "It says here it was a gangland feud. But honest to God, Russ wasn't involved with no gangs. He might have sailed a bit close to the wind, sometimes. Tax and one thing and another. But gangs? What do they know?

"And I told the reporter, Russ didn't have an enemy in the world. He just made it all up."

Jack reached across and squeezed Frankie's wrist, noticing again how slight he was.

"Nice of you to say that, Frankie. How was your journey here?"

"No trouble, Jack. I stopped overnight near Pegasus Bridge. Brought back some memories of when Russ and me took Stan there. Same hotel. I knew they spoke English. Mrs Charlton booked it and everything.

"So all I had to do was drive down to Folkestone, straight onto the train, the train belts under the tunnel and drive off in France. Dunno what they'll think of next."

"Make the most of it, Frankie. It'll all change once we leave the EU."

The crunch of footsteps on the gravel announced that Ali was back from the village with fresh baguettes from the baker's and a bag of mussels from Yann. Hopefully that would draw a line under talking about who might have shot Russ.

Ali gave that smile that Jack had come to love.

"Frankie, you're here already," she said, hurrying across the grass. She thrust the bag and bread into Jack's hands and hugged Frankie close. "So lovely to see you, Frankie. Are you alright?" She let him go and gave Jack a peck on the cheek. "Take those inside and give them a good scrub can you, Jack, love, while I show Frankie the house and where he'll sleep. Are you OK with mussels, Frankie?"

Ali ushered Frankie to the front door. Jack picked up the newspaper and followed them inside. Already he loved this house. The heavy old furniture, the tiled floors, the scent of years of polish.

He went to the kitchen and began to run cold water into

the sink. He spread the newspaper on the draining board and tipped the mussels out. From the window he looked down to where a strip of river at the bottom of the wooded valley reflected back the sun, already high in the sky.

Outside, Frankie's dark blue Jaguar sat behind the car Jack had rented at the airport.

Yann was coming over for supper, with his niece. Frankie had promised to stay for a few days until it was time for him to drive them all home for the funeral.

And by then *Duchesse Anne*, newly painted and with her rusted plates replaced, engines serviced and batteries charged, would be waiting back on her mooring, straining at the warps with every tide, ready to go.

9 October. John Lennon's birthday. He would have been seventy-seven.